Erisha and the Realms

A. B. Holmstedt

For in fire, gold is refined.

Thank you to my family, my friends, and my editor (you know who you are) for all the help in making this dream a reality.

Book cover © 2025 Nani.
@naninanidraws

ISBN-13: 979-8-9993706-0-0

First Edition.

Contents

Pronunciation Guide

Erisha [eh-REE-sha]

Dumur [deh-MUR]

Esirim [ES-sir-im]

Ansira [AN-see-ra]

Semirra [se-MEER-ra]

Anarim [AN-ar-im]

Abkur [AB-kur]

Girisu [GEAR-i-su]

Sidukur [si-DOO-kur]

*Esasag (Furun) [ES-sa-sag]

*Lekur (Felrisa) [ley-KUR]

*Fasur (Semusak) [FA-sur]

*Lerisaba (Abaki) [ler-IS-aba]

* Hursaga (Zari) [her-SA-ga]

Realm Colors

Felrisa – black and silver and blue

Furun – brown and gold and green

Zari – grey and crimson

Semusak – bronze and yellow

Abaki – white and purple

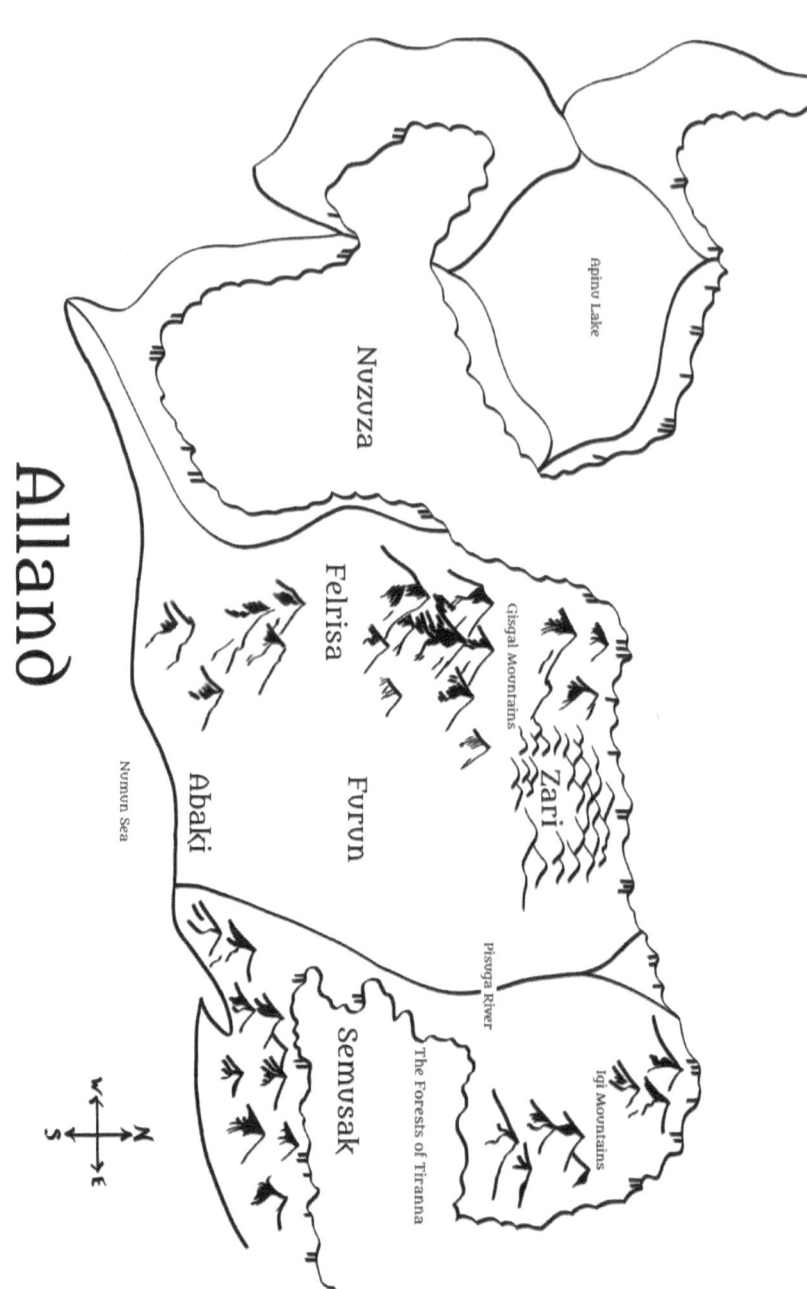

ERISHA AND THE REALMS

CHAPTER ONE

THE KING'S SUMMONS

It was the night of Lady Erisha of Furun's nineteenth year. The Hall was brightly lit by small lanterns lining the walls. The cool night air floated in from the opened doors, yet the breeze could not rid the room of the pleasant smell of ale, wine, and food. Laughter and song swept throughout the Hall while couples and groups danced in the center, tables pushed to the sides. The spirit of celebration and fellowship seemed to bubble over in each occupant's heart.

Erisha Sadurra danced in a group of young people, her elder brother Esirim at her side as her partner. A lively smile graced her face as she successfully completed the quick steps and clapping involved in the dance. As the song finished and the dance ended, she hugged Esirim and rested against his arm as they thanked the other dancers and laughed together. They walked off the designated dance floor, arm in arm, and made their way to their parents.

They chatted gaily until they glimpsed their father and mother. Lord Ansira Sadurra, the Steward of Furun, held a letter in his hands. He studied its contents while Lady Semirra's gaze fluttered from the letter to her husband's face. Lord Ansira stroked his greying beard, a sure sign of his being deep in thought.

"What is it?" Esirim asked as the siblings approached.

His father looked up and was quiet for a moment in the voice-filled Hall. "We will speak later," he finally said, shifting his gaze from his son to his daughter. "The festivities are not yet over." He smiled and welcomed Erisha's arm to link within his own. He led her back through the crowd, Lady Semirra and Esirim following, and weaved their way through the dancers to the very center of the Hall.

"Friends!" he cried, his voice booming through the room.

The musicians quieted, the dancers paused, and the conversations ceased. Dumur Sadurra, the youngest of the Sadurra siblings, appeared beside Erisha after having weaved his way through the crowd. All eyes rested on the stewarding family.

Lord Ansira smiled down at his daughter. "Today, my daughter comes of age," he proclaimed to his people. "After nineteen summers and winters, Lady Erisha can declare herself a young woman." He signaled to a servant waiting in a corner of the Hall. "With that in mind, I will have you all know that Lady Semirra and I have considered Erisha a Lady in her own right long before this day. Erisha has proved her goodness thus far and will no doubt continue to prove herself." The Steward of Furun took one of the four glasses that the servant brought up to him, and he handed the other three to his wife and sons. "So, to Lady Erisha of Furun!"

Everyone in the Hall save Erisha grabbed a flask, cup, glass, or whatever was available, and raised them above their heads. "May your summers be wet," they all chanted, "your winters mild, and good fortune granted to you for many years to come." Then, everyone drank in Erisha's honor while she smiled brightly in the center of the room.

The celebration lasted for a while after, but eventually the villagers were gone and the household worked busily to clear, clean, and order the Hall. Lord Ansira sent a page to summon his militant captain, Turin, then led his family into the war chamber. The Steward took his seat at the head of the mapping table and the other occupants seated themselves near him. They waited patiently, although it was late and a few yawns were stifled, as Lord Ansira smoothed the letter out on the table in front of him. Turin arrived with his usual promptness. Lord Ansira had him seal the chamber doors.

Erisha glanced around her as she waited. The council chamber was a closed room except for a few, small high windows. The walls were lined with detailed maps of each stewardship realm of Alland and an expansive map of Alland lay across the table. The lanterns were already lit in each corner of the chamber while some hung from the ceiling. The sun had set long ago, and the humming buzz and chirp of night bugs could be heard faintly from outside. Erisha longed to be out of doors where the cool night air could wash over her and fill her lungs anew, yet she sensed the gravity of the situation at hand and she also wanted an answer that would explain her father's solemness.

The Steward handed the letter to Turin.

"From the King?" Turin asked in surprise after skimming the letter.

"A summons," Lord Ansira said. "An inspection for war."

"An inspection?" Dumur asked. "I thought that was still to come. It's only annual."

Lord Ansira nodded. "It is, but I'm sure the King has his reasons."

"Being?" Erisha interjected.

"There has been some tension between the realms recently," her father replied vaguely. "The King is a man of peace. If anything unpleasant arises I'm sure he would desire its swift end."

"Where are we to meet him?" Esirim questioned as Turin read over the letter.

"The West border," the Steward answered.

"Felrisa," Turin echoed.

Erisha found the realm on the map of Alland. Felrisa swept up into the Gisgal Mountains in the West where the peoples of Felrisa, the Lekur, made their home. They were a rough people who worked amidst a jagged landscape and unpredictable weather.

"Only a third of the army is required for an inspection and that is all we'll take," the Steward continued. "Not a man more.

And, Turin, you will remain here. If the King is worried about unrest the Esasag will not be left unprotected."

Turin inclined his head in agreement.

"Will I come, Father?" Esirim asked.

"You will," Lord Ansira replied. "I also only want a third of the cavalry with us."

"Yes, Father."

"When do you leave?" Lady Semirra asked.

"The morning," her husband said.

"Then much must be done," she said, rising.

The Steward also stood. "There is. Turin, open the doors."

Turin obeyed as the children stood beside their parents.

Lord Ansira looked to Erisha. "I'm sorry, spirit, but we must be off."

Erisha smiled. "The celebration is over," she admitted kindly.

"Ah, but it'll come again," her father promised.

Erisha laughed then went off with her mother to warn the household of the work that still needed to be done. Lord Ansira went to assemble his own armor and that of his elder son. Turin selected the men who would accompany the Steward for inspection by going about to their houses. Esirim gathered the cavalry men and saddled the horses for an early morning departure as Dumur watched and helped where he could. The Steward pondered the letter in his study before he decided on the path they would take to the border of Felrisa.

Lady Semirra woke Erisha and Dumur early the next morning to see the men off. The Steward and Esirim rode at the front of the company. About forty men marched after them and twenty cavalrymen brought up the rear on their steeds. Erisha, Dumur, the Stewardess, and Cook were standing on the top of the stairs of the Manor with Turin. They watched the men go. The sun was just waking, and the feel of the morning was still dim and cool. The dew blanketed the grass, and the clean smell of a new day had only begun to permeate the air. There were some cows and goats awake grazing, but many of Furun's inhabitants were still peacefully asleep.

The company halted on the outskirts of the village and, from about that half mile, the five figures outside the Manor saw the Steward and Esirim raise an arm in the customary farewell and blessing, chain mail gleaming in the first glow of the rising sun. Although they were uncertain if the men could see them with the dark wood Manor behind them, the two Ladies, the young Lord, Cook, and Turin raising their arms in a responding farewell. Cook returned indoors to begin her tasks in the kitchen while Turin returned to his home, and, after a while, Lady Semirra left the top step and entered her home and sanctuary followed by a yawning Dumur. Erisha, however, sat down on the stair and remained. The light morning breeze pulled her blond curls in front of her face. She quickly brushed her hair back and tied it together, out of her face.

There was something about this morning that irked her. She watched the sun rise and turn the fields of green grass emerald and the fields of wheat golden. She marveled at the beauty and strength of Manor's horses as they were brought out to graze by a particularly responsible stable boy, and she reminded herself to tell her father of the boy's merit. Far off, the Steward and his men grew smaller and smaller until they were too distant to distinguish from the landscape.

Erisha's gaze rested on the Gisgal Mountains on the horizon to the West. The range seemed small and humble from so far away, but Erisha knew the truth: their tips towered high, touching the low clouds, and their sides were treacherous no matter one's skill or experience. The Mountains gated the five realms of Alland from the untraveled realm beyond named Nuzuza on maps and called the Uncharted by most. The Mountains stretched far up into the thick surrounding Forests of Tiranna in the North and also down into the Numun Sea near the realm of Abaki in the South.

Erisha wondered at the King's summons. Alland was a peaceful kingdom, partially due to the respect the peoples of Alland had for the ruling family, the Askattes, and due to the distance between the realms. Each of the five peoples had their territory and independence.

King Anarim Askatte ruled Alland from the northern realm of Zari, the hill country of the Hursaga. Zari had been the seat of the kingship since the beginning of Alland and the Askattes had done well keeping the realms on friendly terms. There were few laws that were held throughout the kingdom that preserved peace, life, and distance and distinction between the realms.

Otherwise, the Stewards of the other four realms were free to govern as they wished as long as they reported to the King with their code of behavior, untouched or revised, each year so that the King knew how to best handle grave accusations brought before him.

Erisha sat back and rested against the steps. The sun was fully risen now, and the village was bustling with activity. She had never been to the other realms. She had often wondered what their villages were like. She had heard stories from travelers passing through and had read about each people, but she knew it was not the same as seeing the realms or gathering with the inhabitants. She loved Furun, but she wondered if she would ever travel and roam. In her dreams, she would often wander to the Gisgal Mountains where she would climb to the top and look over into the Uncharted, or she would be on the edge of the Sea, looking out over the water where the horizon was never limited by mountains or trees. The part of the Tirannan forests across the Pisuga river where the Fasur lived in the East, in the realm of Semusak, was more mysterious than the rest of Alland wished it to be. The tale told was that the forests were enchanted and more than just the Fasur and the beasts they hunted lived within. Erisha wished to visit the forests to experience so many trees growing near one another that they created an everlasting canopy over the land. She dreamed of climbing a particularly tall tree and reaching the top to look out over the sea of leaves that stretched on almost as far as the Numun waters. Then there was Zari itself, the hill country. Erisha did not know if she yearned as dearly to see the home of the Hursaga, the hill-dwelling people. The hills sounded rather familiar; they were like the fields in Furun except molded up into knolls, mounds, and ridges. From what she had been told and seen on several maps, the northern part of Zari dipped down into the forests but on the southern side it opened out to look over the rest of the land which was the primary reason it was the home of the King. The only features Erisha desired to experience in Zari were the majestic home of the King, the White Palace, and the northern breeze among the hills. The breeze was said to have a musical quality in the way the Forests of Tiranna were said to be enchanted. This was something Erisha firmly believed in since she felt that sometimes when she was out dancing in the fields she could hear the soft, lilting voice of the wind as it passed her by.

It called to her.

The time passed quickly. Within a few days, the fields were ready to be harvested and the village banded together to help several farmers finish their fields each day. Then, after all the village fields were done, the Manor's fields were left. Cook and her apprentices, at the Stewardess' request, prepared large feasts for midday and for the evening for three consecutive days. These days at the Manor were some of Erisha's favorite of the year because everyone, no matter who they were, aided in the fields at some point. She would walk through the tall grasses, her long skirt rustling against the stems, and sing or laugh with the others around her as they all bent, crouched, or knelt, using their hands and their tools to harvest what the land had given them. The village worked the Manor's fields at an admirable pace and finished after the three days. Lady Semirra was grateful and tried to thank each and every person individually with the help of Erisha and Dumur. Erisha was sorry that her father and her elder brother had missed the harvest.

Erisha and Dumur watched from the high Manor steps as everyone filed through the village to their homes and shops and barns. Dumur's gaze wavered over to the West. Erisha saw his brows furrow. He breathed in and sighed.

"Erisha," he began, "five days have passed. How long does it take to reach the Felrisan border?"

"About a day and some at a good pace," Erisha replied quietly, now staring at the western horizon with her younger brother.

"How long does an inspection take?" Dumur continued.

"From how Father talked, the King may have had more to discuss than simply an inspection."

There was a pause. "That's true."

Erisha sympathized with the boy's discomfort. Lord Ansira was not gone for long periods of time expect for the annual trip to Zari and during war. Regarding war, in Erisha's lifetime, her father had only ridden off with the risk of not returning twice. Both had been long ago, one to quell a small militant uprising in Felrisa and another to subdue the Lerisaba in Abaki. Yet, this present outing was not specifically related to war. As far as they knew.

"Maybe we could go scouting," Dumur said, his eyes suddenly alight. "We could ask Mother and ride about half a day's distance to see what we might find."

"Dumur," Erisha said uncertainly.

"We need to try, Erisha."

"We need to wait and have faith. Father and Esirim will return. Nothing is wrong."

"No, Erisha," Dumur said firmly, meeting her gaze. "Something is wrong. I must know."

Erisha hesitated — Dumur was right. Lord Ansira would not be away this long without sending word, and the calculated way he prepared to leave by only taking so many of the men had been cautious. Erisha watched as the sun began to set in the West. The breeze cooled her face and tugged at the wisps of hair that had fallen from her braid.

"We cannot alarm Mother," she finally said. "We may ask her before we sleep, but don't be sure she'll agree. If Father has not sent word, it could be dangerous."

Dumur nodded. "Agreed," he said. He looked up at her. "Thank you."

Erisha smiled. "All will be well," she said, echoing her parents' usual comfort.

After they spent time with their mother by the fireside in the study, Erisha requested an outing for Dumur and herself. Lady Semirra instantly rejected the idea. She looked at both her children, a firmness setting upon her mouth that told Erisha and Dumur that she would not yield on the point.

"Your father has not sent word," their mother stated. "He has not explained his prolonged absence. We do not know what happened."

Her children were silent for a moment.

"Could we send a scout instead then?" Dumur asked slowly.

"Dumur, your father would send a messenger back to us if anything was truly wrong," Lady Semirra replied.

Erisha sensed Dumur's rising passion and signaled for him to remain quiet. Thankfully, Dumur listened to her gesture. He slumped back into his chair, cozily defeated in the firelight.

"Very well, Mother," Erisha said soothingly. "We only wanted to see if we could glimpse the men."

"I understand," Lady Semirra replied, "but I think such an action would be ill-advised."

"Are we at such an uncertain state?" Erisha questioned in disbelief.

Her mother stared into the fire for a few long moments. "I don't know," she admitted.

Erisha looked over to where Dumur slouched. He gave her a pointed look. She shook her head and attempted a smile. She stood and went over to her mother.

"What comes is what comes," she said gently, putting her arms around her mother.

Lady Semirra hugged her daughter close. "True words," she agreed but her expression did not soften completely.

ERISHA AND THE REALMS

Erisha kissed her and wished her mother goodnight. Dumur followed suit and the siblings left their mother by the fire. Neither of them spoke except to wish the other a good night's rest. A heaviness hung in the air. It was late when the household was finally all asleep.

Erisha awoke and her eyes opened to darkness. Someone was calling her name. She blinked until her eyes grew accustomed to the lack of light. She knew it was early. She sat up and leaned against the head of her bed. She did not normally wake up before the sun. Her name was not called again in the stillness. She tried to convince herself it had been a dream, but her heart was uneasy. She swung her legs off the side of her bed and stood. She tiptoed to her bedroom door, eased it open, and peered down the hallway. All was quiet.

Erisha stepped out into the hallway, a feeling encouraging her out of her room. The hallway was dimly lit by a couple small lanterns. The warm orange glow was calming, and the carpet underneath Erisha's bare feet was soft. She passed by her parents' room first and waited beside the door. Nothing seemed amiss. She carefully opened the door and peeked in; there was the figure of her mother sleeping peacefully in the light of the room's small fireplace. She closed the door and moved on. She felt fully awake by this point and thought about how she could remedy the morning by going to watch the sun rise. Erisha neared Dumur's room, and her body stiffened before her mind understood why. Heart frozen in her chest, she pushed open the doors. The fireplace was dark, but her eyes were accustomed enough to recognize that the bed was empty and made — maybe never slept in.

Erisha ran into the room and realized that Dumur's satchel and boots were gone. Also, she did not see his sword or bow strewn about anywhere like they usually were when they were not on his person. Without a thought dedicated to anything else, Erisha ran from the room and down the hallway. She raced through the Hall and out of one of the Manor's side doors that opened in the direction of the stables. Her feet were wet and cold on the early morning grass, and it was still so dim that she relied more on instinct than sight to lead her, but Erisha flew over the yard and lunged into the stables. After a mad search of the lantern-lit stables, Erisha knew Dumur's horse, Sisi, was gone, as were Sisi's saddle and a pack. She hesitated for a single moment as the horses snorted irritably at being woken likely for the second time that morning. She wondered about leaving Dumur to return on his own, yet a feeling deep within Erisha fought against this decision.

She retraced her steps to the Manor. She crept about stealthily now and made it back to her room. She dressed warmly, with layers for the morning cold and for riding. She filled her satchel with her maps, a journal, ink and pen, and two short knives. On her person, she strapped a long knife around her waist, a small sword across her back, and her bow and quiver over her shoulders. Afterwards, she left a short note under her mother's door to pacify her then she slipped as quietly as possible through the hallways and into the kitchen. She sighed when she saw that Dumur had already raided part of the pantry, and she went through and packed some food good for sustenance and travel. She grabbed two flasks of water and, on her way through the Hall, she grabbed a blanket from one of the side benches. Her father was always mentioning the wind's severity across the flatlands when he traveled, and she was certain that Dumur had not dressed properly.

Out in the stables, Erisha saddled her horse, Kuranga, and strapped on the blanket, her satchel, her sword, and one of the prepared packs that hung at all times on the stable walls. She led Kuranga out of her stall and out of the stables. In the crisp morning air, she lept up onto Kuranga's back and decided in which direction Dumur had headed. She settled herself to the West and urged Kuranga into a run. She did not know how far Dumur had already gotten and she did not know when he would stop.

CHAPTER TWO

RIDERS AND WARRIORS

K uranga galloped hard before Erisha slowed the noble beast to a trot. The horse breathed heavily as Erisha absently stroked its neck and studied the landscape shining in the sunlight in front of her. She was glad morning had not been too far off and Dumur had not decided to leave in the middle of the night. She knew this much because Sisi's tracks were fresh, and, now being able to find them, Erisha followed the trail. With every passing moment, Erisha's confidence in finding Dumur grew. The boy was not stupid, she knew that much, but that also did not mean he had not made a horribly foolish decision that morning. Dumur would receive one tongue lashing from Erisha before they both received one from Lady Semirra.

The sun continued to rise as Erisha continued to follow Dumur's trail — she would have to speak with him about covering his tracks. Out in the open fields away from the village and in light of her mother's worries, Erisha felt bare and unprotected. The trees were sparse and the rocks and brush were too short to block one from sight for long. She focused mainly on following the trail but would look up from time to time to see if she could glimpse anything in the distance in front of her or around her. About midday, when the sun's rays beat down upon her head during the unusually hot autumn day and she was lamenting her over-preparedness in her clothing choices, she saw a figure on horseback ahead of her. She spurred Kuranga onward and reveled in the feel of the wind whipping past her and pulling at her hair. She approached the figure within a few moments and could rightly tell that it was Dumur. Her brother was keeping his horse at a stable, slow trot and he turned back in his saddle to watch her approach. He smiled and greeted her with a raise of a hand. Erisha grabbed her bow and rushed past him momentarily, smacking him over the head with the top side of the weapon. Then she turned Kuranga about and the horse reared in front of Sisi.

"What was that for?" Dumur cried out angrily, rubbing the back of his head.

"What do you think?" Erisha replied hotly. "How could you? When Mother strictly forbade it?"

The siblings now rode beside each other, their horses slowed to a walk. Dumur leaned back in his saddle, and he stared up at the blue sky. Erisha waited for his explanation, her hand still gripping her bow.

"It may be foolish, Erisha," Dumur finally admitted, "but I want to know where Father and Esirim are. If I was five winters older like you, there would be no questioning my desire to organize a scouting run. As it is, I am still thought to be young and my concerns go uncared for."

"Because there are still certain things you lack," Erisha countered. "Like judgment."

She meant for the comment to sting and sting it did. Dumur set his jaw and looked away from her. Viewing his profile, Erisha wondered at how much he looked like their father. She lamented causing him distress, but his impulsivity was uncalled for. Neither spoke for a while until, just when Erisha decided to turn them back towards the village, Dumur said one word.

"Go," he said softly.

Erisha was offended and annoyed until Sisi charged ahead at breakneck speed, and she realized that the word had been a command for the horse. As she spurred on Kuranga, Erisha bemoaned the fact that she had not trained her horse as well and as closely as Dumur had Sisi. Both horses were female so there was no physical advantage between the creatures, but still Erisha spent most of her time with Kuranga out on trots or short-lived sprints while Dumur and Sisi often trained with the cavalry where the horses were taught quick verbal and gestural signals.

Sisi remained ahead of Kuranga, and the horses were running too fast for Erisha to call to Dumur. It was a battle of endurance now and Erisha was afraid her horse would lose. After what felt like an eternity of crouching down against the horse's back, Dumur slowed to a trot again and Erisha caught up. They were atop a small grassy mound where the land swelled up a little and Erisha rode up beside Dumur who had dismounted and was letting Sisi rest.

Erisha was so angry she nearly fell out of the saddle dismounting, but before she could yell at her brother she glanced in the direction he was frowning at. Her eyes found small dark specks in the far distance: a group of riders coming their way.

She calmed and watched for a few more moments. "I wonder who they are," she mused lowly.

"It's too far to tell," Dumur stated. He turned to her, his expression hopeful. "Shall we wait?"

Erisha sighed and glanced up at the sun overhead. If they turned around now, they would probably return home before dark. Yet, the riders were likely Furunian and then they could return home with protection and information.

Erisha looked down at Dumur. Her anger was now balanced by her hope. "Very well."

Dumur smiled. He looked about and focused on a small cluster of trees back down the mound in the direction they had come. He pointed. "Those trees?" he suggested, leading Sisi back down the mound.

Erisha followed and they made their small camp under the four trees that gave them some shade. Erisha ate from her pack while Dumur ate from his. She was impressed by his level of preparation, but she was vindicated by the fact that he was not dressed warmly enough for now a northern wind had arrived and swept against them, stealing the sun's warmth from their skin. They were also not moving now except to scamper up the mound routinely to gauge the distance of the riders. Erisha gave Dumur the extra blanket and her brother was grateful.

Upon another peek over the mound a while later, Dumur gestured to Erisha for her to join him. Erisha rose from tending their small fire and joined Dumur. They both lay down on the mound and stared out and over.

"There are more riders," Dumur announced, pointing North to where another small group of horsemen were approaching from a distance.

"Odd," Erisha murmured. "Friend or foe…"

Dumur nodded. "It's hard to decide where this new group is headed because they could change directions, but the first has always been headed here."

"They'll be here soon," Erisha replied, nervous for a moment before she calmed herself.

"I still can't tell who they are," Dumur said, irritated.

They returned to their camp and waited. They spoke quietly and quickly when they did speak. For greater lengths of time, they simply sat in tense anticipation.

It was Erisha's turn to check next and she carefully crawled up the mound and realized she was treating the situation more like a game than anything. She shook herself — she was no longer a child. When her face came up high enough to look over, she started. She could not see either group of riders. She looked about carefully and studied the different clusters of greenery or stone, but she could not see any person or creature. She called to Dumur and he raced up the small hill, recognizing the distress in her voice. He dropped down beside her and studied the landscape as she pointed out the obvious.

A sinking feeling settled upon Erisha. "We need to go," she whispered.

Dumur nodded. "Agreed."

The siblings tumbled down off the mound and ran back to their camp. Dumur put out the fire as Erisha packed up their satchels. They were about to mount their horses when a group of men rode around from behind the trees and thundered about them. They were not warriors from Furun, and the siblings gripped their weapons. Dumur drew his sword and Erisha notched an arrow. The riders wore silver, black, and blue, the colors of Felrisa.

The leader of the group, wearing a grey instead of black cloak wrapped around his shoulders, dismounted and began to approach. He stopped when Erisha raised her bow. He raised his hands in a peaceable manner.

"Are you children alright?" he asked.

Erisha eyed the four other riders then returned her attention to the leader. Neither Dumur nor she spoke.

"Are you lost?" the man attempted.

"We're leaving." Dumur replied and Erisha was surprised by the confidence in his tone. She moved over to Kuranga while continuing to face the men and keeping an arrow ready.

"Where are you from?" the man asked. "Where are you going?"

"We'll keep our plans to ourselves, thank you," Erisha answered coolly. "We are in no need of assistance. You may go on your way."

"Fine breeding," one of the riders remarked.

Erisha and Dumur tried not to react.

"We want to escort you both home," the leader announced. He mounted his horse swiftly and looked at the siblings expectantly, "to make sure you're safe. Wandering about is ill-advised."

Erisha's heart beat wildly. She sensed that these men were not well-intentioned, and it would not be smart to lead them to the village. On the contrary, the village had to be warned that there were rogue Felrisan riders roaming nearby. Erisha exchanged a glance with Dumur. He sighed and nodded curtly. He mounted and Erisha followed suit. Dumur glanced at Erisha again and Erisha knew what he was about to do. It would be the most foolish thing he had done that day, but there was no way to stop him. So, she had to go with him.

Dumur spoke to Sisi and the horse sped away with Kuranga right behind. Erisha heard the leader shout, and the riders charged after them. They would not be able to outrun these men, but Erisha had no idea what to do next. An arrow whizzed by Erisha's shoulder and turned her blood cold.

Dumur pulled up a little and rode beside Erisha.

"They're trying to kill us," Erisha shouted.

"No? I thought the arrow was meant as a gift," Dumur yelled sarcastically. "I have an idea." He pulled out some rope from his satchel.

"Why do you have rope?" Erisha exclaimed.

"Why do you not?" Dumur shot back.

Erisha was about to laugh when Dumur cried out — an arrow had nicked his arm.

"Here." He handed her one end of the rope. "We're going to turn around and separate and ride back at them."

"Trip them?" Erisha said indignantly.

"Do you have a better idea?" Dumur retorted over the wind.

Erisha grumbled but gripped her end of the rope. Together, the siblings pulled up and turned their horses about. They nodded to each other and thundered back towards their pursuers. An arrow pulled at Erisha's hair as it flew by. The siblings rode apart but kept the rope low. The riders tried to slow down but everyone was going too fast. The rope hit the legs of the Felrisan leader's horse and the horse tumbled, the man flying out of his saddle. Erisha, however, held on to the end of the rope for a moment too long and was pulled from her saddle as well. She fell through the air then slammed into the ground and rolled over and over on the tall coarse grass.

Her lungs felt as if they were on fire and she could not draw a breath. Her shoulder that had been jerked by the rope throbbed. She heard yelling and shouting and she thought she heard someone calling her name. She tried to sit up and find Dumur, but she only managed to roll over.

"Erisha, get up!" she heard Dumur yell.

Erisha breathed deeply, forcing her lungs to inhale, then willed herself to rise. She found that Kuranga was standing beside her, and Erisha grabbed onto the saddle to steady herself, wincing as her shoulder pinched. She heard many grunts and shouts around her and the clash of metal against metal rang in her ears. She looked about, still gripping to Kuranga, and saw not five riders but ten now. Another group of men, perhaps the one that had been coming from the North, had arrived. They were dressed in dark, earthy, indistinguishable colors, though by their show of military prowess, they were obviously warriors of some sort. The Felrisans were locked in combat with the new riders, but Erisha's eyes searched for Dumur. Finally, she saw him: he was no longer on horseback but was standing against a man twice his size.

Erisha fumbled for her bow and quiver, but Dumur was knocked down before she could notch an arrow. She struggled to lift her bow. There was a shout nearby, but she felt a hard, heavy something smack against her head and all went dark.

Erisha awoke to her head throbbing excessively. Her eyesight focused in and out and she heard herself groan. A figure appeared in her line of sight. It was a man and he knelt down beside her. He was slightly unkept in appearance with a beginning of a beard and his dark hair hanging free, but his expression was not unkind. The memories of what had passed slowly began to return to the forefront of Erisha's mind. She squinted and tried to turn her head, but the throbbing thwarted her.

"Close your eyes," the man ordered. He placed a hand over her eyes, and she closed them under it. "Breathe."

Erisha breathed deeply several times, and she felt her mind begin to clear. "Who are you?" she asked warily, realizing she might need to be afraid.

The man lifted his hand and looked down at her. "You may call me Anarim," he said and for some reason the name held significance in Erisha's mind. "You are Lady Erisha Sadurra. Your brother Dumur is also awake."

"Where are we?" Erisha asked, looking up at the trees they were under and glimpsing the early morning sky through the leaves.

"About half a day's ride from the Furin-Felrisa border," Anarim replied. "Can you stand? The others are waiting."

Erisha sat up lethargically and Anarim helped her stand. Her head felt light for a moment then it cleared again. She stood back from Anarim and rolled the shoulder that had been yanked. It felt alright now.

"We reset your shoulder," Anarim stated.

"Thank you," Erisha said. She looked up into Anarim's face and realization dawned on her. She had seen his face before, once in person when she was young and he had come to Furun with his father and routinely in her peripheral vision as she passed his portrait that hung in the Manor's library. She gasped softly and fell back down to her knees, yet Anarim grabbed her as if she were falling.

"Your Majesty," Erisha exclaimed as she was returned to her feet.

"There is no need for that here," the King replied, steadying her. "We are here secretly and the ruler of Alland is still in the Palace in Zari by all accounts." He raised his eyebrows, awaiting her response.

Erisha stepped back again. "Yes, my lord," Erisha said, but she also caught herself. "I mean… my apologies." She felt herself blush, but she raised her chin and held the King's gaze.

The King smiled kindly. "You mean Anarim," he said.

Erisha nodded, berating herself for acting a fool.

"We are heading out," Anarim said, guiding her from under the impressive grove of trees they had found. "Do you think you can ride?"

"Yes," Erisha said firmly.

"Good," Anarim said.

They approached four men and Dumur already mounted on their horses. The men all inclined their heads respectfully towards Erisha. She nodded in return and looked to Dumur who was dismounting. He hurried over and gave Erisha support. He smiled reassuringly.

"Morning, sleepyhead," he said quietly.

"I'd rather not talk about my head at the moment," she replied dryly.

Dumur gave her a side glance as the King began talking.

"This is Girisu," Anarim said, gesturing up to a rider with bright eyes and light hair pulled back to the nape of his neck. "He is my chief tracker and a close friend." The King raised a hand toward a tall, burly man with a long dark beard and who

26

initially appeared intimidating before Erisha saw the kindly twinkle in his eyes. "Sidukur is a renowned warrior in my army and the finest teller you'll ever meet."

Erisha managed a smile before her attention was shifted towards an older rider with shaggy grey hair and a silver beard. His eyes, she knew, had seen much and were now scrutinizing her. His face was weathered and wrinkled and he had a piercing gaze, but the obvious laugh lines around his eyes put Erisha at ease.

"Abkur," Anarim introduced. "One of my most trusted advisors on my counsel and a personal mentor. And this is Kas."

Erisha took in the last rider who appeared to be fairly youthful, yet his eyes held sign of great wisdom and knowledge. Erisha instantly sensed an atmosphere of mystery and secrecy about this man, but it was not a malicious suspicion. Kas had light hair and grey eyes. All of the riders wore the earthy, dark colors Erisha had glimpsed the day before and all seemed very comfortable in their practical clothing and gear, including Anarim. Erisha both struggled to look at the King but also desperately wished to study him. No one would have expected the King of Alland to be roaming the realms and certainly no one expected to meet him roaming.

"Where are we headed?" Erisha asked, looking to Anarim. "You mentioned that we're near the border."

"Erisha, he's looking for Father as well," Dumur interjected excitedly.

"We should ride, and I'll explain as we go," Anarim replied.

The King lifted Erisha into Erisha's saddle while Girisu held the horse's reins to keep the creature steady. Being helped up on to the horse so easily made Erisha feel like a young girl again. She straightened her back and composed herself.

Girisu handed her the reins. "Are you well, my lady?" he asked. "I can lead Kuranga for a while if you wish."

"I am well," Erisha said firmly but with a smile. "Thank you. Did Dumur reveal everything including our horses' names?" She glanced over at her brother ruefully.

Girisu smiled and the veil of his stony expression lifted. Erisha guessed that he was younger than the King and his other companions yet a little older than Kas appeared to be. "Your brother has been conscience for a while longer than you have, and he has told us many things."

"Oh dear," Erisha lamented. "I hope he's behaved himself." The group started out across the expanse of tall grasses that was gradually becoming rockier.

"He's an admirable youth," Girisu said. "Very just and passionate. He will make a good warrior one day."

Erisha smiled. "I hope so."

Dumur fell back beside Erisha. "Are you well?"

"I think so," Erisha replied as Girisu rode up farther by the King. "Are you alright?"

"Yes, I'm alright," Dumur said. "A bit banged up, but it's my fault."

Erisha noticed his arm wrapped tightly where he had been nicked by the arrow. "What happened? Why are these men here and what does it have to do with Father?" Erisha asked.

"Sire," Dumur called through the group to Anarim as they trotted along at a steady pace. "Would you mind recounting your purpose and what happened yesterday for my sister?"

"Not at all," the King said. He reined back his horse until he was beside the siblings. "To start at the beginning, Kas approached me four days ago, informing me that a royal message had been sent to Lord Ansira and that Furunian troops had been ordered, by me, to go to the Felrisa-Furun border. I sent no such order. I have a good idea of who did forge the message, but I needed to make sure first. I did not want to alert or intimidate any enemies of the kingdom yet, so I chose some of my most trusted and skilled men and we headed towards the border to scout out the problem and see if the situation could be rectified. We were about a day away from the border when we saw the other group of riders, Felrisan warriors in Furun. They were not travelers. Sensing something was amiss, we decided to follow them. Then," and here Anarim glanced at the siblings, his green eyes bright with amusement, "we came upon you two. The Lekur were attacking you. When this young man, Lord Dumur, saw us approaching he had sense enough to call out to us and tell us who he was. Upon hearing that you were both children of the realm's Steward, we rushed to your aid with greater freedom than we had been before. In the skirmish that followed, all but one of the Felrisan warriors were cut down. They would not relent. Abkur was wounded, but other than that we did not suffer any injury."

Erisha nodded sympathetically, now noticing the makeshift cast that held up Abkur's left arm under his coat.

"We are tracking the last Lekur. He fled as his comrades were dying and headed back West. We are hoping he leads us to some answers involving your father and his men," Anarim finished grimly.

CHAPTER THREE

A MOMENT OF TRUTH

T he landscape was quiet in the early morning as they rode along. It was a misty, damp morning and the birds were sleeping in longer than usual. The fog was thick enough that Erisha could not see the Gisgal Mountains, still far in front of them. As time passed by, the sun rose high enough and burned bright enough to dissolve the fog and it was soon a clear day.

The Sadurra siblings listened to conversations between Girisu and Sidukur who rambled on about previous adventures and missions that they had individually or jointly completed. When they talked about individual experiences, there seemed to be a friendly competition and rivalry underlying their comments, and, when they talked about their outings together, they were fondly reminiscing even if one of them had been nearly killed. Abkur chuckled and shook his head often, interrupting whenever the men recounted their stories inaccurately. Anarim did not usually engage but smiled at all the right moments which showed that he was listening even if he looked preoccupied or lost in thought. Kas, Erisha noticed, hardly spoke or reacted except for a few times when the men laughed about some memory and Kas' eyes lit up and a small smile appeared on his lips.

Erisha and Dumur grew comfortable in the group: Dumur fairly quickly and happily and Erisha as much as she could with being the only woman present. During one of the rare times that Kas actually spoke, he informed Erisha that a Felrisan horse with a note had been sent to the village of Furun for her mother to ensure the Stewardess of her children's whereabouts and safety with the King. Kas explained that if either of the siblings had been conscious they may have sent them back, but knowing that there had been Felrisan warriors headed towards the village with unfriendly motives, the men had deemed it wiser to take the two wounded with them since they did not want to lose the deserter's trail.

"But how would the horse know the way?" Dumur asked. "It's never been to the village."

"I have a gift with animals," Kas replied simply and modestly. "I'm sure the horse and message will reach your ailing mother."

Erisha glanced up at him sharply, realizing that their mother likely was worried for them. They had been gone for more than a day now. "Thank you," she said quietly, thoughtful.

The horses' ears began to perk and their noses began to flare as the sun neared the center of the sky. Anarim and Girisu had taken turns tracking the fleeing Lekur. At the moment, Girisu was leading the way. A dark lump lay in the grass in front of them before a small hill. They approached and looked down at a dead man wearing black, blue, and silver. Erisha recognized him as one of the Lekur who had attacked them.

The King sighed. He dismounted and pulled the dead man over to a sole tree that offered some shade. He arranged the body with one hand over the chest and the other on the man's sword hilt: a warrior's burial position. The King stood and looked down at the man for a moment then returned to his horse. He mounted his horse.

"Fell out of the saddle?" Abkur mused.

The King nodded. "He was wounded," he said.

"We can't bury him?" Dumur asked, disconcerted.

"We do not have the tools to bury him," Anarim replied solemnly. "But it has been discovered throughout Alland that warriors left in the burial position remain untouched. So, it is the best practice for such instances."

"They are left completely untouched?" Erisha asked.

"Completely," Girisu echoed affirmatively.

The siblings glanced at each other, impressed.

The King looked to Girisu. "Let's explore the area and see if we can figure out where he was headed."

Girisu continued on at the head of the group. Soon, they were climbing the small hill. Girisu paused cautiously near the top, dismounted, and looked over.

"Halt," he said lowly. He continued to stare out for a few moments longer. He looked back down at Anarim and gestured to the King with a tilt of his head.

The King responded instantly and urged his horse to the top of the small hill. Erisha and Dumur were at the back of the line now, having been left by Anarim. The hesitancy and secrecy alarmed Erisha. When she steered Kuranga about, Sidukur stopped her.

"Wait, my dear," he said softly.

Erisha stared at him. He nodded at her and smiled gently. A horrible feeling had settled in her stomach, yet she waited. She looked over at Dumur, but she could not read his expression. He started then slid off Sisi and rushed up the hill. Without another thought, Erisha followed suit.

Anarim and Girisu reached for the siblings, but they avoided their grasps and raced down the other side of the hill. Erisha finally looked up and the sight sickened her. She gasped as she stumbled down the hill and reached the bottom. There was a terrible smell, but Erisha's eyes began to water for a more serious reason. The ground swayed beneath her as she joined Dumur. The tears came swiftly but they could not wash away the images now in her mind.

The field sprawling before them was blanketed with fallen warriors. The colors of Furun, brown, gold, and green, covered the grass as dead men lay in their own blood. Erisha was certain the whole company had perished. Drops of blue and silver mixed with the brown and gold, but the field mainly glistened gold in the midday sun.

Shocked tears continued to flood Erisha's cheeks. Where did the bodies of her father and brother lay in the aftermath of such a massacre? They would never be able to find them. She felt Dumur fall beside her and hug her close. She felt his own tears on her cheek as they gripped each other.

As quickly as the tears had come, Erisha stopped crying. Her whole being felt limp, lifeless. She breathed slowly, staring out over the field as her head rested on Dumur's shoulder. What would they do? Her mind was blank, everything was numb.

"Erisha," Dumur said sharply, his eyes also drying now.

Erisha sniffed but closed her eyes, wishing she was still home and asleep in her bed and with her mother. Oh, her mother! Her poor mother!

"Erisha!" Dumur exclaimed.

Erisha pulled away. "What?" she asked weakly.

"Listen," Dumur ordered.

She listened and the sound floated across the field feebly. Erisha felt blood rush through her body again. Her eyes snapped to Dumur.

"That's…" he said.

"Our signal!" Erisha said.

"Esirim," Dumur agreed.

The siblings looked about wildly. Esirim's bird call whistled out again from across the field and from over by a small grove of trees.

"What does the signal mean?" Abkur asked as the men joined them, leading their horses. All their faces were grave as they took in the scene before them, but the King's was particularly pained.

"It's our brother's," Dumur explained.

"It's a warning," Erisha added slowly, realization dawning. She stared out over the field, puzzled.

"Perhaps we should heed it," the old man said, eyes scanning cautiously.

"But he's alive somewhere," Erisha replied. "We must find him."

"He'll be able to tell us what happened," Sidukur offered.

"Whatever we decide, a decision should be made soon," Kas said, his voice calm yet also holding a sense of urgency that confused Erisha for a moment before her attention returned to her unseen brother.

Dumur pointed toward a grove of trees to their right ahead of them. "The call is coming from over there."

Anarim gestured for them to lead the way.

Erisha and Dumur headed quickly toward the trees, their horses faithfully following them. The most efficient way would have been to walk through the battlefield, but Erisha and Dumur knew that not only would the attempt be miserable but also disrespectful. As they neared the trees, Erisha almost broke into a run but was stopped by Abkur.

The old man held her back with his uninjured arm. "Young lady," he said sharply.

"Wait," Anarim ordered simultaneously while they were still a few paces from the grove. "I'll not have us drawn into an ambush.

Erisha looked up at Abkur and paused.

A few tense seconds passed, but then a figure appeared from within the brush. The young man limped drastically, and his left arm hung at his side. Erisha stared at him.

"Esirim," she cried.

Her elder brother looked towards her, and she rushed to him. Esirim clung to her with his good arm, but, as she was holding him, Erisha realized how wounded he really was. Cuts, bruises, and dirt covered his face and his clothes underneath his pieces of armor were dried stiff with blood. He was dirty and disheveled and felt thin and weak. She took a few steps back and could only stare at him.

"What happened, man?" Sidukur asked despairingly as they entered the grove after Erisha.

Esirim straightened. "And who are all of you?" he returned, his hand resting on his sword hilt.

"King Anarim and this is my small company," the King said, stepping forward.

"I would kneel, but I would remain on the ground if I did, sire," Esirim replied, inclining his head.

The King acquiesced with a short wave of a hand. "I'm here to discover the origin of the false summons."

"False indeed!" Esirim spat out angrily. "We were welcomed by the whole Felrisan army after we had set up camp for the night and the darkness had fallen. We were slaughtered. That my father and I are alive is laughable and only due to the extreme loyalty and love of our men."

"Father's alive?" Erisha and Dumur exclaimed.

"Where is he?" Dumur demanded, stepping to move past his brother.

Esirim stopped him. "He is alive," he said, "but that is all. He is no longer responsive."

Erisha stared at Esirim then looked passed him into the brush as Dumur took a few numb steps back. "I want to see him," she said.

"No," Esirim replied.

"Why not?" Erisha demanded.

"It would only do you harm," Esirim said. "He is not well, Erisha."

Erisha felt a wave of anger wash through her and stiff her whole body.

"You all should leave," Esirim said before she could speak. "There have been scouts about these past few days. I've lost much blood. We will die amongst our men."

"I think not," Anarim replied. "If the Steward still lives, he must be gotten home. Along with you."

"Agreed, my lord," Abkur said. "I will head back with them as guide and guard."

Anarim nodded. "Very well." He turned and stared back across the field as they stood in the shade of the trees. "Lord Kankal's intentions must be discovered."

"I imagine they are nothing but antagonistic, sire," Esirim said dryly.

Anarim eyed him sharply but inclined his head in agreement. "There is no doubt," the King replied. "I meant his strategy."

Esirim bowed his head. "My lord," he acquiesced.

"These two will return with you," Anarim stated, looking to Erisha and Dumur.

Both Erisha and Dumur looked to the King, and Erisha felt relief spread throughout her body. She would be able to see her father. And if this was adventure and seeing the realms, she did not want it — death, battle, pain. They would be returning with their father, but Dumur's expression darkened. He would be restless when they returned.

"We are not alone," Kas said suddenly.

Everyone stilled and Girisu looked out into the open field after eyeing Kas.

"He is right," Girisu said a moment later. "There are at least three riders coming from the North."

"You cannot lead them here," Esirim demanded. "It'll be the end of my father."

Anarim nodded. "We will meet them," he said. "We will not risk hiding here with so many people. Abkur, stay with the Steward and his son and lead them to their home once the way is clear. There is no room to decently hide more than two horses here. The young Lady and Lord must rush across to the trees on the other side and hope the Lekur fail to see them." He looked to Erisha and Dumur. "Now," he ordered.

Erisha took her pack and weapons from Kuranga's back and mounted on Sisi behind Dumur as they silently decided to leave Kuranga with Abkur for Esirim and their father. Esirim raised his arm in salute and farewell. Erisha raised her arm, but Dumur refused to. With one sweeping look over them all, he ordered Sisi into a sprint and Erisha gripped around his waist.

They bent down low against Sisi's back and prayed the horse would not trample or trip over any of the bodies. They made it across, however, without difficulty. Erisha slid out of the saddle, breathing heavily. Dumur jumped down and led Sisi into the shadows and hid behind some brush. Erisha followed and they waited.

The King and his company, excluded Abkur and the two horses, rode around the field to the front at the North to the edge of the battle's aftermath. They waited and spoke amongst themselves before turning away and putting their backs to the potential enemy.

"Fools," Erisha heard Dumur mutter.

She glared at him reprovingly.

"They're putting themselves at greater risk," Dumur retorted.

"For us and father," Erisha hissed.

Dumur sighed and his expression softened.

Two Lekur rode up from around a rocky mound and approached the King.

Erisha exchanged a glance with Dumur, and they grabbed their bows and notched arrows. She heard Dumur breathe deeply beside her, and Erisha reminded herself to take a breath. They squinted through the shadow and the sun glinting off the men's armor to watch how the situation would unfold.

All of a sudden, everyone drew their weapons. Erisha bit her lip. Dumur raised his bow.

Erisha gasped and grabbed to lower it. "What are you doing? Will you have blood on your hands?"

"Is it not my fate to have them bloodied eventually?" he asked. "Also," he said gesturing ahead of them to the men, "he is our King."

"To kill from a hidden location, from so far away, in such a manner, is not honorable," she replied. "They can take care of themselves."

Dumur lowed his bow, chastened.

One of the Felrisans raised his sword high and it shone in the sun. The siblings watched tensely, but no blows were exchanged. There was the sound of thunder, but the sky was clear. Then Erisha realized it was not thunder, but horses' hooves. From several directions, more Felrisan riders appeared until there were at least a dozen surrounding Anarim and his men.

Loud, hard words were said then there was the clash of metal against metal.

"Now?" Dumur asked irritably, his bow raised long with his eyebrow. "This is clearly unfair." He hardly waited for her nod before he loosed an arrow.

Erisha raised her bow and aimed but hesitated while Dumur loosed another shaft and another man was punctured.

There was a loud yell, and a few riders turned in the direction of the siblings' hiding place.

"Erisha!" Dumur commanded as the riders raced towards them.

Erisha raised her bow and released. Her arrow sunk into a man's shoulder between the pieces of armor. But the riders kept their pace. Dumur shot the other two while Erisha struck the same man again.

Finally, after Dumur shot him through the eye, one man fell. The other two, however, were already upon them. A sword swung down at them. The siblings ducked, but part of Dumur's bow was clipped and the weapon was broken by the blow. Sisi reared and whinnied as the two riders, injured but clearly unfazed, rode about the Sadurras.

Erisha shot the man who had swung at them, but her arrow only buried in his side. The other rider grabbed Dumur, but the boy had drawn his knife and the man dropped Dumur after his hand was severely cut. A hand came down on Erisha's head as she had just notched another arrow and a rider pulled up on her hair harshly. Erisha's eyes watered as she cried out in pain.

She dropped her bow, and her hands grasped the man's arm. Dumur froze but eyed both men.

"Stand down, boy," the rider who held Erisha said. "Drop the knife." He raised the sword toward Erisha's neck.

Dumur clenched his jaw but obeyed.

The man slowly lowered Erisha. She dropped back down onto her heels and rushed over to Dumur. The riders circled them.

There was a yell from where the main fight was happening. The men paused.

"Come with us," the rider with the injured hand ordered.

Erisha and Dumur exchanged a glance then swiftly grabbed the packs from Sisi's back before following the man's horse while the other rider came after them.

"Hurry up," the man behind them growled and they were forced into a run.

They were herded over to where Anarim and his men were standing, having been overwhelmed. Sisi tried to follow but one the riders shot at her warningly. Dumur turned on the man who had shot the arrow.

"Shoot at my horse again and I'll kill you," he snapped, advancing fearlessly up to the man on horseback.

The man backed away but sneered at Dumur.

"These were the sneaks," one of the riders announced to the leader of the group.

Two Felrisan warriors had been killed by Anarim and company, but the rest sat tall on their beasts. The King and his men appeared alright other than being at the mercy of such brutes. Erisha and Dumur lowered their heads as they joined the small group surrounded by the Lekur.

"Are you hurt?" Anarim asked them.

"No," they replied quietly.

He nodded and looked up at their captors.

Erisha felt the cold tip of a sword suddenly under her chin and it raised her face up as the King and the others all stiffened. The leader of the group studied her for a moment. He laughed.

"A woman," he said. "We were attacked by a woman in hiding. And by a small youth with spirit and a loose tongue. Where is your honor, boy?"

"At home. Where's yours?" Dumur retorted boldly.

Sidukur knocked Dumur's head warningly.

The leader's eyes narrowed thoughtfully. "Don't worry. We will not tell Lord Kankal about your lack of manliness. We will, however, bring you all back to speak with him. I think he will be interested in questioning such curious travelers like yourselves. Tie their wrists and string them together. There is still quite the journey ahead of us before nightfall."

Two men dismounted and went about with a long rope tying everyone's wrists together and leaving a length of line between each captive. The rope was tied tight, and Erisha grimaced when her wrists were yanked and sinched together roughly. Dumur also winced, but Erisha guessed his wrists were tied even tighter. Their packs were left behind and each captive was stripped of their weapons. Erisha studied each of the riders surrounding them. There seemed to be a shadow over many of their grim faces. They were dressed warmly for the sun shining down on them so strongly. Many of them were wounded, a ruddy, dark color seeping through their layers of blue and black but they all sat proudly in their saddles.

The Lekur organized themselves and set off towards the mountains. Six of the riders, including the leader, rode in the front of the captives while four riders rode behind. Thankfully, they did not pace the horses too quickly so the captives walked at a comfortable step. Everyone was quiet for a long time.

"I hope Sisi and Kuranga make it home," Dumur eventually murmured to Erisha.

"I think they will. They seem to be wiser than us sometimes," she replied. "You acted with honor aiding in balancing an unfair fight, Dumur. Don't listen to them." She eyed the riders darkly.

Dumur nodded but his expression did not brighten.

"The horses will be safe and will return to their stables," Kas said softly behind them. "And you, Lord Dumur, did well for if it wasn't for one of your arrows your King might have died."

Dumur's blue eyes shone, pleased momentarily, since there was something about Kas which ensured that whatever the man said was sincere and true. Erisha watched Kas as they walked, but she could not place him. There was something foreign about Kas which she had never experienced before.

They trudged on until nightfall. There was not much said among either group and hardly anything passed between the groups. Once it became too dark to see anything, they were told to settle down for the night. Two fires were started as the wind's strength began to rise and the temperature decreased, one strong fire for the Lekur and a meager one for the prisoners. But Erisha was grateful for what they were given because it was quickly getting colder. Anarim and his company blocked the wind as best they could, sitting around Erisha and Dumur who were nearest to the fire. Exhausted, Erisha fell asleep soon after eating a little bread and dried fruit that the Lekur threw at them.

They were all woken when the sun rose the next morning, and they trekked on. The day passed slowly and, as the ground grew more rocky and jagged and hilly. The mountains grew larger and larger as they continuously approached. Erisha had to look up to see the tops of the mountains now. In the afternoon, they began to ascend the mountains, and Erisha could no longer see the tops. At this point, she could not gaze up at the towering tops since she was focusing on where to step so not to twist an ankle or damage her boots. Dumur and she travelled in a state of wonder, trying to study the thin mountain paths and the coarse mountain vegetation. The wing was dangerously strong and biting at times and they marveled at its frequent energy here. The Lekur had all dismounted and were leading their horses while all travelled in single file.

They made their way up slowly on a path that went back and forth, and Erisha enjoyed, during the few times she felt safe enough, looking out to the East to the low, wide valley below that stretched out into the open field country. The fading, deep golden sunlight washed over the green expanse below which stretched across a long way to the Igi Mountains on the other side in the far East. She would have loved to just stop and sit and stare with the wind whipping her hair about to take in the beauty and elegance of the low country that was her home. Yet, her slight hesitation to steal a glimpse caused a disruption in the line so she quickly pushed such longings away.

As the sun began to set, Erisha started to worry about having to traverse the rocky, unstable mountain paths in the dark.

"I don't know how we'll make camp up here," Erisha said to Dumur, hoping her voice was loud enough over the wind for him to hear but not to carry to everyone else.

"I'm sure they do," Dumur replied unconcernedly, looking at the Lekur. "It'd probably be fun. We've never seen anywhere like this. Did you see the view?"

Erisha smiled. "I did. It was incredible."

"I could get used to a view like that," Dumur remarked.

Erisha nodded slowly. "Home is down there though."

Dumur's smile faded. "I hope Mother is alright." His attention snapped back to Erisha, his eyes wide and she suddenly knew what — or, rather, who — he was thinking about. "I wonder…" He nearly tripped and Erisha helped steady him.

She leaned forward and said near his ear. "I hope so."

They hiked quietly again for a while until, just as the last rays of sunlight were fading, Erisha noticed that the leader at the front disappeared with his horse around a corner that did not seem to exist. Another rider and his steed disappeared into the mountain. As she neared the area, she realized they were entering a tunnel in the side of the mountain. The entrance was dark and small, just tall enough for a horse standing up to enter.

She heard Dumur take a shaky breath as he followed Girisu in, and she wished she could pause and obtain a greater feeling of courage before she followed. But there was no stopping: into the darkness they went.

CHAPTER FOUR

UNDER THE MOUNTAIN

It felt like a long time before Erisha's eyes grew accustomed to the darkness. Once she finally felt she could see a little, she realized there really was not much to see. They continued on a fairly level path that contained sudden turns and bends in the road. She sensed, however, that with every few turns they returned to the general direction in which they had started in by heading straight into the mountain. Yet, Erisha did not really know: she was in a dark mountain tunnel, one hand on her brother's shoulder in front of her for comfort, and her sense of direction could be inaccurate.

She only really heard the steps of the men and the horses on the rock floor and the breathing of all as they marched on. It felt like they had been wandering for a long time when Erisha seemed to see light ahead of her on the path. She blinked and realized what she saw were small lanterns hanging on the walls. Inside the lanterns, there were large, slowly burning candles and their soft glow was bright enough for Erisha to see Dumur's golden curls encircling his head in front of her. Her eyes adapted to using such light so that she could see a few people ahead of her in the line.

The tunnels appeared to be widening and soon Erisha could walk beside Dumur. A low noise that was not the sound of footfalls or breathing began to prick her ears. It grew steadily louder as they travelled on until it was loud enough for Erisha to realize it was the drum and din of activity. Before she knew what was happening, the tunnel opened up and light flooded in from a huge open space that was so much larger than the Hall back in Furun. If Erisha took time to think about it, she would have realized that the room was actually closer to the size of the village in Furun than the Manor.

People filled the wide, open space in the mountainous rock they were in. Children ran around, laughing and playing, while adults worked right before everyone's eyes, butchering, blacksmithing, cobbling, carpentering, sewing, cooking, and so many other activities. A few young men ran up when the Felrisans entered and took the horses from the warriors. Erisha watched as they guided the animals to the far end of the room where it looked like they had set up their stable area.

"This is extraordinary," Dumur whispered. "They carved out the middle of a mountain."

Erisha looked up and the ceiling was high above their heads. Yet, it looked flat and there were large holes every now and again.

"For the smoke," Sidukur said behind her. She looked back at him, and he gestured over to the large fire pit nearby that contained a warm, raging fire. "Smoke rises and it can't stay in here."

Erisha followed the embers rising above the bonfire with her eyes and watched as the smoke rose and flowed toward the closest opening in the ceiling. Huge makeshift chandeliers hung from the ceilings and could be hoisted down and back up with ropes secured on the walls. She realized she was gaping, and she quickly lowered her head and closed her mouth.

The warriors led their captives across the room and some of the Lekur they passed by looked up from their work or play. Some faces wore curious expressions as they momentarily took in the strange prisoners, but most looked disinterested. The floor was smooth and clean underfoot. Scattered through the expansive area, thick pillars stretched from the floor to the ceiling and also seemed to be used as dividers between different types of activity. As they approached the other side of the room, Erisha saw they were headed towards another tunnel with a large opening. There seemed to be several different tunnel entrances in the walls of the room. They entered the one tunnel and Erisha lamented leaving the magnificent area behind her. It was so full of laughter and activity that a sense of comradery seemed to permeate from it so that even though they were all under a mountain and had no natural light Erisha did not feel trapped.

It grew quiet in the tunnel again, but this section did not last long. The main tunnel branched off several times in different directions, but they continued on. Soon, they were in a normal-sized room with a long table and many chairs on one side of the room and one large chair separated from the rest and at the back of the room. It functioned as a throne, and a large grey-haired man was seated in it. Two men spoke to him from a distance. Their conversation stopped as the captives were ushered in.

"What is this?" the grey-haired man asked curtly.

"Skilled warriors, my liege," the leader said. "We found them examining the dead Furunian warriors."

There was a pause. "Bring them forth," the enthroned man commanded.

The prisoners were shoved forward, and they all walked up to the man in the chair and his face was stern. Erisha saw the grey-haired man's eyes alight with recognition once Anarim was near enough — the room, like every other space so far, was lit by many torches and lanterns hanging from the walls.

"Ah," the man sighed complacently.

"Lord Kankal," Anarim greeted flatly.

Erisha and Dumur exchanged a glance.

Lord Kankal Nidugul raised a hand and looked to his warriors. "Leave us," he ordered.

"Sire, these men are more than adept at defending themselves," the leader began.

"I said, leave us," Lord Kankal repeated icily.

Without another word, the warriors left the room, and the other two men approached Lord Kankal again.

"Your majesty," Lord Kankal greeted amusedly. "This is a surprise. You leave your haven in Zari and come to visit me here?"

"Do you expect me to ignore the fact that a whole company of men lay dead on Felrisan-Furunian border?" Anarim replied coolly.

Lord Kankal sighed. "I know. I do not like the loss of life either, but they were a necessary sacrifice. Furun has always been too loyal to the ruling family."

"You have slaughtered some of my people, Kankal," Anarim growled. "You lured Ansira into a trap under false pretenses, forging my signature. Your sins must be and will be dealt with."

"Not while you're under my roof, I'm afraid," Lord Kankal said. "You see, my people do not know much about you, intentionally. You have no power here because no one, except a special few," he gestured to the two men, "like my advisors, will recognize you or believe your claims if you tried to convince them."

"You forcibly have your citizens live under a mountain, blind, deluded, and naïve," Anarim accused.

"They are not unhappy," Lord Kankal said with a wave of his hand. "But I am unhappy. With you. You do not deserve the throne in Zari, Anarim. Your father may have died, but you are young and inexperienced. Your mother is dead as well, yes? So, you have no one wise and practiced enough to advise you. You are not fit to rule."

"Do not disrespect my parents by invoking them in such a conversation," Anarim replied coolly. "And refrain from disrespecting my advisors who have been sources of great wisdom even before I was crowned."

Erisha eyed the King. It was true that his ascent to power came at an unusually young age, but it had not been Anarim's choice. His father had died prematurely, his mother following soon after. Thus, though new Kings were coronated around the time of their forty-fifth spring in the past generations, Anarim had been crowned fifteen springs earlier than most and after a period of great mourning. Some realms like Furun and Abaki had welcomed Anarim Askatte as their King while the others had remained quiet. The views of the Fasur in Semusak were normally mysterious, but they responded when needed and acted respectfully. The Lekur were a loyal, hot-headed people, and they had respected Anarim's father, so their silence had not been interpreted as a threat. Erisha's father had been impressed with Anarim's management so far in his reign; he praised the young King's confidence and humility when dealing with small conflicts and organizing the annual gathering of the Stewards. Anarim was known as a wise, clear-sighted warrior who had led the suppression of the Lerisaba's rebellion in Abaki a year before the previous King's death, and the people of Alland had no reason to doubt Anarim.

Lord Kankal, however, seemed to be an exception to this assurance.

"I held your father in high regard, Anarim," Lord Kankal continued, ignoring Anarim's comment. "I did not always agree with him, and he could become annoyingly inquisitive. Yet, he led well. But you… your situation is unheard of. We have never even had a Steward in power as young as you are, and we were expected to simply accept you. I think not."

"So, you have poisoned your people against my existence," Anarim answered, "and are bent on destroying my closest allies. Then, I assume, destroying myself?"

"That sums it up nicely, yes," Lord Kankal said, looking pleased.

"I had made no ill-advised or faulty choice in my rule," Anarim exclaimed. "You have no grounds for such base, traitorous actions."

"I have my reasons, Anarim. My choices are not unfounded. Yet, I personally do not think I need to explain myself, least of all to you," Lord Kankal said. He paused and, as Anarim studied with narrowed eyes, a small smile stretched across his face. "I have long wished, and, it has been a wish of my family, to see a member of the Kidugul dynasty on the throne in Zari. And, as I have no daughter of my own to entice you with, this seems a far better course in such time of opportunity. For you are young and, ultimately, merely tolerated by the realms since you are untried. And, at this moment, I believe you have made your first mistake by leaving your home without its King and by allowing yourself to become my prisoner. Your reign, my dear boy, looks to be over. Very short indeed. And quite nice for me since you are without heir or wife. Less death. Now, evening is upon us so we should show you to your quarters for the night while I decide how to execute you all tomorrow." He looked to

Erisha. "I'm sorry, my dear, but I'm afraid you've joined the wrong group of people. Maybe if you begged prettily and renounced the King, I might let you live…"

Erisha raised her chin. "I'm quite sure when I belong, thank you," she replied.

Dumur stood nearer to her while Sidukur placed a hand on her shoulder.

Lord Kankal's eyes narrowed curiously. "Your names, children," he required.

Erisha swallowed, unsure, but Dumur answered for her.

"We are Sadurras," he said proudly, "and you will answer for what you did to our father and his men."

Lord Kankal was silent for a moment. "Kian!" he suddenly called, and his voice echoed about the room and down the tunnelway.

Everyone waited then heard the echo of someone hurrying through the tunnel. The leader of the riders who had captured them appeared.

"Kian, how did these children come to be with this company?" Lord Kankal asked, and Erisha could not read the older man's expression.

"I don't know, my lord," Kian replied. "We found them hiding in the brush while the others were out in the open. They killed Namus."

"A woman attacked you?" Lord Kankal mused, eyes alight oddly.

Kian hung his head while Erisha debated if she should interject. She looked over to Anarim and he subtly shook his head to warn her from speaking. Erisha pursed her lips and looked down.

"A young swordswoman," Lord Kankal stated.

"Archer, actually," Dumur corrected, breaking the silence.

Lord Kankal's attention flickered to Dumur for a moment. "Quiet, boy," he ordered. "There is no honor in hiding behind a bush."

"You're hiding in a mountain," Dumur retorted but then he closed his mouth as Anarim placed a hand on his shoulder.

"Kian, summon Mita and clear the arena," Lord Kankal said, returning his attention to Erisha.

The warrior left to obey.

"Kankal," Anarim said warningly.

In response, Lord Kankal let out a yell that caused them all to jump. It was a terrible, loud scream that seemed to reverberate through the whole mountain. Erisha wanted to bend down and cover her head, prepared for the ceiling to cave in. But the ceiling did not fall. Instead, warriors poured into the room and stood at attention before Lord Kankal.

"Let us escort our guests out to the arena," Lord Kankal said calmly, and his gaze rested on Erisha again.

Anarim stepped in front of Erisha as Lord Kankal stood from his chair. "Kankal," he said again, a low growl in his tone.

Lord Kankal gestured to his men and within moments each member of the King's company including the Sadurra siblings were in the hold of two warriors.

"Peace, Anarim," Lord Kankal said dismissively. "It is an act of mercy."

Anarim and his friends struggled against their captors while Erisha and Dumur were hurried out of the room behind Lord Kankal. They were brought back into the huge room and Kian was shouting. The people slowly who rose from their work and play. Furniture and tools were moved and before Erisha could rightly assess the situation, she was brought into an open circle while Dumur, Anarim, and the others were held back on the edge in front of the growing crowd.

Lord Kankal entered the circle and all the Lekur pressing in quieted their cries of confusion and interest. A young woman near Erisha's age waiting on the edge of the circle answered the silent beckoning of Lord Kankal's raised arm in her direction. She tried to mask her confusion, but Erisha sensed she was as perplexed as herself.

"My Felrisans," Lord Kankal's voice boomed in the wide openness, "today my daughter, Mita, will best this," Lord Kankal pointed to Erisha, "ignoble young woman who killed one of our men, Namus, in hiding."

Erisha looked about in shock and the room was horribly silent.

"This match," Lord Kankal said, a hand on Mita's shoulder, "will be to the death."

"No!"

Erisha looked over to where Dumur was struggling valiantly against two Lekur. They both punched him in the stomach and Dumur crumbled to his knees. Anarim, Girisu, and Sidukur all looked at her, their faces contorted in anguish, but they were already subdued by several men. Anarim, the King himself, had been gagged. Kas watched everything unfolding with a puzzled expression on his face.

The warriors holding Erisha released their grasp and cut her bonds. Then one warrior handed her his sword. Erisha, stunned, held the heavy weapon in her hand. She knew how to wield a sword. All women in Furun were taught at a certain age how to defend themselves with most weapons, but Erisha's father had always emphasized that to see a Furunian woman in battle would be a time of swiftly approaching tragedy.

Erisha looked over across the circle at Mita. The young Lekur was pretty with soft brown hair pulled back, intelligent eyes, and an attractive mouth. Yet, when Erisha's gaze met hers, Mita stepped into an attack position. Her eyes apologized to Erisha and revealed her own fear, but the young woman swung her sword in her hand nonetheless.

Lord Kankal approached Erisha. "Your time has come, my dear," he said, and he stroked her cheek with the back of his hand. His touch was rough and cold. Erisha turned away. He did not react except to say: "It's a pity. Blue-eyed, golden-haired. Such beauty gone to waste." He turned away from her and joined the crowd outside the circle.

Erisha looked over to Mita again. The two young women began to circle one another. Erisha tested the weight of the sword in her hand. It was heavier than any weapon she normally used, and she wished for her own sword. Erisha did not want to kill Mita; she did not want to kill anyone.

Mita's hesitation seemed to suggest the same sentiment.

"Mita!" Lord Kankal demanded.

The young woman's shoulders dropped and she breathed shakily. Then, fast as could be, she tensed and ran at Erisha. Erisha raised her sword to parry Mita's blow and she swung hard. The blades met with a deafening clang and then a scrape as they slid apart. Erisha backed away and studied Mita, her focus narrowing to ignore the crowd around them. She clenched her jaw and blocked another of Mita's blows. She swung her sword and Mita parried her blade. Erisha's sword was ridiculously heavy in her hands as she gripped it tightly: she would not be able to keep this up for long. Mita swung again and Erisha ducked and spun back, feeling the swish of air from the blade passing by above her head.

Erisha made a critical decision. She dropped the sword and dodged another of Mita's attacks. Without carrying the sword, Erisha felt lighter and more energetic. She spun down onto her hands, and, swinging out one of her legs, she tripped Mita. Mita fell, her sword clanging down loudly on the rock floor. Erisha leapt up and hurried placed a foot over hilt of Mita's sword. Mita groaned as her hand was pinned under the hilt.

"Leave it," Erisha ordered.

Mita eyed her then swung her legs up, smacking Erisha in the back. Erisha jerked forward with a cry. It was enough movement to release Mita's sword, and the young woman dragged the blade away from Erisha as she stood. They glared at each other, waiting. Erisha eyed her sword but knew she did not stand a chance either way. Mita charged.

"Stop!" came a loud demand.

Mita halted mid-swing as Erisha rolled to the side. Both young women looked over at Dumur. Everyone looked at Dumur, but Dumur kept his eyes on Lord Kankal. Before the old man could grow angry, Dumur pleaded his case.

"I killed your man Namus," Dumur said. "I was the one who convinced my sister to help me shoot your men. I am the one with the Felrisan blood on my hands." Dumur glared at the Steward under the mountain. "I will fight to the death. Not my sister."

Everyone held their breath while Lord Kankal deliberated.

"You're only causing your sister more misery, boy," Lord Kankal said, but he gestured to the warriors who held Dumur.

The warriors released Dumur and shoved him into the circle. The sword was retrieved. Erisha was seized and dragged out of the ring.

"Wait," she argued. "Dumur. Let me go! Dumur, stop!"

"Silence her," Lord Kankal ordered.

Erisha was swiftly gagged as she twisted and pulled against strong, rough hands.

The sword was thrown back into the circle. It clanged on the stone floor. Dumur stooped down and picked up the weapon, weighing it in his hand. His gaze shifted from Erisha to Mita, eyeing his opponent cautiously.

Mita looked to Lord Kankal and then to a young man on the edge of the ring, but when no help came from either she rolled her shoulders and began to walk about the circle. Dumur also eyed Lord Kankal then took a deep breath and walked to meet her. The crowd remained quiet but soft whispers began to pass among the people. Erisha risked a glance over at Anarim and his friends. They still stood tense but some of the agitation had left their faces. Even Kas looked relieved. Now, they all watched Dumur's and Mita's steps intently.

Mita positioned herself to swing but Dumur anticipated and was already swinging. Mita managed to block his blow and try at him again, but Dumur parried hers and struck hard against her blade. Mita backed away and they circled each other. Dumur was at least a few years younger than Mita, Erisha thought, but he had been trained well. Erisha did not know anything about Mita's training but, having met Lord Kankal, Mita would not be easy to best. Yet, she also knew that Dumur, a hard look in his eyes now, would not give in.

The two struck back and forth many times before Erisha realized that Dumur was not using his full strength against Mita. There were openings he purposefully missed. The crowd soon knew it too.

"Quit messing with her," someone shouted.

Even Lord Kankal was irritated. "Kill, boy!" he said.

Dumur lowered his sword. "Will you have your own daughter die?" he asked in disbelief.

"I have no children," Lord Kankal replied coldly.

Mita swung while Dumur was distracted but he noticed and reacted in time as the crowd all gasped. Dumur gave a series of blows back and forth and Mita lost her balance and fell with a cry.

"Yield," Dumur said as he pointed the tip of his blade at her neck.

Mita glanced up at him and she rolled away and got up onto her feet. She sliced her blade against him with renewed vigor, but soon her energy gave way and Dumur had her on her knees again.

"Yield!" he yelled.

Mita looked up at him, breathing heavily. She rested her forehead on the wide part of Dumur's sword blade. He waited, poised. A moment later, Mita's sword fell from her hand onto the floor. The clang echoed up to the high ceilings.

"I yield," Mita said clearly.

Erisha breathed a sigh of relief.

The crowd erupted while Dumur lowered his sword and surprised Mita by helping her up. Yet, with an angry cry from Lord Kankal, Dumur was seized by a warrior again and the captives were forced through the crowd.

"Put them away for the night," Lord Kankal declared. "They will be gotten rid of in the morning." He pulled Kian aside for a moment, eyes on Erisha, and whispered something in his warrior's ear. The way Lord Kankal stared at Erisha made her blood run cold.

They were shoved down a different tunnel. They trekked along in the dim firelight. It felt like they were descending, and they walked for a while. Finally, they stopped but there was no doorway or break to a different tunnel. Kian pointed to a large hole at the bottom of the right wall.

"In you go," he said. He turned to the warriors who held Erisha. "Take her to a different cell."

"What?" Erisha panicked, her voice muffled by her gag.

The tunnel was suddenly filled with voices as everyone shouted and argued. Sidukur somehow freed himself from his captors and managed to free Erisha. He placed her behind him, protected. The Lekur drew their weapons and positioned themselves around the small company.

"Alright!" Kian cried, raising his arms. "Never mind. Everyone, get in."

The tunnel quieted.

A different warrior brought up a rope ladder and dropped it down the hole. Anarim was ungagged and untied, and he stepped forward to go first. Carefully, he tested the warrior's hold on the ladder then he slowly climbed down into the hole. Dumur followed after a weary look around. Erisha tensed as she watched him ascend but she was suddenly ungagged and pushed forward. She felt like crying, the shock and exhaustion from the day settling in. A dark hole was the last place she wanted to go, but she descended next.

The cool rock walls surrounding her seemed to close in, but the hole was more than big enough to fit her. Holding onto the rope for dear life, she carefully felt her way down with her feet onto each new rung below. Finally, her foot reached rock.

"Who is it?" Anarim asked in the darkness.

"Erisha," she replied.

There was silence for a moment. Someone moved beside her as her eyes adjusted to the darkness. A hand reached out and touched her arm, and Erisha felt Dumur's hand. Erisha pulled him into a hug, and he gripped her tightly.

"Thank you," Erisha whispered. She brushed his curls back as he relaxed slightly.

Kas was descending, however, and they had to move. Both siblings moved around their prison, and Erisha kept a hand on Dumur's arm. They made their way over to a small hole just big enough for a face to look out. It pointed straight out like a window and Erisha smelled the fresh night air. The moon's light was shining across the sky, but she could not see the moon. The little window was deep and hardly helped to light the room. Their prison remained dark and dusty.

Erisha moved away from the window as Dumur looked out. Girisu and Sidukur had joined them.

"They pulled up the ladder," Girisu informed.

Something came bumping down the passage and suddenly a torch fell onto the ground with a sputter, sparks flying. Girisu picked up the dying torch and they looked around the chamber. It was not very wide, but it was long. Kas pointed out a small lantern by the orifice. Girisu lit the lantern after a few attempts then handed the torch to Anarim.

Erisha felt better having the light from the lantern, no matter how weak the flame was. She could at least see everyone's faces now if they were facing the lantern. She sat down by the window and Dumur joined her. They leaned against one another, and Erisha felt her heartbeat slow for the first time that day.

Anarim wedged the torch between two rocks on the other end of the chamber. The floor was not polished out like the floors in the tunnels or other rooms they had been in thus far. The men eventually sat also, and it was quiet for a spell.

Erisha watched the torch burn and flicker. The bit of smoke produced rose and found its way to a small hole in the ceiling of the chamber. Erisha rose and made her way to stand under the opening, but she did not see any stars.

"They wouldn't want rain pouring in, lass," Sidukur said. "Nor would they want the smoke that escapes to alert outsiders of the real whereabouts of their rooms."

Erisha returned to sit by Dumur.

"You seem to know an awful lot about how things seem to have been constructed here," Dumur stated, and Erisha could not tell if the comment was merely curious or accusatory.

"I've heard tales about the mountains here," Sidukur replied. "I knew they had a tunnel system through the Gisgals, but

I had no idea they had built their whole community under here." He turned to Anarim. "Kankal means business, Anarim. The man controls the people well. We have trouble on our hands."

Anarim looked across at him for a moment then nodded.

"I'd say we have more than trouble," Dumur said. "From how it sounded, we're all going to die tomorrow." His voice was loud but shaky.

"No one's fate is certain," Girisu replied quietly.

"But—"

Anarim interrupted Dumur. "Boy, you need to learn how to hold your tongue," he declared.

It was quiet for a moment and Erisha felt the tension rising.

"I know how to hold my tongue," Dumur retorted, "when it really counts. You, on the other hand… do you know what you're doing at all? We are trapped here, waiting to die, and you're supposed to be leading us!" Dumur was on his feet at this point.

"Boy," Sidukur warned.

"Dumur, you haven't an idea of the gravity or scope of the situation right now," Anarim replied, his own voice rising.

"No, I don't," Dumur admitted.

"If you had listened to me and remained hidden, you wouldn't be here," Anarim said.

"Maybe," Dumur agreed, "but all I know that it feels like I've been the only one *doing* anything! My sister might have died. I stepped in. You would have died if I hadn't loosed an arrow!"

"Dumur Sadurra, sit down!" Sidukur bellowed, rising to his feet.

Dumur took a couple steps back from where he had been advancing on Anarim.

"No, he speaks truth," Anarim said with a sigh. He looked over at Dumur. "You are right. I owe you my life for your arrow did save me from a blow that may have been lethal."

Despite being validated, Dumur hung his head. "I'm sorry," he apologized. "I shouldn't have spoken like that. I shouldn't have spoken at all." He fell back down beside Erisha and hid his face.

The King rose and moved to kneel beside Dumur. He put a hand on the youth's shoulder. Dumur lifted his face and Erisha and Anarim saw the tears in his eyes. At such pain, Erisha felt her own eyes water.

"You did well in the ring, Dumur," Anarim said softly, shaking Dumur slightly. "You saved your sister and you saved me. Do not lose hope. The sun will rise tomorrow, and I am still King of Alland no matter what Lord Kankal says. I have made a mistake, but we will figure something out."

Dumur nodded and put his hand on Anarim's arm before the King stood.

"We should sleep," Anarim said. "We are all tired and we do not know what will happen tomorrow." He sat back down where he had been with Kas.

ERISHA AND THE REALMS

Kas watched the children sitting at the end of the chamber then he turned to Sidukur. "Perhaps," he said, "you know a lullaby."

Sidukur smiled gently and nodded. "Indeed," he replied. He sat back and thought.

Erisha relaxed as well as she could against the stone with Dumur and stared across at the torch's flickering flame.

Taking a breath, Sidukur began to sing, his voice low but pleasant to hear:

The night has come, the stars awake,
Yet it is time for us to sleep;
The sun will rise at dawn's break
And we have promises to keep.

The animals need brought to graze.
The fields need plowed, children need fed.
All to guard against hunger's daze
And the weather's cold before bed.

Such toil bends backs and brings tears,
But our spirit is hard to destroy;
For, although we are burdened by such cares,
We are gifted with laughter and joy.

So, do not weep when the stars wake
Because it is the time to sleep.
The sun will rise and you will ache
While thinking of the gifts you keep.

Erisha's eyes began to close as Sidukur sang. She breathed deeply and suppressed the fears of tomorrow. She leaned against Dumur and soon she was asleep.

CHAPTER FIVE

OUT THE FRYING PAN AND INTO THE FIRE

E risha's eyes fluttered open and the chamber felt cooler than it had been the night before. She arched her back into the rock wall behind her and rose quietly so not to wake anyone else. She turned and looked out the little window. It was still early morning outside, and Erisha breathed in the fresh air that flowed in. She looked back around the prison and realized that the torch had burnt out, but the lantern's small flame still wavered and licked faithfully.

Some of the men stirred and Erisha looked back out the window where she could see the grey sky and bit of the faraway fields through the trunks of trees. She leaned against the wall and rested her head on the edge of the window. There was movement behind her and soon Anarim stood beside her.

"Good morning," he greeted quietly, looking out the window.

"Good morning," Erisha whispered.

They were silent for a while as they stood there, and Erisha thought about home. She hoped that Esirim, Abkur, and her father had made it to the village and her father was still alive. She hoped they had brought her mother news of Dumur and herself. Although, now, if news could have been sent to them it would not have been good news. She sighed and her thoughts wandered to the fields and the warm sun beaming down in the afternoon and the harvest moon festival that was quickly approaching before the first snow came. Would she live to experience these things again?

"Are you afraid?" Anarim asked, watching her.

Erisha looked up at him. She paused, thinking, then shook her head. "I do not fear death," she said softly. "In life, the gods can punish us as well as bless us. We can feel pain and loss here. When we die, what do we feel? We don't know. What is there to fear? I suppose, only the unknown. I believe I have lived a decent life that I hope the gods will be pleased with." She paused. "Are you afraid of death?"

He studied her for a moment, a look of admiration visible in the quiet light of the morning by the window, then he lowered his head. "No, I do not fear death," he said. "I fear failing my kingdom."

"You haven't failed," came Dumur's voice from below. The youth rose to stand beside Erisha. "We will help you escape, somehow, no matter what happens."

Anarim shook his head. "I am not leaving without all of you," he said. "Especially you two. I must return you to your parents."

Sidukur yawned loudly and Erisha jumped in surprise. Dumur and Anarim grinned at her, amused. Sidukur stretched and groaned.

"Nothing like sleeping on stone," Sidukur said. He looked over in the trio's direction. "Is it morning already?"

"I suppose it must be with you blabbing on," Girisu grumbled, sitting up.

Kas stood and stretched. "The sun rose on a new day," he said.

"Indeed," Sidukur said, also rising.

"The light is not shining through the window yet," Anarim reminded.

They waited. Soon, they were trying to think of likely execution ideas to make light of their situation. The musings and wonderings about Lord Kankal's twisted mind soon devolved into more stories from Sidukur and Girisu.

"This chamber reminds me of the Loman adventure six summers ago," Sidukur said. "Do you remember it, Girisu?"

"Remember it?" Girisu exclaimed. "The chamber was so small Anarim and I had to basically sit on top of you."

The men laughed.

"That was a close shave," Sidukur chuckled. "If it wasn't for old Abkur, we might still be sitting in that chamber."

"Well, you got to trade that one for a bigger one," Kas said with a smile.

Everyone laughed.

"I do believe that's the first joke I've heard from you, sir," Sidukur declared.

Kas smiled but didn't reply.

"Abkur often came to our aid when we were young," Girisu said fondly.

"He still comes to our aid," Anarim said.

"How long have you all known each other?" Erisha asked.

"Well, while this one was growing up as a Prince under his father," Sidukur said, gesturing toward Anarim, "I enlisted once I was old enough to be with my father. He was a high-ranking cavalry man in the old King's army."

"A good man," Anarim said gently.

Sidukur nodded. "Yes, he was," he echoed. "I rode with him often and trained with his company outside of my regiment's training hours. I saw Anarim some and we would speak. Then, my father grew ill and died. It happened so quickly it was hard to accept at first and I swore I could hear him some afternoons barking out orders to his men. But the young Prince, here, kept me grounded. Befriended me and helped me along until I was back on my own two feet. Then, one day, this man," he clapped Girisu on the shoulder, "just appears from out of the forests."

Both children exclaimed in surprise and Girisu smiled, putting his hands up.

"I am not a Fasur," he explained. "My blood is Zarian. These two were out romping—"

"Romping," Anarim laughed, incredulous.

"—one morning and I was out hunting," continued Girisu, "I have no fear of the forests. When I was a babe, my father and mother needed land of their own and they couldn't afford to stay in the city, so they travelled to the outskirts where the farmers lived during all seasons except the winter. They negotiated for a plot of land and my father took it upon himself to build a house. He looked to the woods. He hadn't an axe big enough to cut down a tree, but he went in hoping to find some fallen trees or branches to use. He pulled back a long trunk that day and began to build. Each day until the house was completed, he entered the forest and came out with a log or two that had fallen. He never had to try to cut down the trees. The forest provided. Thus, I have never been afraid of the Tirannan forests. But these two were riding along, saw me exiting the forest with my kill, and demanded answers."

"Soon, we realized Girisu's gift as a tracker and hunter," Anarim said. "He was caring for his parents, and they were living quietly in that house built long ago. I brought him to meet my father, but we should have wandered through the woods first because, although he was impressed with Girisu and his courage, my father did not trust the Forests of Tiranna. He wanted his people safe. So, he forbade entering the woods and offered Girisu a position as a tracker and messenger."

"I accepted so to give my parents a chance to move back into the city. The home made out of Tirannan wood now houses Sidukur's family," Girisu said, smiling at his friend.

"That is does," Sidukur confirmed, "and my Nami and I will be forever grateful to you."

Erisha turned her attention to Kas. "And you?" she asked. "What is your story?"

"Indeed," Sidukur said, hunkering down for a nice long telling of a life. "Tell your tale, man. We know close to nothing about you except that you're a skilled warrior and you appeared before the King as if coming with the wind."

"It is as you said. I came in the wind," Kas said with a sly smile.

Before anyone could encourage Kas to elaborate, there came a call from through the orifice. An end of the rope ladder dropped down to them. No one moved at first.

Anarim raised his head and went over to the ladder. He pulled down on it and it hung firm. He paused and everyone was quiet. He looked around at the chamber's inhabitants and he nodded. He climbed up.

Kas followed the King. Sidukur and Girisu had Erisha and Dumur go next. Erisha gripped the ropes and slowly pulled herself up. Once she was visible to those in the tunnel, two Lekur men grabbed her and hoisted her out. Erisha looked at those aiding her and recognized one of them as the young man Mita had silently appealed to the night before. The young man steadied her and placed her with Anarim and Kas.

The group awaiting them was made up of a dozen Lekur. Some wore warrior attire, others did not. Erisha saw Mita among the group but did not recognize anyone else. Studying Mita and the young man who had helped her, Erisha decided the two must be siblings or cousins. The young man's hair was fairer and his eyes were dark, but their features were strikingly similar.

Dumur appeared and he hoisted himself up out of the hole. Erisha noticed that young man's hesitation before he offered Dumur a hand. Dumur stood and glanced between the young man and Mita before moving to join Erisha. Mita's eyes followed Dumur for a moment longer than everyone else's and Erisha struggled to place the young woman's expression. There was a mixture of curiosity, disapproval, and something akin to admiration perhaps on her soft face.

Girisu and Sidukur arose from the depths and once the Lekur had them grouped in the middle between their company, the young man related to Mita led them through the tunnel. They marched along, silent. They made it to the big open room and walked through the quiet, less bustling activity of the early morning. The individuals who were awake and at work looked up at they passed through, even those far on either side of the room.

They reentered the tunnels and still no one told the prisoners anything. Erisha walked on, head down as she watched her steps. The tunnel's light gradually grew dimmer along many turns and corners and Erisha noticed that they began to ascend. It grew darker in the tunnel and there was a short period of being in utter blackness again before Erisha saw a whiter light ahead of them: the sunlight outside. She breathed in and tasted the outdoor air instead of the stagnant air inside the tunnels.

Everyone trooped out into the morning. They were higher up on the mountain and there were more trees scattered about than there had been lower down. It was rockier and steeper as

well. They came out and everyone blinked. The Lekur moved
about and soon encased the King and his company into a sem-
icircle while the captives' backs were still to the tunnel.

"I am Lu Kursignirgal," the young man related to Mita
said. "I am Lord Kankal's heir, and I have been tasked to lead
you to the top of the Gisgal range where you will meet your
fate." He looked mainly at Anarim as he spoke. "Do not try to
escape as we hike. You are not mountain people and would not
get far. Also, most of my group will be armed and ready. You
will meet death in one way or another. Am I clear?"

"Lead on," Anarim said with a gesture of his hand.

Lu hesitated then started up a trail that steadily ascended as
far as could be seen through the trees. Mita and another Lekur
followed Lu, and Anarim followed then after no one else made
to move. Erisha and Dumur fell in behind the King and his
friends followed them. The rest of the Felrisans brought up the
rear.

It was cold and Erisha was glad that they kept moving at
their brisk pace. She moved her fingers often to keep them from
feeling numb and touched any tree near enough as they passed
to steady her. Their breath came out in little white puffs as they
progressed. Every now and again when the trail began to become more difficult, the trail turned back on itself and forged a
path higher in the opposite direction. Erisha slipped a couple
times, but Dumur and Kas were always there to steady her. The
one time Dumur tripped both Lu and Mita instinctively made
to help him before Anarim steadied him.

They hiked in silence until the questions in Erisha's mind forced her to speak, breaking the peaceful tension.

"Are you siblings?" she asked.

Lu and Mita looked back and found Erisha watching them. They were quiet as they turned forward again and continued, but Erisha waited.

"We are twins," Mita said finally.

"And the son and daughter of Lord Kankal though he said he had no children?" Erisha offered.

The Kursignirgal twins exchanged a look, and Erisha saw Dumur put his head down in front of her. She knew he was smiling; he was not the only one who could be impertinent if desired.

"The Lady simply desires an explanation," Anarim soothed.

"We are going to our deaths after all," Dumur said. "Might as well get our last questions answered."

Erisha poked Dumur, not wanting trouble, but then she glimpsed Anarim's slight smile and she did not berate her brother further. They all waited for a response from the leaders of the Felrisan pack.

"Why do you care?" Lu asked irritably.

Erisha shrugged. "Curiosity," she admitted, "and a distraction from thinking about other, more prominent things."

Lu sighed. "Our parents are imprisoned by Lord Kankal because he believes they're a threat to his authority. It happens every now and again, imprisoning people in the mountains," he said dryly. "They are allowed out only as a part of the Felrisan army which they are required to serve in." He grew quiet.

Erisha watched as Anarim glanced back at his friends concernedly.

"Lord Kankal took a liking to us though," Mita continued in her brother's stead. "Lu is a skilled warrior and a clever planner. I came along being Lu's twin."

"My sister was chosen by Lord Kankal in her own right. Having a pleasant, intelligent young woman to call his daughter made him more accessible to his people."

"You're very forthright with this information," Anarim commented, looking back at the rest of the Lekur who were hiking and who appeared to be quite unfazed by such brazen honesty about their Steward.

"Would you have preferred dishonesty?" Lu questioned coolly.

"We don't... love the Steward," Mita added. "We respect and follow him."

Anarim inclined his head in acquiescence.

Erisha realized that Mita was referring to the Felrisans as a whole. The idea of not honoring or admiring your Steward was foreign to her, yet her Steward was her father. Most of Furun, she thought, admired Lord Ansira. There were not many complaints nor any hidden quarrels that she knew of. Yet, again, she was beginning to see that in more than a few ways she knew very little of the world she lived in.

They travelled on and the sun's growing warmth as it rose softened some of the painful cold. Their breath was no longer visible, but Erisha noticed that the tip of her nose, numb by now, did not grow any warmer. She looked up and thought she saw where the top of the mountain rested in the blue sky above, but she was not certain.

"Do you take this path often?" Dumur asked suddenly.

"No," Mita replied after a moment.

"Good," he replied. "I like being special," he added.

Erisha longed to smack him although under more comfortable circumstance she would laugh at his presumption. Afraid he would fall down the mountain, she refrained from hitting Dumur. She looked warily up at the twins in the front and was surprised to see a bright, amused smile on Mita's face while the glint in Lu's eyes betrayed that he was entertained. The twins exchanged glances, however, and their expressions sobered.

"You are going to die, boy," came the voice of the Lekur with the twins. "You'd be better occupied praying to the Master of the Heavens for mercy in the afterworld than talking smart."

"Peace," Lu demanded. "Let the youth enjoy himself while he can. He could also be praying; he could not be. That is not our concern."

Dumur looked back at Erisha, and she glanced at him. He shrugged. They marched on for a while in silence.

The sun was shining through the trees' last few bunches of leaves that had not completely blown off yet. They had to climb up a pile of stones jutting out to get up to the elevation above.

Erisha carefully grasped with her hands and placed with her feet, desperately afraid to fall but not wanting to ask for help. She made it up finally, Dumur helping her rise, onto a small plateau. The sight that awaited them as they looked down the other side of the mountain took Erisha's breath away as they were now at the accessible top, the raging wind whipping about her. She looked down first. The plateau stuck out a little and the side below was very steep. The side was treed all the way down and at the bottom the rocky land was cut into sharply by a large river rushing along the range towards the sea. After the river lay thick forest, but Erisha also thought she saw a glint of water in the far, far distance. She stared at the horizon and realized she was looking at the Uncharted realm, Nuzuza. Not many people had seen what she was viewing now.

Anarim and his friends also stared in awe at the grand, unsettled expanse. Dumur's gaze stretched to the most western side of Alland, to what Erisha wondered was a twinkle of the sea. Dumur turned about and Erisha looked with him to discover that the Lekur were surrounding them again, weapons at the ready. The small group of unfortunate travelers waited.

Lu and Mita stepped forward.

"Your sentence is to be banished to the Uncharted to meet the fate that the gods have in store," Lu announced. "We offer you weapons."

Three Lekur who had been carrying large packs came forward and drew out six swords and six bows and full quivers. Anarim and his friends quickly strapped on their weapons and shouldered their bows and quivers. The Sadurras held their weapons, trying to internalize what was going to occur.

"You'll stand at the edge of the precipice, and I will push you off to meet your fate one by one," Lu said.

"What?" the Sadurra siblings exclaimed.

"You're not serious," Sidukur demanded.

"I'm afraid we are," Lu said. He turned to Anarim. "You, sir, are first."

Anarim studied Lu then looked out into the Uncharted realm. He walked over to the edge of the plateau and Lu followed. Erisha held her breath and grabbed onto Dumur's arm as Anarim's gaze dropped down to the rocky landing that lay below him. Erisha watched as Anarim looked over Nuzuza, a strange, pained expression on his face. She wondered at his look.

The King turned about, and Erisha looked with him over her shoulder. There lay what they knew. There lay the way down the mountains, the fields of Furun below, the forests across where the Fasur lived. The hills to the North and the way to the sea in the South. There lay their home.

"No," Anarim said in the quiet of a moment of the wind dying down.

"I'm afraid you don't have a choice," Lu replied with a scoff.

"I'm afraid, young man, I do," Anarim countered.

"And what makes you think that?" Lu asked warily, drawing his sword.

Anarim glanced at the weapon but made no move to draw his own even though Sidukur's and Girisu's hands went to their hilts. "Because I am Anarim Askatte of Zari," Anarim answered firmly, holding Lu's gaze, "Steward of the Hills, Lord of the White Palace, and King of Alland. And I say no one will die this day."

Lu stared at the King, but his raised sword lowered. He studied Anarim for a long while as the wind rose again and whipped fiercely at their clothes and hair. Finally, Lu raised his sword but the hilt was up and the blade was down. He placed the tip of the blade onto the stone of the plateau, and Lu kneeled before Anarim. Slowly, the rest of the Lekur followed suit and all knelt before the King. Erisha and the others moved to kneel as well, but Anarim stopped them with a wave of his hand.

"Rise," he told Lu, stepping forward and touching the young man's shoulder. He looked down at the youth curiously. "Lord Kankal said you would not know me."

Lu stood and stared at Anarim. "I do not know your face," he said with a shake of his head. "But I have longed to know you. We all knew there was a King in the White Palace, but no one knew who you were. Were you just and kind, or cruel and violent like Kankal?" Lu looked down, and Erisha wondered if he was hiding glassy eyes. "You, sir, have the air of a man who is honorable and just and wise. I would want you as my King."

Anarim put his hand on Lu's shoulder again. "I'm here to help," he told him. "Help me, and I will free your parents."

Lu nodded, shallowing.

"Thank you," the King said. He looked at the rest of the Felrisans gathered about. "Should I fear these people?"

Lu shook his head again. "I was to handpick a group of my own. All here are friends of ours," he explained as he gestured for Mita to come to his side, "and are silent dissenters against our Steward."

"You are all fairly young," Anarim stated.

"Lord Kankal has imprisoned most of our parents and others who were not careful enough to hide their differing opinions," Lu said.

Erisha shuddered at the thought of dozens upon dozens of people confined within the mountain.

"You must leave now," Lu announced. "Mita will be your guide."

The young woman's eyes widened. "I will?" she asked.

"You wander the mountains often," Lu replied. "If I returned late and Lord Kankal suspected, I would be killed. He likes you better. You'd only be whipped."

Mita raised her eyebrows and gave her brother a sharp look.

"We cannot ask one of them," Lu said quickly, and Erisha recognized his referring to the other Lekur. "Kankal will definitely suspect something if they don't return this day. And they," Lu gestured to the King and his company, "will not make it down alive without one of us. I would go and take the thrashing if I wasn't sure it would mean death for me. And my death is not something I will stand for, leaving you under Lord Kankal alone. I will fabricate something that he will fall for and our friends will help convince him if need be. You may not even be punished if you make good time and leave now."

"If the young lady's wellbeing is at risk," Anarim interjected, "we will make our way alone."

"You will die," Mita said with a wave of her hand. "Lu is right. The mountains are a harsh, unforgiving home."

"It is also growing colder, and we have no food or water to give you," Lu said giving his sister a pointed look.

"Do not vex me further," Mita shot at him. "I will decide. I am the elder."

Lu shrugged and waited.

Mita looked at the small group whose fate rested in her hands. "I will take them," she said with a nod then she looked up at her twin, "but your heroic act is not far off, I promise you."

Lu's brows furrowed but Mita gave him a quick hug and marched across the plateau. She nodded her farewell to her friends then looked to the King and the others expectantly. She raised her eyebrows, not about to shout at them above the wind.

Dumur strapped on his sword and shouldered his quiver, bow in hand, and followed Mita. Erisha looked to the King, but Anarim was shaking Lu's hand and telling him something quietly. So, she went after Dumur and Mita.

CHAPTER SIX

THE NEW PATH

Mita did not lead them back down the way they had come but she led them along a slim path that descended slowly and travelled along the high ridge they were on. They walked along between the trees and when Erisha looked back once, Anarim and his friends were following. From then on, her focus was forward or on her feet.

"You seem upset," Dumur said to Mita as they began to descend more extremely on a path that folded back and down.

Mita stopped and stood at a cross section in the path, and it was not clear where the new path led. "I'm trying to figure the best way down," she replied absently.

"I meant more about you having to help us survive, not about losing the path," Dumur explained.

Mita looked back at him with an expression of utter disbelief. "I have not lost the path," she retorted. She started walking forward again, gripping onto trees nearby so as to not slide down the steep incline.

"But you are upset," Dumur said after they reached more level ground again.

"I'm not upset to be helping you," Mita said. "You all seem to be more than decent people. None of you are cowards. You didn't try to attack us once we gave you weapons, and you didn't beg for your lives. You saved me and your sister." She glanced back at the Sadurra siblings as they listened. "I don't know how you got yourselves into such a predicament, but I owe you my life. So, I'm happy to help you save yours."

Erisha and Dumur nodded.

"I'm assuming your siblings," Mita said apologetically.

"We are," Erisha replied with a smile.

"You didn't explain why you're upset," Dumur pushed.

"Dumur," Erisha chided.

"I'm thinking," Mita replied, a scowl returning to her face.

"About?" Dumur continued, gesturing for her to go on.

Mita looked back at him, obviously not knowing whether to laugh or snap at him. "Is he normally like this?" she asked Erisha.

"Sometimes," Erisha replied, embarrassed. She smacked Dumur's arm. "Why are you being annoying?" she asked in a hiss.

"Look," Dumur said, speaking at a normal volume, "I'm tired, I'm cold, I'm hungry because we haven't eaten in what feels like an age, and we're precariously climbing down a mountain. I'm trying to make conversation so I'm distracted."

Mita coughed and Erisha thought it sounded suspiciously like covering a laugh.

"He's hungry," Erisha told her.

Mita hid a smile, and the two young women shared a knowing look. "Here," Mita said, pulling something out of the small satchel she carried on her back. "I brought this since we started out so early this morning."

Dumur shook his head and looked away. "I don't need to take your food from you," he said quietly.

Mita stopped and put the large pieces of bread and dried meat in his hands. "Eat it," she said.

Dumur took it. "Thank you."

Mita smiled before forging ahead again.

Just as Erisha was beginning to realize how hungry she felt as well, Dumur held out a ripped piece of the bread to her. She took it gratefully and bit into it. Nothing had ever tasted better, she thought. Dumur gave her some of the meat too, and that also tasted good though it was a little chewy.

"Where are you both from?" Mita asked.

"Furun," Erisha said between bites.

"The low country," Mita mused. She paused. "Are you of high standing?"

Erisha looked at the back of Mita's head as they trekked on. "How did you know?" she asked.

Mita shrugged in front of them. "Something about how you walked," she said. "Also because you are travelling with the King."

"Oh, well, the King isn't a clue at all," Dumur said. "It's all an accident that we're with him."

Erisha smiled gently at him.

"But you are, say, the Steward's children then?" Mita asked.

"Yes," Erisha admitted. "We're like you."

Mita laughed humorlessly. "I have no desire to be affiliated with Lord Kankal," she said. "Our position as his heirs has been useful but that is all it has been."

They were quiet for a while.

"Do you ever get to see your parents?" Erisha asked cautiously.

Mita shook her head. "Only from afar during random training exercises," she said. "Lu and I have searched the tunnels and the different prison chambers, but we haven't ever been able to find them. Lord Kankal also keeps careful watch over us, or at least did for a while. We have belonged to him for five autumns now and have learned how to handle him to an extent. He trusts us some now."

"How old are you?" Erisha asked.

"Nearly eighteen winters," Mita said. "You?"

"Nineteen harvests," Erisha said.

"And you?" Mita asked, looking back at Dumur.

"Sixteen winters," he said.

"We have an older brother who is three summers older than I," Erisha said.

Mita nodded, thoughtful.

"You obviously don't like Lord Kankal," Erisha said. "Why do you suffer him?"

"If people overthrew their Stewards simply when they disagreed with him, there would be chaos," Mita said. "That is not justice."

"Agreed," Erisha said, "but Lord Kankal doesn't seem to be ruling you justly either. He keeps truths from you."

"Order must be kept," Mita replied hesitantly.

"Tyranny and authority are not the same thing," came Anarim's voice from behind them.

The children paused and looked back at the men as they caught up to the three younger travelers. Mita started off again, brows furrowed in thought.

"How long have they been exiling people in that way?" Anarim asked curtly.

Mita hesitated, surprised then wary. "I don't know," she replied finally.

Anarim eyed her.

"Lord Kankal is a strange man and a hard man," Mita said. "I admit that, but he does keep order in the mountain."

"And yet you fear him," Girisu said quietly.

Mita started and grew pale. "We could not leave if we wanted to," she said passionately after a moment. "He would not stand for it."

"Do some people leave?" Anarim asked before the Sadurras could.

Mita nodded. "Some do," she said. "Especially the young people. They leave quietly and marry in the other realms and stay there."

"That breaks the Nitadum Pledge," Girisu stated.

"Well, can you blame them?" Mita questioned, waving her hands anxiously. "The King himself suggested that Lord Kankal is a tyrant."

"But part of the problem lies in the failure to follow the Pledge," the King replied. "The young man ought to join his wife's community and help improve it. There is a balancing effect, a principle at work."

Erisha saw Mita lick her lips, agitated.

"Isn't the King exempt from the Nitadum pledge?" Dumur asked.

"For obvious reasons," Anarim stated, giving Dumur a raised eyebrow. "It would be impractical to have the ruling seat move with every new generation."

"It may be true that the Nitadum Pledge is an important practice, your Majesty," Mita spoke up, "but there is a sufficient part of the community who still support the Steward and approve of his forcefulness. How do you know these men we might bring into our realm would not be snuffed out by Lord Kankal and then we are left with young widows?"

"How do you know that would be, lass?" Sidukur said gently.

Erisha looked back at the men and Anarim's gaze met her. She shook her head slightly. He seemed to understand her gesture and he remained quiet. No one pressed the matter further.

Mita looked back at them all, her eyes cautious and apprehensive.

Erisha sensed her distress and put a hand on her shoulder. "None of this is your fault," she said.

Mita looked ahead as they hiked down, side by side now. "I cannot fix it," she said, her eyes glassy. She sniffed and the tears disappeared. She quickened her pace, and the rest struggled to keep up with her for a while.

Finally, Mita slowed and soon they stopped for a break. They each found a rock to sit on or a tree to lean against. Mita passed around her water flask.

"We seem to be angling to the South more then we need to be," Girisu stated.

Mita nodded. "You're right."

"The reason being?" Girisu asked.

"I am getting you as close to the Abakiti border as possible," Mita answered.

They all cried out in protest and confusion, but Mita raised her voice above theirs.

"Lord Kankal is planning to attack the Lerisaba next," she said. "He leads a large troop out tomorrow. You must warn them. The Esasag were slaughtered. Lord Kankal returned and demanded celebration. Lu and I were not informed of the attack upon Furun until after the fact. Then Lord Kankal announced his plan to us. I will not stand by and let another realm be overwhelmed and crushed. You must warn them in Abaki and defeat Lord Kankal."

They all stared at her as birds tweeted above them cheerfully. The wind's strength had subsided as they had descended the mountain. Now, it was closer to a blustering breeze than a robust current. There were a few squirrels who chattered and rushed about on the nearby trees' branches or scurried across the rocky surface of the mountain. Erisha, along with everyone else, looked to Anarim who was sitting on a large protruding rock. His expression was grim but thoughtful.

"Lu has talked for the past few days of trying to rally the like-minded Lekur," Mita continued, "but I do not think it would succeed. It would mean death for many—"

"It may still mean death for many," Anarim interrupted.

Mita looked to him. "We need help," she said simply. "More importantly, if you are King and I am willing to believe you are, your people need help." She paused then pressed on. "What say you?"

"I say yes, of course," Anarim said, rising. "I just do not see the way clearly yet."

"I know how to help you on your way at least," Mita said. "Shall we go on?"

Anarim nodded though Erisha could see already that he was trying to discern the best way to subdue Lord Kankal. They followed Mita at a consistent pace now and Erisha felt that they were making good time. The sun was overhead after a while, but they continued to race along the mountain paths at a fast walk.

They were finally out of the treed area of the mountain for the time being and Erisha enjoyed being able to see everything about her. She could look out over the fields or up along the mountain. Or she could look ahead and see how their trail curved and arched with the rocky surface. She felt a tiredness growing in her legs, but she would not stop. She managed, one step after the other, to keep up behind Mita and Dumur. Dumur was in a far better mood after eating a little and he entertained Mita with stories of their life in Furun. He was a lively and competent storyteller and even Sidukur asked questions or seemed drawn into the short tales of little nothings.

Mita laughed often and drank in Dumur's works. Dumur told of how the village was situated and the different festivals that were put on throughout the seasons. He told amusing tales of when he trained with Esirim and the cavalry. He relived the time when Erisha and he were young and had snuck out in the evening to go stargazing: the whole village had gone out to look for them and further chaos had ensued that night because the stars had burnt bright and flown across the night sky in a way that only happened rarely.

Mita told of how her parents used to bring Lu and herself out to camp and stargaze. She had loved sleeping outdoors and staring out into the open air. Her father had also taught the twins to build a small tree house which they could escape to during the day if they wished, because, funnily enough, when most Lekur left the mountain, they did not look up since they were not used to anything worth looking at being above them. These were a few of the things done by her parents that Lord Kankal had been suspicious of.

"I still sneak out sometimes at night, though," Mita admitted, "and I look up at the stars. Lord Kankal has learned to put up with any short disappearances. I think it amuses him now. It's like how Lu doesn't speak often. Lu hardly ever responds to Lord Kankal with more than a word. It infuriated the Steward at first but it is one thing that Lu has never given up. He has become the Steward's head errand boy, his spokesman, and his second-in-command for our army. But he will not converse with Lord Kankal. He just lets the man talk."

They went on for a bit longer, but Erisha noticed that Mita kept looking up at the sky in the direction of the sun. They stopped for a rest and Mita looked preoccupied for a long time, her lips pursed together in a frown. Eventually, she took a breath and moved passed the group back the way from which they had come.

She faced them. "I must head back now. Follow the trail until you're off the mountain then continue South. You'll find your way, I'm sure," she said quietly. "I wish you safe travels and success." Mita nodded in farewell and looked to Dumur and Erisha last.

Erisha was upset to see fear and something that looked like longing in Mita's eyes, but the young woman quickly turned away.

"Thank you for your help," the King said.

Mita smiled. "Thank you for yours," she said. She turned to go but paused. She looked to Dumur again. "Thank you," she said, "for sparing me."

Dumur watched her. He replied with a nod.

Mita spun about and marched away back down the path.

They all watched her go. Something inside her did not feel right and Erisha stood from where she had been sitting on a rock. She deliberated, knowing she probably would not get her way and she did not want to cause trouble. But she looked to where the figure of Mita was becoming smaller and smaller as the young woman trekked back over the mountain.

"She's afraid," Erisha said finally. She looked to Anarim. "She doesn't want to return."

"Her brother awaits her," Anarim replied. "I doubt Lord Kankal will guess what they have done. He will be occupied organizing his warriors for their march on the Lerisaba. She will be fine."

Erisha looked to Dumur for help. She knew he had seen and felt what she had. He may be male, but he was not senseless.

Dumur hesitated. "She should come with us," he finally said.

"Why?" Anarim asked dubiously. "We cannot invite every lost person we meet to join us."

The Sadurras looked at one another and Dumur pressed on.

"I cannot explain it," he said honestly, "but she belongs with us, at least for now."

"She is close to this realm's Steward," Kas said, speaking suddenly. Anarim turned to him in surprise. "She could have information on how to handle Lord Kankal that could be invaluable."

"Could," Anarim reiterated.

"We are also not off the mountain yet and I haven't traversed this landscape much," Girisu said. "I'm sorry, Anarim, but I think the children are on to something. Mita may prove to be an important asset of which she herself has no idea."

"We are going on an inkling that this girl may help us further," Anarim countered.

"Is that not all one has sometimes?" Girisu challenged.

"Always idioms, Girisu…" Anarim looked at all of them. "Sidukur," he said, "you have not spoken yet."

"Because I am watching the girl," Sidukur replied. "She is getting farther away. You best make your decision soon."

Anarim sighed. He looked to Kas and the man nodded encouragingly. "Very well," the King said.

Erisha smiled brightly as Sidukur shouted after Mita.

"Dumur, run after her," Sidukur ordered.

Dumur stood and chased down the path. "Mita!" he called.

They waited patiently until Dumur returned with Mita in tow.

"It took a bit of convincing," Dumur announced.

"I still don't quite understand," Mita said.

"Neither do we," the King admitted, "but I'm sure we will eventually. Are you with us, my lady?"

Mita nodded. "I am with you. I don't know the whole way to Abaki," she said, "but if we keep heading South…"

Girisu nodded. "I have been there before."

"As have we," Anarim said, gesturing to Sidukur. "Once we get far enough, we will figure out where we are. Just get us off the mountain safely." He smiled.

Mita grinned. "Very well," she said. "Shall I keep leading at least until then?"

"Of course," Anarim said.

Mita started off and smiled shyly as she passed Erisha. The Sadurra siblings fell in behind her again and off they all went. Soon, they had fully descended the mountain slope. Mita led them well down a steep incline that was less steep than any way down nearby. They pushed farther away from the mountain and were soon marching through grassy fields. The sky was blue and the leaves on the few trees they saw scattered about back down in the low country were beginning to turn colors. Birds flew overhead from time to time, and little scurrying creatures dove sporadically through the grass in front of their feet.

Dumur, growing hungry again as the sun began to shine on their right, notched an arrow and succeeded in obtaining a couple unlucky, wandering rabbits. He strung them up and flung them onto his back, proud of himself. Sidukur shot down a small deer afterwards and carried it over his shoulders. The tales of hunting expeditions began, and all the male company was soon occupied. Erisha, glad to not be the only woman anymore, walked at the front with Mita.

"What do you think will happen when you don't return?" Erisha asked.

"They may send out search parties," Mita replied. "Lord Kankal will be busy organizing the warriors so I doubt he'll pay much mind, but I don't know if Lu will suspect what I've done. I wish there was a way to get word to him, but there isn't."

"He'll be relieved, at least, when he sees you again," Erisha said.

Mita smiled. "Yes," she agreed. "Hopefully, he does not lose heart."

Erisha stared up at the blue sky and appreciated the gentle breeze that caressed her cheek. She sighed. "A couple days ago if you had told me I'd be travelling with the King to Abaki having just escaped from Felrisa, I would have laughed at such a tall tale. Yet, here I am. Isn't it odd?"

Mita looked thoughtfully ahead of her. "Life is strange," she agreed. "I find if I try to understand it or think about it too much or too hard, it only gets more confusing." She looked over at Erisha, looked a little abashed. "I took a risk today. I'll be the first to say I've spent years worrying about what each day will bring concerning the fates of my parents and Lu and myself. But when Dumur came after me and gave me the choice to join you and he kept trying to explain the reasoning, I decided to leap. And it was the first time I have made such an important choice on instinct. I hope it does not bring misery." She shook her head. "I'm sorry. I've let my tongue run."

Erisha laughed. "Of course not," she said. "All you said, I agree with. You were very brave. At the beginning of this adventure, I had no time to think. My only focus was to go after

Dumur and find him before he did something foolish. And there have been consequences and probably will be more for our rashness, but now that the decision is made and it wasn't a wrong decision, I cannot go back. I can only go forward."

Mita nodded slowly.

"Did I hear my name?" Dumur asked, walking up beside them.

"You would," Erisha teased.

Dumur smiled. "Kindness, please," he pleaded, eyes twinkling.

"And what are our young guides discussing?" came Anarim's voice.

"The beginning of our adventure," Erisha replied, gesturing to Dumur.

"Oh yes," Sidukur said. "We haven't heard the story of you two yet."

"Do we want to hear it?" Kas asked, an eyebrow raised.

Erisha looked back at him and searched his face and person for a clue as to why he would speak so critically.

Dumur, however, seemed to understand Kas better. His smile faded. "It was my fault," he admitted. "I did something foolish."

They were all walking in a group side by side now. The men listened to Dumur as he told the tale. Anarim looked to Dumur questioningly once the young man had given them the facts of the matter.

"I was worried about my father and brother and the men," Dumur explained. "I was convinced something was wrong. So, I took matters into my own hands. I ran away from home and after them. And Erisha came after me to stop me."

The men were listening so quietly and their apparent allowance of Dumur to blame himself completely irritated Erisha.

"But something was wrong," she added. "You were right."

Kas looked over to Dumur and Dumur's gaze went from Erisha to Kas to the ground.

"It caused a lot of pain, Erisha," he said. "And we've almost died multiple times. You've almost died."

"So, do you want us to turn around now and go home?" Erisha asked, anger rising.

Dumur shook his head. "No, we're helping now," he said, "but that doesn't mean I won't face consequences for my actions eventually."

"I believe you already have in many ways," Girisu said quietly.

Erisha looked about at them all then turned to Dumur. "Well, I followed you," she said. "I'm here too. It's not all your fault."

"I disobeyed mother, and you followed," Dumur said.

"You were trying to do a good thing," Erisha demanded.

"Do you think we will not face judgment for our bad decisions?" Anarim asked her.

Erisha turned to face him, feeling hostile. They were encouraging Dumur to blame himself only. They were ignoring the fact that he had saved her life, the King's life, and arguably Mita's life. Dumur was a good young man, and something *had* been wrong. Ultimately, they had found their father and Esirim and the men because of Dumur.

"It does not matter if you have good intentions sometimes," Anarim said. "There are consequences that cannot be escaped."

Erisha stopped in her tracks and stared at the King. "Just because you are King—" she began.

"It does not matter that I am King," Anarim said, halting as well and facing her. "You are speaking untruth."

"I refuse to believe—" Erisha began, noticing in her peripheral vision that the others were continuing without them.

"The truth," Anarim said firmly, taking a few steps nearer, "is that, ideally, you and your brother would not be here right now. What must be dealt with is not something a child or a woman should have to deal with. It is dangerous and often fatal. Your brother's impulsive decision is understandable in some sense, but it has led to near-death experiences that you both will remember for the rest of your lives."

"I admit, of course, that it is not wonderful," Erisha replied, "but are we going to complain every time something uncomfortable or scarring or bad happens to us?"

"I am not referring to that aspect," Anarim stated sharply. "I am referring to how Dumur has to take responsibility for his actions because, whether or not you want to recognize it, his choice has put his life and, more importantly, your life under threat. That is his fault, and it will be his responsibility, not only as your brother but as the instigator, until we get you both home safe. And there is no guarantee that you will make it home safely or at all. He is being mature and accepting that he was foolish and disobedient. Do not hinder his growth."

Erisha glared at him but then looked away, hiding the tears welling in her eyes.

Anarim's manner softened. "Erisha, I'm sorry," he said, placing a finger gently under her chin for a moment to tilt her face up so she had to meet his gaze. "This is also my fault. I decided to bring Dumur and you and now Mita with us because I was afraid of the potential danger against each of you. But if I took the risk and took more time to discern, none of you would be here. You would be safe in Furun with your family. I am sorry."

Erisha furrowed her brows. "I have made my own choices," she replied.

Anarim raised his eyebrows then sighed. He looked at her and Erisha felt, looking into his eyes, that he was trying to tell her something without telling her. Erisha did not look away but searched his face, bewildered by his manner.

He smiled sadly. "Let's go on," he said.

They hiked after the group who was a ways ahead of them now. They plotted on silently for a few moments. Erisha tried to piece together everything that had just transpired and kept stealing glanced at Anarim.

She finally worked up the courage to speak. "You think I am naïve and overwrought," she lamented quietly.

Anarim glanced over at her. "On the contrary, I am thoroughly impressed by you," he stated.

Erisha looked over at him in surprise and the King laughed.

"You have been amiable and uncomplaining," he said, "and valiant. You have dealt with everything that has happened admirably. I'm quite impressed."

Erisha looked over at him and felt her mouth smile. She looked down then forced herself to look back towards him. "I'm sorry for losing my temper," she said resolutely.

But all Anarim did was stare at her and a smile broke onto his lips.

Erisha blushed, feeling like she was still acting childish somehow.

They quickened their pace and rejoined the group. No one spoke as they pressed on. Slowly, the sun began to set, and the bright, yellow glow faded into gold then bronze. Before the sun had set completely in the West, they stopped and set up a camp. Girisu and Kas began setting up a fire while Anarim and Dumur looked for wood. Sidukur skinned the rabbits while the women search for a stream or brook to fill Mita's flask.

When they had all returned, Girisu had the flames burning brightly and Sidukur and Kas were roasting the rabbits. The King and Dumur proclaimed their success, and Erisha and Mita drank their fill before returning with a full flask of water for the men. They were all quiet as they watched the rabbits cook.

CHAPTER SEVEN

THE CALL OF THE SEA

I t was quickly growing colder, but Erisha stood and moved away from the fire. She walked a bit and allowed the rising wind to fold around her. Some early, brighter stars shone down on her from within the night sky. She stood and faced the direction of Furun. She wrapped her arms around her waist and breathed in deeply. After a moment, she sat down in the grass, the tips of which nearly reached the height of her shoulders as she sat, and looked off across the country. Admittedly, the situation was troublesome, and Erisha felt as if she kept making it worse. She was supposed to be a young woman, but she felt like she kept acting like a child. She had embarrassed herself multiple times and had now encouraged Mita to walk into danger with them. Her mother was probably still sick with worry, and what if her father and brother were dead? Lord Kankal was carefully planning a further attack on innocent people and, from what she knew of the Lerisaba, they could not be sure they would rally together, heed their warning, or help them.

Erisha lay her head down in her hands and felt the tears on her palms. She lifted her head again and wiped the tears away. She sniffed.

"This won't do," she chided herself.

There was movement behind her, and she looked up to see Kas. Without a word, he sat down beside her. Erisha wondered if she ought to be ashamed that he found her crying, but, oddly, she felt no discomfort.

"You'd probably feel better if you let yourself cry," he advised.

Erisha looked over at his profile in the last bit of daylight. "Do you cry?" she asked.

He nodded. "Yes."

She sniffed again. "Why?"

"For the same reasons most cry, I suppose," he said, looking over at her with twinkling eyes.

Erisha smiled, despite herself. A couple tears fell down her cheeks. Then, inexplicably, Erisha began to sob silently. Kas sat beside her as she cried, and he offered her a clean handkerchief when she was done.

"I suppose Anarim is right," she said.

"I would say he is more often than not," Kas replied.

Erisha sighed. "It is irritating to always be wrong," she said.

"Are you?" Kas asked in surprise.

"It feels like such," Erisha said.

"Well, you are not," he said. "In my experience, it is merely that life's difficulties that make it seem like one is failing. There are many who feel or used to feel like you do. Even Anarim."

"And he does not now," Erisha added.

"Because he has grown enough to trust himself," Kas said, "and to trust his gifts. You are not far behind. On the contrary, as most females are, you will be ready far earlier than Anarim was."

"So, you pretend to trust yourself until you do?" Erisha mused.

"You try," he said, "and if you fall, you get up."

They looked at one another. Erisha studied him. He allowed himself to be studied.

"Who are you?" Erisha asked softly.

Kas met her gaze, but he did not speak. Erisha's eyes never wavered but they grew round for a moment then her brows furrowed. What Erisha had read in Kas' gaze was an explanation he would or could not properly put into words. And, after a little while of searching as far as he would let her, she began to see. The sky darkened and the sun set. The multitude of stars began to twinkle like minuscule gems sewn into the dark flowing quilt above.

Erisha sat back in the darkness. "You're not from here at all," she murmured.

"I am a messenger," he said, watching her.

Erisha nodded. "How do you know this place if it is not your home?" she asked.

"I've travelled about here many times with many different faces."

"Different faces?" Erisha asked concernedly.

"Some with beards, some without," Kas said with a small smile. "Some with bigger noses or ears."

Erisha grinned and shook her head. "I don't understand," she said, staring out across the fields.

"You won't," he said. "But you needn't be afraid of me. I'm still like you all, in a way."

"You don't belong here," Erisha exclaimed incredulously.

"I am not of this land, but it is not your place to decide where I belong."

"You were sent."

"Yes. I am an emissary from the Master."

Erisha hesitated then she looked back behind her to where the small group sat around the fire chatting. "To warn Anarim."

"Yes, and to aid him if need be," Kas said, watching her look back at the King. If one had been looking and had looked closely enough, one might have seen something akin to sorrow in those eyes that held more and had seen more than any other's eyes.

"You care for him," he said simply.

Erisha turned back to him in surprise. "I've been about him four days," she stammered. "I hardly know him." She paused. "Am I that easily read?" she asked ruefully.

Kas smiled. "Openness is not a bad thing," he told her. "But I am also better at seeing than most."

Erisha shook her head. "It is no matter, he is the King," she said, looking away.

"Ah, wisdom," Kas mused. "Yet, from what I have seen and known, it is often that the heart refuses to be wise."

Erisha looked over at him. "Do not torment me."

"I did not mean to torment," he replied.

Erisha held his gaze. "I will not be foolish," she admonished.

"By all means, do not be a fool," he said.

"Does he care for me?" she asked gently after a moment.

"Oh, I think his affection and respect is obvious," Kas said, "as is the rest of the group's liking for you and your brother. But you are really asking about love, and I do not think you and your peoples have the ability to read the heart and see the future."

"No, we cannot," Erisha lamented. She looked over at him hopefully. "But you can?"

Kas laughed. "Dear Lady, it is not my duty to tell you of his heart, but your chance, if you wish, to discover to it. You must wait and be patient to see what fate will bring about."

"So, fate may guide?"

Kas was quiet for a moment. "If depends on how much we care," he revealed. "And even then, you and your peoples have the ability to work against fate and you all often do."

Erisha was quiet. "I suppose fate isn't the right word."

"No, I don't suppose it is."

"Will you both join us?" Anarim called from the fireside.

Erisha and Kas looked at each other in the glint of the starlight.

"Your tears have dried," he said.

Erisha smiled. "Thank you."

They stood and made their way over to the rest of the group. The air was warm and dry by the fire and Erisha felt her senses calm. She sat down near Dumur and Anarim.

"Are you well?" Dumur asked softly in her ear.

Erisha smiled at him. "Yes," she assured.

"The King has called for a story," Girisu informed Erisha and Kas as they both received a piece of rabbit from Sidukur.

Erisha took a bite of meat and grew comfortable in the fire's glow. She felt her eyelids grow heavy with another bite.

Sidukur stood, having finished his meal. "A story," he mused. He paused and paced about. "This might not be what you had in mind, but what of the Account of the Usuma?" He looked to Anarim.

"Usuma?" Mita exclaimed, eyes wide. "But surely, it is only a creature from the minds of tellers!"

"What is Usuma?" Dumur asked curiously.

"We have one who thinks it's a falsity and two who have never heard of it," Sidukur lamented. "I must and will tell the tale."

Erisha and Dumur exchanged confused glanced while Mita kept her eyes on Sidukur warily.

"With the twist of its scaly back in the deep, blue waters,
The men at the shore hid their wives, sons, and daughters,
For close by, not far from where water breaks, waits the enigma,
And this is how it starts, the story of the Usuma.

A. B. HOLMSTEDT

As long as the beach is wide, the Usuma could lay,
And in the deepest fathoms is where it spends its days.
Only a few times has its back or side been seen
And only once has its head reared up in front of man, displeased.

Displeased by the people and their brawls,
Since its job is to bring true chaos, thunder and squalls.
The Monster will not stand for much fury that is not his own;
If he finds you, the sounds that follow are true cries and groans.

He has sunk ships of poor fishermen, the boats empty,
Yet he has also led others to catches aplenty.
They say he cares not for the creatures above
And others say he punishes out of a strange love.

But I say he sees more than is told
And is encouraged to interfere where he thinks swell.
Whether that means death or life: one never can tell.
The being would be fearsome to behold
And the few who have seen have never been the same.
His world and ours hardly collide but it is disastrous if they do.
For although he may help the ailing boatsman
He may not have a liking for you.

And before you know it, clasped in its jaws and dragged into the sea,
Your fate is decided by the gods that be.
And this little tale I've just told is quite the drama

Of the fierce, elusive beast named the Usuma."

The group all shuddered in unison as Sidukur finished his narrative.

"This thing lives in the sea?" Erisha asked.

Anarim nodded. "That's what is said."

"Does it still live?" Dumur asked.

Girisu shrugged but the atmosphere remained heavy. "The Usuma hasn't been seen for years. Before any of our grandfathers' time was when it was seen last."

Erisha looked over at Kas. After a moment, he saw Erisha's gaze, a small smirk resting on his face. Erisha was not satisfied by what his look said.

"Ought we really travel to Abaki?" Mita asked, but she stopped herself. "Never mind. There haven't been reports of mysterious deaths or sinking boats. It does not matter."

Kas nodded. "I think worry is quite useless in response to a creature like this," he said.

"To be eaten by a sea monster would be a terrible way to die," Girisu remarked.

"It is not the Usuma who judges or rewards," Kas answered.

Erisha looked over to Anarim and he glanced at her.

The King studied Kas and Kas held his gaze.

"Is there a reason to doubt?" Kas asked.

"In the existence of such a beast?" Sidukur asked as Anarim inclined his head.

"There are many things to fear in this life and to doubt their existence would be folly." Kas paused. "I'd be grateful that you are gifted with joys as well as fears. One must believe in the existence of both."

"Yes," the King replied before anyone else could.

"Anxiety is useless," Kas repeated, looking to Mita.

Mita held his gaze for a moment before looking into the fire.

"I thought it sounded quite interesting," Dumur said. "Fascinating really."

Kas laughed and the mood lightened instantly.

Dumur grinned, abashed. "Well, we've never heard of such a creature," he said, gesturing toward Erisha.

Erisha smiled. "What will we discover next, I wonder?"

They woke before daylight the next morning and trekked on. Mita was sure, from what she knew about the Felrisan army and the paths they took down the mountain, that if they continued at their current pace they would stay ahead of Lord Kankal. Erisha travelled beside Mita most frequently though Dumur would often join them in their discussions throughout the day. Erisha and Mita kept up a steady flow of conversation and shared many details of their respective lives. Erisha soaked in Mita's stories about life in the Gisgal Mountains and Mita was just as interested with life in the low country.

The men were quieter unless Dumur engaged them in conversation. Then, they would happily humor him and answer his questions about Zari or the royal military or the Forests of

Tiranna, though upon the last topic they knew only a little more than him.

They rested in the middle of the day and ate some of the rabbit they had saved from the night before. Sidukur still carried the deer over his shoulders. They continued and Erisha refused to allow herself to think about how tired her body was and how much her limbs ached.

The day was cold at first and the cool temperature aided them in their steady march. The breeze's strength grew in the latter half of the day but so did the warmth in the air. Erisha began to smell a sweet, sharp fragrance in the air she had never smelt before. She breathed it in and wondered what it could be.

"What is that smell?" she finally asked.

Anarim smiled at her. "The sea," he said fondly, looking ahead.

Erisha looked from him back to their path in front of them, but she could not see any water yet.

"Do you travel often?" Erisha asked, falling back beside him. "I know you've been to Furun as Prince a few times."

"Yes, I used to, but not since becoming King," he said. "That sounds backwards, doesn't it?"

Erisha smiled. "I'm sure you're busy," she said.

He nodded. "I used to travel through the realms annually when I was younger," he explained. "Admittedly, I never went into Felrisa far enough to know that they lived in the mountain. Father knew that Lord Kankal was a crusty, unfriendly old man and he didn't want my appearance in Kankal's stewardship to appear threatening. But I've visited Furun and Abaki quite a few times and Semusak twice." He paused in thought. "I don't remember seeing you during my visits in Furun."

Erisha longed to ask about the forest dwellers, but she grinned. "Well, when we were young, Mother would always send us off so there would be no threat of misbehavior," she said. "And that became the habit until they decided they wanted Esirim to join them in welcoming visitors once he was twenty summers. That age became a silent criterion then, so I would have joined in welcoming travelers this year. Yet, I doubt you've been to Furun for multiple years."

Anarim thought. "Not in seven harvests, I believe," he said.

"Yes," she said with a laugh, "and there was absolutely no interest in welcoming travelers then. Esirim was still with us, and we were out wandering the fields. I have seen you though."

"Oh?"

"Yes, a couple times we hid among the villagers when you arrive by yourself or with your father. We participated in the traditional greeting and neither you nor our parents were ever the wiser."

"Until now," Anarim teased.

Erisha glanced at him but only allowed a small smile. Her mind wandered back to the Tirannan forests, but she decided she should be practical first. "What are the Lerisaba like?" she asked.

Anarim thought for a moment. "Well, they're fishermen," he said. "Like the rest of Alland's inhabitants, they've learned to adapt to the area they call home. But the sea is a little different from the hills or fields or trees or even the mountains. The sea is deep and cold and temperamental. One day it can be calm and clear, dazzling the eye for as far as it can see. The next day it can be fierce and dangerous, drawing a storm inland. The undercurrent beneath the surface will always surprise you and the creatures of the sea are very different from the land beasts. It's a different world in many ways."

Erisha listened to him, enthralled. "Have you ever gone in?" she asked.

"Into the sea?" Anarim asked. "Yes, I've waded in before and swum about. I've also been on their boats once, long ago when I was a boy. I say, Erisha," he continued, a faraway look coming into his eyes, "being out on the open waters is like nothing you can imagine. The waves roll under the boat, and it takes a while until you get used to the sway. And the water leaps up at you, and you're drenched before you know it. Then you get so thirsty being out there, sun or no sun, and you have to turn back when you wish you could keep sailing out to wherever the waters take you, to a new land or the edge of the world."

"And when you step back onto land?" Erisha asked, amused but also impressed by his liveliness.

"When you step back onto land you nearly fall over," Anarim laughed, "because the ground is flat and immobile again. You realize how exhausted and parched you are. And," he looked over at her, "you're happy to be back home."

Erisha grinned.

"I'll–" Anarim stopped himself. "You'll have to experience it all one day."

Erisha's smile brightened. "Oh, I'll have to," she agreed excitedly, "though it also sounds terrifying."

"Ah, but what's life without a little risk?" Anarim challenged.

Erisha laughed. "Well, I'd hope to come back like you did," she said.

"Most do," he replied.

"Not you?" Erisha questioned. "You'd rather travel to the ends of the world?"

Anarim laughed again but his laugh was different this time somehow, younger and higher and sheepish in a way. He looked down and continued to smile. Erisha sensed that his mind was wandering. "Maybe," he admitted. "Part of me would at least."

"But you're stuck here," Erisha said.

Anarim shook his head. "I wouldn't say 'stuck,'" he said.

"Then you don't mind not being able to explore?"

He hesitated. "It is not my lot in life," he said. "I have a bigger responsibility. No, I do not mind." He looked over at her. "And you?"

"Yes?" Erisha asked.

"You seem to want to travel but never have yet," Anarim said.

"Oh, I did want to travel. I mean, I do. Well, I don't know now. I wanted to see everything," Erisha said. "I wanted to go with my brother Esirim once we were both old enough, but he grew too busy with his duties as warrior and heir. So, Dumur and I promised ourselves we would go and roam about once he was old enough. We obviously didn't have to wait that long." Erisha wondered, though, if travelling was so rewarding if one also experienced so much tragedy and pain along the way.

Anarim smiled. "You'll have to see Zari one day," he said.

Erisha nodded. "And Semusak," she mused.

He nodded slowly.

They walked on and the daylight was beginning to fade from gold to a soft rose pink. The salty smell of the sea grew stronger as they drew closer, and Erisha looked up to the horizon and glimpsed the shine of the water ahead. She ran up to Mita and Dumur, and the young people began chattering excitedly. They marched on ahead of the men. They lost sight of the water for a moment then they hurried up a small elevation in the ground. They stood for a moment and allowed the salty breeze to blow over and about them. Erisha's spirit swelled as she gazed out over the sparkling glass and an energy she had never felt before filled her.

Mita breathed deeply. "The Numun Sea. It's so much better up close," she said.

Erisha looked to her as they continued down the other side of the slope. "You've seen the sea before?" she asked.

Mita gestured to Dumur. "As I was telling your brother," she began, "if you climb high enough and to the right spot, you can see the sea from the mountains. It stretches out for forever, there's no end to it."

"I was asking if she had ever seen sign of the Usuma, but she was claiming it was too far to see anything in the waters." Dumur looked dubious.

"And I am correct," Mita replied.

The dirt underneath their feet became grainier as they marched on, and the grass grew farther apart in clumps.

"Sand," Erisha mused, remembering that she had read about the beaches that the Lerisaba lived on.

The land swelled up slightly in some places into low dunes. As they neared the beach, the men caught up to them. Anarim and Girisu led the way while Kas and Sidukur brought up the rear.

The grass became more sparce and the ground grew sandier and more golden in color. Erisha's boots felt odd upon the new type of ground, her foot sliding slightly with every step.

Suddenly, movement stirred around them and, within moments, creatures with horrific faces surrounded them. The men and Dumur brandished their weapons while the young women, admittedly, clung to each other before remembering themselves. Erisha reached for an arrow, but she sensed Anarim relaxing in front of her.

"At least they have sentinels," the King muttered to Girisu. He sheathed his sword and raised a hand. "Peace," he said to the figures who Erisha, upon further study, realized were men clothed in light colors and wearing large masks made from animal skins she had never seen before.

"Good men of Abaki," Anarim continued, "please lead us to your Lord. We come with urgent news."

Surprised murmurs spread throughout the group of seven men as they recognized the King. They all removed their masks and pleasant, normal faces appeared. They all bowed to Anarim.

"Forgive us, your Majesty," one man said, holding a large mask with many pointed bones framing it which Erisha thought looked remarkably like teeth of some beast. "We did not realize it was you."

Anarim nodded. "There is no harm done," he said. "Please, take us to Lord Tubgal."

The Abakiti rose and began to lead the way to the beach.

"You failed to mention that they wear horrid masks," Erisha whispered behind Anarim.

He looked back at her and smiled. "I had forgotten," he said. "Some of their warriors, not all, don masks made from the skins of sea creatures to alarm their enemies."

Erisha nodded but her attention quickly shifted to the full view of the Numun Sea before them as they stepped onto the beach from around a dune. The water rolled onto the shore, the ripples twinkling and sparkling in the fading light, then it slid back out while leaving its wet mark behind. The quiet sound of the waves and their crashing onto the shores was unlike anything Erisha had ever heard. It was soothing and enchanting, and she breathed in the sea air. She sighed, her spirit at peace.

She looked over to Dumur who seemed mesmerized by the view before him. His eyes were on the horizon, and he walked towards the shore. His boots sunk into the wet, darker sand closest to the water and he crouched down onto his heels, fingers reaching out to touch the approaching wave.

There was movement beside Erisha who had stopped to watch her brother, and she found Mita beside her. Mita tore her gaze away from the sea and looked to Erisha then to the men who were walking down the beach to the left where, ahead, there were large firepits and huts arranged.

Erisha understood. "Dumur!" she called.

Dumur looked up quickly and almost lost his balance and his hand fully submersed in the water and down into the sand as he caught himself. He rose and joined them, rushing across the sand and kicking up the golden dust behind him.

Once they rejoined the group, more of the people of Abaki appeared. Many young children, after a few moments of hesitation, wandered up to the men and studied them closely. Once they saw the Sadurras and Mita, however, they quickly decided to interact with those closer to their own ages. They spoke rapidly and excitedly, and the young travelers tried their best to respond to every question.

The children who were not trying to directly talk to Erisha or Dumur or Mita stood a few steps back, whispered to each other and pointing at the visitors.

"They think we're strange," Mita said with a smile. She raised her eyebrows at some of the whispering children. "What?" she asked them. "What's so amusing?"

The Abakiti children all giggled and the travelers laughed with them. There came a deep laugh from within a nearby hut and an elderly man walked out. His smile was wide and white, and he held his arms out welcomingly as he neared the large groups of youths.

"Do not mind the children," he said. "It is not often that we have visitors from the lofty mountains or the rolling fields."

"How did you know where we're from?" Mita asked.

"That you're Lekur?" the elderly man asked. "Through the same observation that is causing the children to study you all so keenly. There is no pale skin here by the Sea. You mountain people never seem to get enough sun. The Esasag," he said, gesturing to Erisha and Dumur, "are light as well but they are outside enough that the sun graces their skin with freckles and their hair becomes the color of the straw they grow." He looked back to Mita. "You, young Felrisan, are pale from the cold mountain life like most hill dwellers usually. At least those who aren't spending their time roaming the land." He looked to Anarim and his friends who were maybe once pale like Mita but whose skin was now tanned and weatherworn. Erisha studied the Abakiti children's dark skin which was not as completely covered. Most of the Lerisaba had dark eyes and hair but their white smiles flashed attractively against the contrast. More adults were appearing and surrounding the visitors.

Erisha wished to touch her cheek to see if it had become rough, but she resisted such vanity. Instead, she smiled at the elderly man. "Lord Tubgal?" she asked.

The man bowed slightly. "At your service," he said, smiling and his worn, sun-seeped skin stretched and created may friendly wrinkles.

A warrior realized that Lord Tubgal was present just as Erisha attempted to begin to explain their presence in his realm. The Abakiti warriors brought the King and his men to Lord Tubgal and the children reclaimed the younger travelers' attention by grabbing their sleeves and dragging them away from the impromptu counsel just as Sidukur was presenting the deer to Lord Tubgal.

CHAPTER EIGHT

NIGHT FALLS BY THE SEA

$\mathcal{E}$ risha tried to listen to what was happening within the group of many men but struggled because of the children's persistence. She overheard Anarim announce Lord Kankal's plan, and she noticed the lack of quick reply from the Lerisaba. Yet, she had to give the children her full attention soon after. They particularly surrounded Dumur and took turns climbing his back and touching his light, curly hair. Erisha and Mita laughed as Dumur good-naturedly struggled.

A little girl came up to Mita and demanded to be held. Another followed suit and Mita directed the waddling child to Erisha who happily lifted her up. The older girls came and had Mita and Erisha sit down in the sand, and they asked a continuous stream of questions which only halted when Dumur and the majority of the children did something particularly funny. Dumur at one point asked to go in the water but the children all laughed at him.

"What?" Dumur demanded, bemused. He smiled over at Erisha and Mita.

"It is cold water now," a boy explained firmly. "And you are not a swimmer. It would not be good for you."

"You would probably drown," another younger boy proclaimed.

"Or get sick," a brave girl among the boys stated.

"I would not," Dumur argued.

The children all smiled.

"You would," a boy stated.

Dumur looked over the water. He sighed as he thought.

"Oh dear," Erisha murmured.

Mita smiled. "Stubborn," she said.

"Quite," Erisha said dryly.

Dumur suddenly looked back at the boys, eyes alight with a thought. "How about a small boat or something?" he said. "Take me out over the water. Show me how it's done."

Some of the older boys looked at each other, tempted.

"Alright," one finally said and the whole lot nodded.

A couple boys raced off as Dumur came over to where the girls sat. He unstrapped his weapons and took off any extra layers of clothing. He put them beside Erisha for safe keeping.

"Making friends quickly," she mused.

"For good reasons," Dumur replied slyly.

Erisha looked up at him as the girls all listened and watched Dumur with a particular fascination. "You really don't know how to swim, Dumur," she warned.

"What?" Mita said sharply. "Then this idea is foolish." She looked up at Dumur.

Erisha also looked to her brother.

Dumur smiled. "I'll be alright," he said. "I'll let them know."

Mita sighed irritably as Dumur walked away and joined the boys who were setting the small flat boat they had acquired onto the water at the end of the beach.

The girls took up their questions again but were distracted every now and again with the boys' progress. The sun was setting now and Erisha worried for her brother. Yet, she was also faithfully trying to pay as much attention as possible to a story told by the little girls surrounding her about a large fish that the men had caught the other day.

Mita was also listening to the story and watching the boat. All talk paused for a moment when Dumur and two Abakiti boys were pushed off from shore. The Abakiti children all clapped. Erisha and Mita watched anxiously for a few moments, but nothing disastrous happened and the boys on the boat with Dumur kept it fairly close to the shore. Some of the women came out by the girls and the children and watched along with them. The mothers were amused by the children's enthusiasm with the visitors. The children continued their stories.

Mita observed that she was not well liked by children as the many girls surrounding them lost interested and went to the shore to watch the boat. "I do not have the charm you and your brother have," she said with an apologetic smile.

Yet, Erisha sensed the pain behind the words. She looked over to where Mita sat, a young girl resting peacefully in her arms and a little boy fast asleep in her lap. Erisha smiled. "On the contrary," she said, "they like you very well. You may not attract the crowds, but you provide the haven."

Mita blushed. "I did not mean to sound self-pitying," she criticized herself roughly.

Before Erisha could reply, many of the children gasped. Erisha and Mita looked up and saw, to their horror, that the boat had overturned! The children around them all jumped to their feet and hurried to the shore. The boy napping on Mita's lap sat up in the confusion and Mita took the opportunity to stand with Erisha.

Heads bobbed up beside the boat, but Erisha could not tell in the fading light where Dumur was. Her heart beat thunderously in her chest and she clasped the child she was holding closer.

"Anarim!" she called, looking back up by the huts. She saw his head turn, but she did not wait to see if he would respond.

Beside her, Mita carefully but hurriedly handed the little girl she was holding to a mother nearby. Mita rushed to the shore. It looked as if Mita was about to jump into the sea, and, indeed, she stepped into the rising waterline. Erisha, however, saw Mita's shoulders sag and Mita looked back at Erisha, her face full of relief.

Erisha looked out again and saw that the boys had righted the boat, and three figures were on it again. She sighed deeply and hid her face with a hand for a moment. She felt movement beside her and Anarim was there.

"What happened?" he asked concernedly, peering out at the boat.

Erisha rubbed her forehead then readjusted the child in her arms who was watching everything with mild interest. "Dumur had some of the boys take him out on a boat and it overturned," she explained.

"It looks to be right side up now," he said.

"It is," Mita said, joining them. "They're coming in and the waves seem to be aiding them. And my boots are now wet."

They all looked down at her sandy boots as Mita squished up to them.

Mita shook her head. "Never mind," she said. She looked up at Anarim. "What does Lord Tubgal say?"

"The Abakiti are debating amongst themselves," Anarim replied. "Lord Tubgal seems sympathetic, but his son was not convinced."

"Not convinced that they need to be prepared for an attack?" Mita exclaimed dubiously.

Anarim sighed. "I know," he said.

Erisha looked back at the large group of the Abakiti men. They were circled together with a few men in the center. Every now and again someone more emphatic spoke loudly and the spontaneous council quieted as he spoke.

"Why was he not convinced?" Mita asked but at that point Dumur and his fellow sailors made it to shore. Dumur came trudging up to them, soaked and grinning.

"Tossed about a bit?" Anarim asked, amused.

"It was fantastic," Dumur replied.

Erisha raised her eyebrows.

Dumur's grin faded a little. "I'm alright, Erisha," he promised. "I'm sorry I worried you, but they took care of me and I'm here."

Erisha took a breath, but she felt Anarim touch her elbow subtly as he crossed his arms. She relented and nodded. "I'm glad you're alright," she said.

Dumur smiled broadly. "You'll have to try it eventually," he said.

"You'll catch a chill soon if you don't change and warm up," Mita said.

Dumur shivered as if on cue. Then he sneezed.

Anarim smiled. He raised a hand. "Come along, young man," he said. "We'll find you a place to dry."

Anarim and Dumur moved away from the shore. The children finished pulling the boat up onto the sand and the two boys who had also fallen in made for one of the firepits.

Mita picked up Dumur's outer layers and his weapons. Erisha handed the little girl off to an older girl and helped Mita by taking Dumur's clothes. They followed in the direction where Anarim and Dumur had headed. They caught up and managed to hand off Dumur's things before he was led away into a nearby hut by an amused middle-aged man.

"Why are we choosing to trust him?" came an angry voice from within the group of consulting Abakiti.

Everyone near enough to be affected by the angry tone grew quiet.

A young man who looked a few years older than Anarim forced his way out of the circle and looked about. His eyes latched onto Anarim when he found him, and he marched toward the King. Kas, who had been by the sea watching the children and their mothers, looked up and watched the man warily. Girisu and Sidukur appeared from out of the group of men on the outskirts and their hands went to the hilts of their swords.

"This could be our chance," the man exclaimed, staring hard at Anarim.

Lord Tubgal appeared from within the group. "Suhu," he warned sharply.

"He hasn't visited us since becoming King," Suhu continued. "His Inim Code demands we report to him, but we don't know what he's doing in Zari! His own forces could be coming to attack and dominate us! He knows nothing of sea-life, of the effort it takes to survive surrounded by sand and water."

"Suhu!" Lord Tubgal demanded. "The annual visits, according to the Code, do not only contain our reports but a tour of Zari and an explanation of the King's own stewardship. You know this."

"We revolted once," Suhu exclaimed, eyes alight. He turned to face his fellow Lerisaba. "We nearly won. We should join Lord Kankal because maybe the old man under the mountain is right. The monarchy needs recast."

"Suhu!" Lord Tubgal ordered in the silence as everyone watched Suhu step closer and closer to Anarim who was standing his ground with great composure. Girisu, Sidukur, and Kas were also slowly moving nearer to the King. "Peace! *You* revolted once, and persuaded others to join you in your rebellion. You were a traitor, turning not only on your King but on your own family. The mercy of the King and his father was the only thing that saved you from execution."

Suhu stiffened and spun to face Anarim. "What do you say, oh wise King?" he spat. "How will you defend yourself?"

Anarim watched the young man but said nothing.

Suhu gave a rageful cry and drew his long knife, but a similar weapon met Suhu's. Lord Tubgal struck Suhu's blade away and smashed the knife from Suhu's grip.

"One more word, boy," the Steward said softly, and Erisha shuddered at the threat in his voice, "and you will spend the rest of your life at sea."

Suhu eyed Lord Tubgal but relented. Lord Tubgal nodded to some warriors behind him, and they came up to their Steward.

"See him to his hut and be sure he remains there," Lord Tubgal ordered, gesturing at Suhu.

The warriors took Suhu away while Lord Tubgal turned to Anarim.

"I apologize for my son's behavior," the old man said. He bowed his head towards the two young women standing behind the King.

"I'm growing accustomed to some hostility," Anarim said grimly. "I'm not my father and there are people who still lament this."

Lord Tubgal shook his head. "Your father was a good man," he told the King, "but so are you. Your rise to kingship has broken tradition through no fault of your own. Some are suspicious even though they have no reason to be." He put a hand on Anarim's shoulder. "You must stand strong. You are not alone. We will stand against Lord Kankal, and I would be honored if you remained and fought with us."

Anarim nodded. "Absolutely," he said.

Lord Tubgal looked across at Mita. "And maybe this young woman could inform us of Lord Kankal's troop tactics and tendencies in battle."

Mita hesitated. "I can try," she said, unsure. "I can tell you right now that he will be here tomorrow evening. He will attack as soon as it's dark."

Lord Tubgal nodded. "We will be ready." He raised his voice and announced his decision to his people. "I suggest we begin our preparations," the Steward advised, "until it is time to sleep." He turned to Anarim. "You and your company need food. Come with me."

Anarim nodded towards Girisu and Sidukur who joined him as they followed Lord Tubgal. Kas came up behind Erisha and Mita, and the group was led into a large hut nearby. Dumur already sat within by the fire with the Abakiti who had been given charge of him. Dumur was enjoying a large bowl of soup, its salty smell permeating the room, and he smiled in greeting as the others entered. He was wrapped up in Abakiti clothes and his own garments hung near the fire, drying.

"Jarmin, would you please serve our guests?" Lord Tubgal asked the man with Dumur.

Jarmin rose and went to work pouring many bowls of soup for the foreigners. Dumur rose and put down his bowl as if to help but Jarmin waved him down.

Erisha and Mita joined Dumur. As they all sat together, Erisha noticed something about her brother. "You've grown," she said.

Dumur grinned proudly. "I know!" he said. "I also just realized today."

Erisha shook her head. "You're *finally* taller than me," she said with a grin.

Dumur looked at her smugly. "I suppose you'll have to get used to being the shortest now," he goaded.

Erisha glared at him but could not hid a smile for long. "You better not grow taller than Esirim," she said. "He already towers over me."

Dumur grinned. "I probably will," he said.

Erisha laughed as Jarmin served Mita and herself after giving Anarim a large bowl.

He served the rest of Anarim's company then brought his Steward a bowl.

"Have you eaten, Jarmin?" Lord Tubgal asked, not taking the bowl.

"No, my lord," Jarmin admitted.

Lord Tubgal nodded at the bowl. "Eat," he said. "I can get my own. You may return to your family now. Thank you for your help."

Jarmin bowed slightly then left the hut as ordered.

Everyone ate for a few moments as Lord Tubgal poured himself a bowl of soup. Erisha looked up at the round hole in the roof of the hut where the fire's smoke and sparks floated out into the night. The sky was dark now and she thought she glimpsed the appearance of a few stars already. There was a consistent flow of voices outside and the noise of weapons being sharpened and carried about. Erisha looked out the doorway and caught sight of men carrying torches passing back and forth as they followed other men around to give them light in the darkness.

"I'm sorry this has come upon you, Lord Tubgal," Anarim said, "but it looks like your men will be prepared to face Kankal tomorrow."

Lord Tubgal smiled humorlessly. "My people are a fierce bunch," he said. "They will not die quickly."

"Not many will sacrifice their lives before I sacrifice mine," the King replied.

The young people looked up at Anarim, but the King's face and the faces of his friends were grave and set. Erisha's chest restricted fearfully. Dumur, soup finished, put down his bowl in the sand that was the floor and cleared his throat.

"I will be able to fight by your side, won't I?" he asked Anarim.

The King looked to him and smiled gently. "You will watch my back," he said.

Dumur set back his shoulder, face alight, and he nodded.

Erisha bit her tongue and did not speak while Mita looked down at her feet.

"My men will stand with me," Anarim said, "and we will all stand with you."

Lord Tubgal looked over the King's friends and nodded approvingly. "All my men will stand," he said.

Mita raised her head and looked up at Anarim. "Where will I go?" she asked soberly.

Everyone looked at her.

"What do you mean?" Dumur stammered.

Mita looked around at each of them. "Your women don't wage war?" she asked.

Dumur looked from Mita to Anarim and back. "Yours do?" he asked. "You do?"

"At times," she said. "Not always, but at times. We're all trained for battle. I haven't been charged yet, but I knew my time would come eventually." Realization dawned on Mita's face as she looked at each of their quiet expressions. "I am trained," she assured. "I am more than able."

Anarim shook his head. "It isn't about that," he said softly. "You and Erisha will stand with the women and children tomorrow night as our last line of defense."

Dumur was glowering at the fire. He clenched his jaw then stood and left the hut.

Erisha and Mita watched him go.

"Perhaps the young ladies would like to be shown to their sleeping quarters so they don't need to be patiently exhausted by our talk," Lord Tubgal said, looking towards Erisha and Mita.

"Of course," Anarim said.

Erisha and Mita rose and followed Lord Tubgal out of the hut after wishing the men a good night. They entered the bustle outside, but the activity had slowed even though there were still men moving about everywhere and twinkling torches all around the beach.

Erisha looked but could not see Dumur anywhere.

Lord Tubgal led them past the hut they were just in and farther from the beach. Grass began to appear again among the sand, but the Steward showed them into a tent before they got too far.

"The women have prepared this for you both," he explained. A small fire was situated in the middle and two thick blankets were laid down on the sand. Erisha was impressed by the coziness of the scene and her body suddenly became very tired.

"Thank you," she said gratefully. "Lord Tubgal, would you mind keeping an eye out for my brother. He stepped out into the night, and I don't know where he is."

"He will be found," the Steward assured. "Sleep well, young ones."

"You as well," Mita returned.

Lord Tubgal smiled then headed back down toward the beach.

The young women fell onto the blankets and grew as comfortable as possible.

Erisha turned on her side and looked into the fire. She sensed Mita looking at her. She shifted her gaze and looked to Mita.

Mita shrugged and moved a little. "Good night," she said softly.

"Good night," Erisha replied.

She lay back and stared up at the stars toward the small hole in the roof. Her eyelashes fluttered several times before her eyes closed. Sleep came quickly.

"Erisha! Erisha!" came Dumur's harsh whisper.

Erisha rolled over towards him. "What?" she asked groggily, not opening her eyes.

"Erisha, wake up," Dumur demanded.

Erisha squinted and saw that it was still dark, and the only little bit of light came from the glow of the embers in the fire pit. The moonlight, however, suddenly streamed through the doorway of the tent that Dumur had left open.

Erisha squinted her eyes shut against the silver light. "What time is it?" she asked, propping herself up and blinking.

"Hours before dawn," Dumur said.

Erisha moaned and laid back down. "You woke me up before dawn?" she complained.

Dumur shushed her fiercely. "I have to tell you," he explained. He shook her. "Erisha!"

Erisha groaned and forced herself to sit up. "What?" she asked, rubbing the sleep from her eyes.

"I saw it, Erisha," Dumur said in an excited whisper as Erisha noticed that Mita continued to sleep on the other side of the tent. "I saw the Usuma."

Erisha's attention snapped to her brother's face and the shock of his statement cleared her mind some. "The Usuma?" she breathed.

Dumur nodded in the moonlight. "I was sitting on the beach," he began.

"Why?" Erisha demanded in despair. "Did you not sleep? Did no one find you?"

"I was eventually found in the crowd after I left you by Lord Tubgal and he brought me to the hut I was to sleep in with the men, but I couldn't sleep," he said. "Honestly, I tried, but I couldn't. It was strangest thing. I kept feeling drawn to the water. I listened to the waves until I answered their call, and I went out onto the beach. I sat down on the sand and looked out over the waters. The moonlight is fairly bright, and I wasn't afraid at first. The water flowed like silver in the light and the sound was so soothing. But, after a while, a feeling came over me. I can't explain it, but I sensed something's presence.

The waves became more violent for a moment and the breeze strengthened. But it all calmed again soon enough except the feeling didn't leave. I wanted to move and go back to the hut, but I couldn't. I was afraid then, but I had to figure out what was frightening me. Then," he paused, and Erisha realized her own heart was beating wildly, "I saw it. The water was barreling oddly a little ways from shore as if something was moving under it. The Usuma swam closer to shore and then its head rose out of the water. Oh, it was horrible, Erisha."

"What did it look like?" Erisha asked breathlessly.

"Its head rose out of the water and its long neck followed," Dumur said. "It was covered in scales and ridges. It was this deep blue and its skin glimmered in the moonlight. Its head was huge, and these spikes seemed to protrude from the skin at the end of the head and around the ears and jaw. Its snout jutted out with its rows of teeth gleaming in its open mouth. It made this strange low chirping sound. It looked about the shore and somehow missed me. Or maybe it didn't miss me, I don't know. But it slithered up on to the shore down the way from me and then suddenly its arms appeared out of the water and stomped down in the sand. I felt the impact from where I sat, and I nearly fell over. Its claws were long and scratched into the sand. It looked about again, its long neck slowly pulling its head about. It kept making the mesmerizing chirping sound, but then all noise stopped. It was looking at something a bit farther from shore — I think that it was focusing on this tent here, actually," he said suddenly. "I wonder…" Dumur's eyes were wide and he stared at his sister. "It wanted you."

Erisha shuddered at the thought of such a creature. "What? Why? Never mind. What happened?" she asked hurriedly.

"It rose up higher somehow," Dumur said, staring out the tent into the moonlight as he remembered. "It was going to attack, I knew that much, but I didn't know what to do. Its mouth opened wide and there was this sound of rushing wind. Then Kas appeared."

"Kas?" Erisha exclaimed in surprise.

Dumur shushed her, putting a hand over her mouth and looking over at Mita. "Yes," he hissed. "He was even more of a surprise than the Usuma in a way. He raised a hand and *spoke* to the Usuma. He told it, 'No, there will be no death or destruction tonight.' The creature looked down at him, but it began to retreat back into the water as Kas advanced. It pushed itself back into the water with its front arms and sank down a bit so that only its head remained above the surface. It continued to watch Kas, and it was quiet.

Then, the most terrible thing happened. It looked at me. I'm sure, actually, it knew I had been there the whole time. All I could do, Erisha, was stare back at the creature. It was horrible. It floated closer and closer to me and Kas followed it along the shore also watching me. It came so close, Erisha. It stuck its head farther out again and neared me. I couldn't move, I could hardly breath. Its snout nearly touched me, and I could smell its salty breath. It snorted at me, wet air hitting my face, and its

A. B. HOLMSTEDT

golden eyes taunted me. I looked into those eyes and terrible, terrible images came into my mind."

"Of what?" Erisha asked urgently.

Dumur shook his head and swallowed. "Finally, I managed to speak."

"You *spoke* to it?" Erisha hissed in alarm.

"I told it to leave," her brother said. "I told it, 'Go!' And it went... I thought it was going to eat me, but if backed away and disappeared into the waves. And eventually the horrible feeling abated and I could only hear the waves again."

Both siblings breathed deeply.

"Kas sat by me for a while," Dumur said. "Neither of us said anything for a long time until he asked me why I was awake, and I told him I couldn't sleep and he smiled. 'Sometimes,' he told me, 'it is better to let go of dangerous, angry thoughts and just to sleep.' I nodded and stood. 'I think I'll sleep now,' I told him, and I thanked him. He told me I had done well, but I can't think of what he meant. I left him and meant to go into the hut, but I realized I had to tell you first. I wanted to make sure you were alright." He finished and looked a little abashed.

Erisha hugged him tightly. "I'm glad you're alright," she said shakily. "And I'm glad Kas was there. I'm fine, don't worry. We should probably both sleep now. You need rest."

Dumur nodded then hung his head tiredly. "You're right," he said and he yawned. He stood and smiled down at her. "Good night."

"I'll see you in the morning," Erisha said, watching him.

142

Dumur left the tent and made sure to close the doorway again.

Erisha lay back down and sighed deeply. Her mind was racing as she went back over everything Dumur had divulged. She shook her head several times and clapped her hands over her mouth once, imagining the creature her brother had faced. She puzzled over Kas' relation to the Usuma, and she wondered if Dumur would begin questioning the identity of Kas as she had.

Eventually, however, her eyelids began to grow heavy again and her heartbeat slowed. She fell back asleep.

CHAPTER NINE

NIGHT DARKENS BY THE SEA

S he awoke this time to Mita's gentle voice calling to her. Erisha opened her eyes and bright sunlight greeted her. She groaned and rolled over to face Mita. Her body subtly ached everywhere. She closed her eyes and raised her eyebrows, wondering how she ever got herself into such a strange situation of trekking across Alland with the King and his close friends to stop a manic Steward.

Her facial expression must have been expressive enough because Mita laughed. "Good morning," she said cheerfully. She held out a bowl to Erisha. "Here is your breakfast. I managed to grab some for you."

Erisha sat up and took the bowl. "How late is it?" she asked.

"The sun is high in the sky," Mita replied, "and the beach has been a flurry of activity for a while. Eat," she encouraged. "Do you feel poorly?"

Erisha shook her head and drank the warm liquid in the bowl. It was salty and Erisha realized there was something in the bottom of the bowl. "I'm just tired," she said. "What is this?"

"Boiled seaweed," Mita stated. "I was hesitant as well. It doesn't look pretty but it tastes fine."

"And I supposed..." Erisha trailed off, lifting a wary hand towards the bowl she had set down before her."

"Yes," Mita said with a nod. "You just... use your hands. After you've drunk all the water."

"Oh," Erisha said. She picked up the bowl again and took another drink.

"Here, I'll grab you some water to actually drink," Mita said, standing. "You'll need it." She left the tent as Erisha continued to carefully sip from the bowl. When Mita returned with a large wooden cup filled with fresh water, Erisha had drunk most of the sea water and was mentally bracing herself to pick up a piece of seaweed.

"So, I just eat it?" she asked Mita.

Mita nodded. "Just shove it in your mouth," she said grimly. "It's the only way." She smiled. "You should have seen the men this morning. They handled themselves wonderfully, but none of them really liked it. Dumur nearly choked at first."

Erisha looked up, soft, slippery seaweed between her fingers and before her mouth. "He choked?" she exclaimed, looking critically at the seaweed.

"It's alright!" Mita laughed. "It's his own fault. He stuffed too much in. Try it."

Erisha looked at her uneasily but dropped the seaweed into her mouth and chewed. Then she swallowed. She shuddered, imagining green sea slime sliding down her throat. She took a breath.

Mita raised her eyebrows expectantly.

Erisha took another breath. "It's alright," she finally said, forcing herself to pick out another strand.

"Just be happy you weren't eating with all the Lerisaba watching you," Mita teased.

Erisha grinned and downed another piece of seaweed.

"When you're done, drink the water then come on out," Mita said, rising. "We need to figure out what's going on."

Erisha nodded her agreement and Mita left the tent. Erisha hurriedly ate the rest of her sea plant breakfast then thoroughly enjoyed the fresh water. She stood and felt refreshed. She brushed herself off and arranged her clothes properly. She smoothed back her hair and re-braided it. She grabbed the dishware and left the tent.

The sun welcomed her and warmed her face although the day was chilly and breezy by the seaside. A few Abakiti passed her and greeted her. Erisha asked one woman where she should put the dishes and the woman asked her to clean them in the sea then the river inlet a little further down the beach. Erisha gladly complied, sensing the activity in the community. As she grew closer to the beach, the noise of men's voices grew louder and the sound of metal hitting metal alarmed Erisha.

She rounded a hut and came upon the sight of many different groups of men training. The archers were practicing with their bows and fashioning arrows. The swordsmen were sparring under Sidukur's watch. Girisu and Dumur were with the small group of horsemen. The women were busy making the midday meal and moving belongings from the huts to the places farther back from the beach nearer to the riverside. Children were the only ones unworried, keeping their distance from the busy adults but playing lightheartedly.

Erisha did not see Anarim about but realized after a moment that he was probably with Lord Tubgal discussing defense and attack strategies somewhere. She went to the sea's edge and let the waves wash over the dishes. She rose after they were clean and stared out over the water, thinking of Dumur's story from the night before and marveling that such a creature could live in something that looked so beautiful. Yet, she supposed, the sea was wild and brutal too.

"Good morning," came a voice behind her.

Erisha was quietly pleased with herself for not jumping in surprise because she had sensed him approaching. "Good morning," she replied, smiling back at him.

Anarim stood beside her. "Are you well?" he asked.

She nodded. "Just tired," she admitted. "Are you well? I must go bring these to the inlet," she explained, moving to head down the beach. "May you walk with me?"

"I may," Anarim said with a smile, but his step fell alongside hers.

Erisha took in his appearance. He was not wearing his outer coat nor his cloak. His shirt sleeves were rolled up. His sword was tightly strapped around his waist and he had cloth wrapped around his palms. He was slightly sweaty and dirty already. "You have been busy," she said.

"I have," he replied as they walked. "We gathered all possible weapons we could and have been trying to prepare the men for every possibility we can think of. I've been rotating between training with the men, discussing possible positions with Lord Tubgal, and scouting the area."

Erisha nodded, feeling guilty that she had slept in. "And?" she asked.

Anarim shook his head. "I do not know," he said. "Mita hasn't an idea of how many warriors Lord Kankal will bring. Our biggest advantage will be being prepared and hopefully we can surprise Kankal."

Erisha nodded, glimpsing the inlet ahead. "Are you well?" she asked again. "I didn't give you a chance to answer before."

Anarim hesitated for the shortest moment. "I am well," he said.

Erisha studied his profile, but they came to the river of fresh water that flowed into the sea. Anarim took the bowl and they both knelt down to wash out the dishes. Erisha kept stealing glances at him, thoughtful. After a couple of swishes around in the water, Anarim handed the bowl back to Erisha and he splashed his face with water.

Erisha stood and watched him patiently. Her brows furrowed and her lips pursed, but she turned away as he stood. They began to walk back.

Erisha paused and worried, but she forced herself to speak her mind. "You are not well," she stated.

Anarim looked to her, taken aback, and she set her mouth and looked back. He was silent but his eyes searched hers. She raised her chin and kept her mouth closed against an apology for speaking so bluntly.

They looked ahead again and walked on a few paces in silence.

Anarim sighed and Erisha turned to him. Yet, he continued to hesitate. He stopped and she stopped with him. He looked to her then looked away. Finally, he shook his head.

"I will not worry you," he said, moving to walk again.

"You are worrying me," Erisha pointed out, remaining where she was.

Anarim stood. He gazed steadily at her and sighed through his nose. "I am afraid," he said.

"Of Lord Kankal?" she asked gently, moved by his admission.

"Of what may happen tonight," Anarim explained. "People will die tonight and I do not want them to. We may best Lord Kankal, but he very well may best us. I am at a lost for what to do and how to stop him. I don't know if I can stop him."

"Maybe not alone," Erisha agreed slowly. "But you are not alone." She touched his arm. "You will stop Lord Kankal. You'll find a way."

"I can see a way ahead if we get through tonight," Anarim said. "We must get through tonight first though."

"We will." She smiled up at him encouragingly. "Is there anything I can do to help?"

Anarim shook his head slowly. "No," he admitted. "Not for this type of task."

Erisha nodded, quiet.

He took her hand from his arm and squeezed it. "We will make it," he said firmly.

They walked back together then parted ways. Anarim went to look over the men before the midday meal and Erisha found Mita. The young women helped the Abakiti women dish up the midday meal and hand out the food to the men. Then they sat down to eat as well.

The day was quiet for a while after the meal. Everyone rested and Dumur found Erisha and Mita. They sat on the beach in the sun and by the water, talking and laughing lazily. Dumur told them of the small cavalry's progress proudly and the young women had Dumur show them the dunes that were to be the look-out spots come evening. They climbed up a dune together and looked over the country that shifted from sandy grass into wide, green fields with mountain ranges in the West and the river to the East. Beyond the river was a smaller range of mountains called the Igis that also led down to the sea. Erisha declared she saw the beginning of the Forests of Tiranna in the far Northeast across the river, but Dumur and Mita were not as sure.

They descended the dune and went to rest in the shade now. Dumur ran to find them all some water to drink and Erisha dozed off in the coolness of the shade for a while. When she awoke, Dumur and Mita were sitting at the edge of the shade, chatting.

"You'll have to visit Furun someday," Dumur was saying to Mita. "We'll show you all our favorite spots and we'll show you the village. And you'll have to be sure to come for a festival so you can experience a real celebration."

Mita smiled. "I would like that," she said, but her smile faded slightly.

"And I could come visit you in the mountains," Dumur added.

"Oh, yes, and I can take you to the highest peaks and we can look down over Alland," Mita said, but although her tone was happy Erisha sensed her fading spirit. It puzzled Erisha.

Erisha sat up and they greeted her. They all sat and allowed the salty breeze to ruffle their hair. Men began appearing on the beach again and Dumur left quickly to see if he could aid Girisu further with the horses.

Erisha and Mita watched the men organize themselves. Erisha wondered about how there was nothing she could do to help. She realized that what happened tonight would influence so many lives, and she had not done much during this journey. So much had happened to Erisha so far yet these men around her were preparing to face a traitor while she appreciated the beauty of the shore.

"I've been so passive," Erisha murmured. She stared out at the water washing against the sand. She had seen numerous sights in the past few days filled with similar beauty; her dream of travelling the realms was being granted. Yet, the realms were more than beautiful places to see. They were homes and they were being threatened.

"Do you think we have a chance?" Mita asked Erisha suddenly.

Erisha looked at her profile. "I would think you'd have a better idea than me," she replied.

Mita played with the sand and scratched at the tiny grains with her fingers. "I don't know," she finally said, "but I have this feeling that if anyone can beat Lord Kankal it is the King."

Erisha nodded. "I think you're right."

"I don't have too much hope."

"Neither do I, but, sometimes, isn't hope all we have?"

"Hope breeds strength," Mita said absently.

"And perspective breeds wisdom," Erisha said.

Mita looked at her.

"It's as my grandfather used to say," Erisha explained. "We live for the day and in the day, but, after years pass, the day's pains will not be felt, only half-remembered."

"Unless you die," Mita said numbly.

"Especially if you die," Erisha countered, "because you will not be here anymore at all."

Mita stared at her and shook her head in disbelief. "To have so much suddenly and know that it might all be taken away," she said. "I would never have thought I'd find people like you. I call you my friend and do so proudly."

Erisha smiled. "I call you my friend as well," she decided.

Night approached quickly. Food was passed around as soon as the sun began to set noticeably. The community was tense and quiet now. Erisha spoke in hushed tones with Mita or any of the children who came up with a question. The children were full of anxious energy. They all talked in loud whispers and passed about or rocked absently as they sat on the ground.

The first group of scouts were sent off and Sidukur arranged the archers. The horses were brought out to the men and one creature's reins were given to Anarim while Lord Tubgal was given another set of reins. They walked about the set up with their horses following them as they checked over all the men.

Finally, the women were sent back far into the small village with the children. They were told to remain in the huts for protection. Erisha looked about for Dumur but could not see her brother anywhere. She cursed that fact that he had been involving himself so much and was now tall enough to be mistaken from the back as any other warrior. Mita waited beside her as the Abakiti women and children disappeared from the beach.

Anarim advanced towards them with his horse trailing behind him. "Mita," he said, "would you remain hidden in the nearest hut? We may have need of your assistance if we think of any last-minute problems or questions."

Mita nodded. She lifted her chin, but Erisha felt the fear rising in her.

"May I remain with her?" Erisha asked.

Anarim hesitated. "Of course," he said curtly. "Stay hidden."

Erisha nodded and Dumur came rushing up. She pulled him into a hug. He held her tightly.

"I love you," Dumur said, stepping away.

Erisha sniffed and refused to cry. "I love you too," she said. "Be careful." She looked up at Anarim for a moment but could not add anything.

Dumur swallowed but stepped back as Anarim mounted his horse. "Stay safe," he said. "Both of you." He stepped away, watching them for a moment, then he turned and headed back towards the small cavalry.

Anarim steered his horse about as the darkness fell. "Mita, we will come to you," he said. "Stay hidden."

Both young women nodded.

"We will," Erisha promised.

Anarim nodded and rode away.

Erisha and Mita exchanged glances then headed into the nearest hut. Erisha looked at the waves which glowed purple and red in the faded light, and she was reminded of the embers of a fire as they burned out but still had the power to spark into a bright blaze if stoked right. She blinked and followed Mita into the dark, murky hut.

They stood by a window, each on either side of the opening, and they carefully peeked out. They were able to watch the men farther down the beach, torches lit and swords at the ready. The only sounds heard on the beach were the rolling of waves and the sporadic neighing of the horses.

Everyone waited as the sun set completely and the shadows engulfed the seascape. The moon was mostly hidden behind clouds and Erisha and Mita squinted in the dark to distinguish the men before their eyes grew accustomed to the lack of light.

Time passed in quiet tension. Erisha had to keep reminding herself to breathe and to ease back her shoulders. She thought she heard Anarim speak to the men a few times, but she could not be sure with the splashing of the water in the background.

There was sudden movement and Erisha heard Mita gasp in surprise across the window frame. There were voices but Erisha could not make out what was happening. She thought she heard the sound of thunder and she looked at the clouds above the sea. She realized, however, that the rumbling was not thunder but the sound of many horses' hooves rushing across the ground. Riders appeared from around the dunes, and they reared up at the sight of Anarim and the Abakiti army. The thundering did not end but quieted as warriors ran onto the beach behind the riders.

Erisha saw the gleam of raised weapons in the torches' light.

"What is this?" demanded an angry voice and Erisha recognized the voice of Lord Kankal. She looked over at Mita and saw the girl tense.

"Lord Kankal," came Anarim's voice clearly. "You are ordered, by your King, to leave."

There was a silence then a loud, cold laugh rang out.

"I see, Lord Tubgal," came Lord Kankal's voice, "that our dear King has gotten to you before I have."

"A blessing," Lord Tubgal retorted coolly.

"Are you sure?" Lord Kankal shot back. "You would rather trust a young fool than an old, trusted friend?"

"The days of our friendship are over, Kankal," Lord Tubgal announced.

"Is that so?" Lord Kankal mused.

Mita turned to Erisha suddenly and, in the dim moonlight that was struggling to break through the cloud cover, Erisha saw the terror in her eyes. "He will kill them," she whispered tightly. "All of them." Her voice did not tremble.

"Leave my realm, Kankal," Lord Tubgal countered as the two armies, the Felrisan troops swelling out behind their horsemen and ready to overwhelm the Lerisaba, faced each other.

There was a pause. "How did you know I was coming?" Lord Kankal questioned, pulling up his horse.

Erisha looked over at Mita and sensed a moment before it happened what the young woman was going to do. Mita made to move and turn for the doorway, but Erisha reacted and grabbed her before she could show herself.

"Mita, no!" she hissed in her friend's ear.

Mita was breathing heavily. "They will all die because of me," she cried.

"They will die if you go out there," Erisha demanded. She intuited the young woman's desperate course of action and decided against it.

"Answer me!" Lord Kankal yelled furiously.

At that moment, Mita broke away from Erisha and Erisha acted.

"No!" she screamed as Anarim growled for Lord Kankal to leave.

Erisha's scream startled Mita enough for Erisha to grab the young woman and whirl her about and back into the hut. Erisha paused but only momentarily, and she walked out of the hut and approached the armies across the sand.

All the warriors stood frozen in place as she neared. Erisha's eyes sought Anarim. When she found him, his expression was hard. Everyone watched her.

Lord Kankal adjusted himself in his saddle. "This is not a woman's business, young lady," he warned.

"From what I've heard," Erisha replied bitingly, turning to face him, "you do not make that distinction." Yet, she noticed that, thankfully, there did not seem to be any women warriors in the Felrisan group that night. She swallowed and pressed on. "You must leave, Lord Kankal," she continued. "The lives that may be lost, including your own, are not worth whatever your desires are."

"Is this your tactic, your Majesty?" Lord Kankal mocked, looking to Anarim. "Have a woman come beg for peace? Well, let me tell you," the old man said, looking back at Erisha, "I will not agree to peace."

"Your whole purpose is to bring peace to the land," Erisha demanded. "If you war tonight, you disgrace and fail all the

Kidugul Stewards before you and you destroy any shred of honor you still have."

Lord Kankal roared angrily and raised his sword, urging his steed forward. Yells rose from each side. Lord Kankal swung at Erisha.

His blade did not touch her. Its metal struck against metal and Erisha opened her eyes to see Mita blocking Lord Kankal's blade with her long knife. The Steward of Felrisa started at Mita in surprise, but Mita swung his blade away and kicked at his horse roughly. The horse reared about, but Lord Kankal had regained his composure.

"Traitor!" he raged.

Mita screamed at him, a yell so full of fury that it shocked everyone into stillness, including Kankal. Erisha, watching the old man, saw his eyes snap with a dangerous light. His hand moved for his bow. His movement brought everyone out of their amazement.

The Abakiti surrounded but not before Lord Kankal had swiftly notched an arrow and shot at Mita. He directed his horse into his troop of warriors as Mita fell, the arrow finding a mark. The sea dwellers positioned themselves in front of the two women as Lord Kankal arranged the Felrisans. Many of the Lekur stared at where Mita had fallen. Dumur, who had cried out madly when Lord Kankal had aimed at Mita, was by the young women in moments.

The arrow had found its place in Mita's upper shoulder between her shoulder and neck. It lay inches above her heart.

Erisha and Dumur kneeled on the ground beside her. Erisha felt helpless as she watched blood seep into Mita's shirt, but Dumur startled her out of her shock.

"Erisha, help me," Dumur demanded, carefully lifting Mita up by the shoulders. The sound of weapons clanging together and yells of the men surrounding them.

Mita, eyes closed but breathing labored, cried out.

Erisha lifted Mita up as far as she could while Dumur adjusted so he could carry Mita. Erisha was skeptical, but she was thoroughly surprised when her brother lifted Mita up in his arms and made for the hut. Erisha followed, not daring to look back. They entered the hut and Erisha helped Dumur to lower Mita as gently as possible onto the ground.

"I'll find some women to help tend to her," Erisha said. "You guard the way."

Dumur nodded and both siblings left the hut again. Fortunately, a couple of Abakiti were already nearby having heard Erisha's and Mita's screams. They came to help Mita at once and decided to move her back by the rest of the women and children.

Erisha helped them lift Mita up again who, by now, had fallen unconscious. They exited the hut as quickly as possible while Dumur guarded the way, bow in hand as he shot arrows into the fray. Erisha looked at the ensuing battle as the women carried Mita away. She meant to follow them but the fact that she could already see men lying on the beach in dark slumps kept her. Her heart beat in her ears and a terrible, horrible feeling filled her.

Dumur drew his sword and made to rush into the fight as Mita was taken out of sight, but something stopped him. He turned, eyes wide, then he pushed Erisha after the women. He spun back towards the waters, not seeing if she went. He stared at the waves.

He gripped Erisha suddenly. "Erisha, go," he breathed urgently.

She looked at him then at the sea. A large hump of water was racing toward shore. Erisha looked to Dumur again and she felt her heart turn cold in fear. "Dumur…" she said.

Yet, her brother was stepping away from her and raising his sword.

First, the head appeared from out the water. It was huge and scaly with a long snout and wide jaw. It slowed and approached the beach silently, its attention solely on the ensuing battle. Men shouted and cried out, crossing blades and oblivious to the coming, greater danger. Horses began to whinny and buck. Chaos reigned before her eyes. Not one warrior saw the Usuma rising up behind them, its huge forearms stomping out of the water and onto the beach as its long, long tail flicked excitedly back in the water.

Erisha watched as Dumur continued to approach the creature, but then the beast roared. The sound, reverberating out of its mouth as it threw back its head, came out as a blend between a screech and bellow. The air vibrated and those near the Usuma, including Dumur, were thrown to the ground.

There was a moment of complete silence as all the men looked up at the creature staring down at them. Then, real chaos ensued. The Usuma lunged down, jaws opened wide. Men screamed and flung away. The Usuma's snout slammed into the sand, just missing a rider and his horse. It straightened back up and looked down at the warriors who now ran around the beach in all directions. The Usuma bent down and slithered its neck around after frantic men.

Erisha realized that the Felrisans were retreating from the beach with Lord Kankal on his horse at the lead. Most Lekur followed their Steward as best they could while others remained behind to protect their dead and injured.

The Usuma looked after the Felrisans as Lord Kankal arranged a line of archers. The creature rose high, and Erisha thought she heard the sound of air being sucked in. Lord Kankal shouted for the arrows to be loosed. A low rumble came from the Usuma then an ear-splitting crack and the night lit up! Fire burst forth from the Usuma's mouth and brunt all incoming arrows into ashes. Many men fell to the ground and covered their heads. Erisha felt the heat from where she stood. The beach was lit up by bright flames.

The Usuma closed its mouth, and all grew dim again in the moonlight. The Usuma stretched forward toward the Lekur, the sucking sound coming again as the creature opened its mouth a little. Lord Kankal dragged his horse about and, without a look back, thundered away. Those Felrisans with him ran after him.

The sucking sound faded and the Usuma drew back, satisfied in that area of the beach. It turned to the men left. It drew down by Anarim and Erisha wanted to scream but no sound came up from within her throat. Anarim warily stood his ground before the beast. Kas stepped forward and Erisha's heart lept. Yet, Kas did not do anything. Anarim raised his sword and hesitated. The Usuma snapped forward, jaws open, and it was only Kas's quick reaction of leaping onto Anarim that saved them both. The Usuma's head lunged forward above them, barely missing them as it closed it empty jaws.

"Fool!" came Kas' voice harshly.

The Usuma's head swung about, and Kas was on his feet. Dumur, however, had snuck up to the water's edge by this point and he slashed furiously at one of the Usuma's arms.

The Usuma screeched out in pain and took a couple steps back into the water. It arched around and faced Dumur, but Dumur did not hesitate. He swung at the creature's face and stuck it across the jaw. The Usuma did not roar angrily this time. It slowly brought its head back around after the impact of the hit and it stared at Dumur making an ominous chirping noise in the back of its throat.

"Leave!" Dumur yelled, stepping closer to the Usuma's face. "Go!"

The Usuma stared at Dumur darkly.

"Leave!" Dumur demanded, raising his sword again and staring levelly at the creature. "Now."

The Usuma paused then it raised its head and stared up at the clear sky for a moment. It lowered its head and looked to the panting warriors, to Dumur who still stood tall with his weapon raised, and finally to Erisha. Its gaze told her that it had always known that she too had been there.

The Usuma withdrew and sunk back into the sea. Everyone watched the rippling lump of water move away from shore and, when it disappeared, everyone breathed a collective sigh of relief.

The Abakiti confronted the Lekur left and the Lekur dropped their weapons. Everyone tended to their dead and injured. Erisha absently watched Dumur join Anarim and his companions as they helped those lying on the sand. Some warriors ran about to put out the fire burning through the shrubs at the back of the beach where the Usuma had attacked Lord Kankal.

Erisha realized she needed to be with Mita and the women but when she made to move her legs buckled beneath her and she fell onto the sand. Her head spun and she lay here breathing heavily. She forced herself to take deep, slow breaths. Her vision cleared and just before she attempted to sit up an Abakiti neared and helped her up.

"My Lady," he said concernedly as he pulled her up and surprised Erisha by carrying her. "Are you alright?"

"Just faint," Erisha said. "Thank you for your help."

The man began carrying her back toward the women. "Are you injured?" he asked.

Erisha shook her head. "No," she said. "You can put me down."

Erisha fancied she saw the man raise an eyebrow, but he stopped and set her down gently. Her feet touched the ground, and her legs did not give in. Confident, she took a step forward, but she swayed and reached out for help. The Abakiti scooped her back up and continued. Erisha looked back towards the beach and saw Anarim and the others. She locked eyes with Anarim for a moment and sensed his anger.

The women cried out in relief when they saw Erisha. They rushed up and took Erisha from the young man, helping her stand. Erisha heard the sounds of crying and hushing and sniffing and nervous whispering. Before any of the women could ask, Anarim arrived.

"The battle is over," the King said. "The losses are few. There are many injured, but all will be well. Please, rest, and we will take care of what must be dealt with until morning. Then you may take over. Sleep, for we are safe tonight."

Many women nodded and bowed to the King, giving their words of thanks. Anarim nodded respectfully and left without a glance towards Erisha. Yes, he was angry with her. She thanked the man who had carried her before sagging in the women's support, morose. The women reacted by fussing over her and bringing her over near Mita where she lay still unconscious but no longer bleeding. Her shoulder wound had been deftly wrapped and although Mita looked pale her breathing came steadily.

Erisha was set down beside Mita and a blanket was thrown over her shoulders. She was brought water to drink then asked if she needed anything else. Erisha refused, bemused by their attention. She encouraged them to look after those who really needed help as she would be fine, and she offered to attend to Mita for them.

The women with her agreed to this arrangement and went on their way back into the continuous activity of dealing with the elderly, the hysterical, and the young who all needed calmed.

Erisha sat beside Mita and watched the young woman breath a couple times. She looked up at the clear skies and gazed at the sea of stars above. Her own breathing slowed and she brought her gaze down to watch as the women went about successfully creating a peaceful environment. News spread that the Felrisans had been overcome and there had only been a few deaths. There was a quieter worry now because the identities of those who had died were not known, but a stronger feeling of relief washed through the community.

CHAPTER TEN

ERISHA AND THE KING

E risha did not know when she fell asleep, but at some point as the camp grew quieter her head had nodded and her eyelids had closed and exhaustion had overcome her. She woke in the early morning still in her sitting position and her back cramped as she moved. Slowly, she made it onto her feet, and she stretched her aching body.

She looked down at Mita in the dim light of the rising sun. Her friend's skin looked pink and clammy. Erisha fell to her knees beside Mita and felt the young woman's forehead. It was hot to the touch. Erisha examined the area of the wound and gently touched the area. It was swelling. Erisha sat back, knowing that all these signs pointed towards healing but also knowing how uncomfortable Mita would be when she finally woke up.

Erisha checked that the young woman's breathing still came steadily then she quickly made her way around the sleeping people and out towards the river with a large bowl in hand. She trekked to the riverbank and filled the bowl with cold, fresh water and she found some herbs on the way back that she knew had some healing effect. Upon return, she knelt again beside Mita and filled a small cup with some of the water from the bowl. She crushed in one type of herb and lifted Mita up.

Slowly, she poured the liquid in Mita's mouth drop by drop, making sure she did not choke but persisting until all the water was swallowed. She lay Mita back down and used the other herbs to make a paste in the cup with a little bit of water. She gently put this paste on Mita's wound, pulling back the bandage. Mita grimaced and moaned as Erisha applied the paste, but Erisha took the response as a good sign that the young woman was slowly coming to. With the rest of the water, Erisha wet a cloth and cooled Mita's skin.

When she thought she had done all she could do for the moment, Erisha rose and glanced about to see other women waking. Erisha was satisfied that if anything happened to Mita they would be more than equipped, so Erisha made for the beach to glimpse the situation there. A few women spotted her leaving and decided to join her. They crept about quietly and looked around a hut to see out onto the beach.

The men lay about, sleeping on the sand. Horses rested nearby and many warriors slept with weapons in hand or near at hand. A couple fires were smoking lightly, having been started the night before and finally going out now. Erisha looked around but did not see the King or Sidukur or Girisu or Kas.

"Where are the wounded?" a woman whispered beside her.

"Maybe in a hut?" another woman offered.

Erisha led the way, skirting around the hut and not onto the beach. She passed a window and, after an encouraging nod from the women behind her, she carefully peeked in.

The hut was dusky with the morning glow pouring in through the doorway, but Erisha was fairly sure only one man slept within. She lowered herself and told the woman closest to her what she had seen. That woman snuck a peek and declared the man to be Lord Tubgal. They moved onto the next hut and the last before the long stretch of beach.

Erisha braved a look in again and was startled when she glimpsed movement. She hid herself and the women looked at her, eyes wide. Erisha took a breath and shook her head. She raised herself up and looked in again to see men lying on the floor. The King and his companions were tending to them, the injured warriors. Erisha, smiling, related what she had seen to the women.

The women rose without hesitation and walked around to enter the tent. Not as confident in this sudden course of action, Erisha followed warily. The women blazed into the hut unannounced and spoke in hushed tones to the surprised men. Erisha remained outside the hut and waited. She leaned against the hut wall and looked out across the sea.

Men slept along the beach, though away from the shore. It looked like they had fallen asleep any place they had found free to rest their bodies. Erisha turned her head when she thought she heard someone at the doorway, but her eyes rested on three figures lying outside the hut but nearby it: the three slain Abakiti men. Erisha stared at the bodies then abruptly looked back at the sea. She breathed deeply and was grateful for the breeze. There was never stagnant air by the sea; everything was always moving and changing. Maybe that's why her spirit did not feel as troubled by the death of these three men because she knew the people here would handle the loss well. Life was always full of little gains and losses, a coming and going. Her throat tightened thinking about such things, but she raised her chin and did not cry.

Kas came through the doorway, and he gazed at the waters before looking around and seeing Erisha.

"Hello," he said, stepping near.

Erisha smiled. "Hello," she said softly. "How are you? Are you alright?"

"I am unwounded," Kas said with a sigh.

Erisha looked at the sea with him. "Somehow, I suspected you would be," she admitted. "I don't worry about you."

Kas smiled but then the smile faded. "No, you wouldn't," he said. "You needn't."

Erisha glanced at him. "Yet, you are still unwell," she said.

"I do not like war," Kas said. "There is so much pain."

"Do you know pain?" Erisha asked.

Kas' eyes widened in surprise and Erisha was pleased to know she was able to cause him to be more interactive and... ordinary. "You thought I didn't?" he said. "We all know pain."

Erisha studied him and he held her gaze as always. "But there is not war or strife where you come from," she said finally.

Kas laughed and shook his head. "You speak of what you don't know," he said.

"Tell me," she said eagerly.

Kas gazed at her but shook his head again. "I cannot," he said.

"Cannot or will not?" she questioned.

"May not," he clarified.

"Oh," Erisha replied. She rested her head back against the hut. She nodded.

They stared out at the waters again.

"I would like to tell you," Kas said suddenly. "But it is not for me—"

"It's alright," Erisha said with a smile. "I'll figure it out someday."

Kas laughed softly. "You'll know someday," he said.

Sidukur came out of the hut and greeted Erisha heartily.

"It feels like an age since I last spoke to you," the large warrior said, looking down at her fondly. "You remind me at times of my little Sagi, my daughter. She's a stubborn lass." His eyes twinkled, yet his face fell soon after. Erisha touched his arm sympathetically. "How is the other woman of our company?" he asked.

"She'll make it, I'm sure," Erisha said. "She's in pain, but I… it cannot be helped."

"No," Sidukur said with a shake of his head. "It cannot. Mita will be well."

"How are you?" Erisha asked the burly man. "Unharmed?"

"Scratched and bruised but well otherwise. Fortunate, I'd say."

Erisha nodded but Anarim and Girisu came out of the hut and distracted her for a moment. Girisu came to greet her, but Anarim merely glanced at her before moving out across the beach.

"Erisha," Girisu said kindly, but all eyes were on the King.

"Hello, Girisu," Erisha said quietly. "Unharmed?"

"Yes," he said with a smile. "And you?"

"Oh, I am well," Erisha said, looking up at him.

"I wish I could say so much for him," Sidukur spoke, eyes still watching the King who was roaming among the men on the beach.

"Is he injured?" Erisha asked sharply, and she sensed Kas tense beside her.

"We don't know," Sidukur replied. "He will not let us attend to him."

"His shirt is bloodied," Girisu said. "But with his blood or another's blood is the question."

Sidukur looked down at Erisha. "You should go to him, lass," he urged. "He may let you minister to him."

One of Kas' hands came down to rest on one of her shoulders. He knew her internal struggle, afraid to anger the King further. She felt some of her stress abate as she looked up at him.

Erisha took a breath. "Very well," she said, stepping away from the hut.

"Thank you," Sidukur said, and Erisha smiled back at them all.

She walked after Anarim. She calmed her heart and was careful not to disturb any of the sleeping men as she approached Anarim. She neared him as he was letting the seawater wash over his calloused hands. Once he finished, he looked up at her in the brightening sunlight.

She looked down at him. "Hello," she managed.

He lowered his head for a moment, but Erisha glimpsed the smile before he could hide it. She pursed her lips and looked out at the horizon. He was laughing at her.

"Hello," he said. He stood and looked down at her. "You shouldn't be afraid of me," he said, walking pass her.

Erisha turned as he passed her. The audacity of this man, King or not King. She followed him away from the sleeping men. "Well, maybe you shouldn't look so fearsome and un-friendly," she retorted.

He looked over at her as she came to stand beside him. "Maybe I shouldn't," he agreed.

Erisha glanced at him. "I know you're angry with me," she said.

His expression became grim. "I am," he assented.

"And I know why," Erisha continued.

"Kankal is not a man to be reasoned with, Erisha," Anarim said. "What you did last night was foolish."

"I understand," Erisha said.

Anarim held her gaze. "Good," he said quietly, not pressing the point.

"Are we friends again?" Erisha asked.

Anarim hesitated. "We were never not friends," he said.

"You were rather hostile," Erisha pointed out.

Anarim studied her then lowered his head, and Erisha wondered at the shift in his behavior. "I'm sorry," he said.

Erisha felt an oddness grow within her. Momentarily, the sea's constant breeze whipped by them more vigorously, and the waves slapped onto instead of lapped the shore. The water splashed up and drops hit Erisha's and Anarim's faces as they watched each other. A restless bewilderment grew in Erisha.

"It's alright," she said quickly, pushing away the feeling. The waters and wind calmed. "The others are worried about you," she continued without taking a breath, "because you may be injured and you're not letting anyone help you. So, I'm here to help you and you must stop being stubborn."

Anarim looked taken aback. "Alright," he said.

Erisha swallowed, relieved he had not sent her away. "Good," she said firmly.

"I'm alright," Anarim assured. "Only my forearm and my back were cut last night. I'm not seriously harmed."

Erisha raised an eyebrow. "The wounds must be cleaned," she said critically. "We must find you a place to sit."

"Right here?" Anarim asked in surprise.

"Well, no, I suppose not," Erisha said. "I'll need fresh water and alcohol perhaps."

"I'd rather not go back by the women," Anarim said, moving to follow her.

"Why?" Erisha asked, amused.

Anarim's expression grew sheepish.

Erisha laughed as they walked along the beach and Anarim grinned. "You don't like be fretted about?" she teased.

Anarim smiled ruefully. "Not particularly," he said.

Erisha nodded. "Very well," she said with a smile, having pity on him.

They went around the beach and Anarim waited by a hut still out on the beach while Erisha went to fetch supplies from the women. She passed by Mita, and she checked on the state of the young woman. Mita was breathing well and had cooled a bit. A woman came over to Erisha and told her that Mita had woken up while she was gone. Mita had seemed in a daze, however, and had quickly fallen to sleep again.

Erisha thanked the woman and found cloth, a bowl of fresh water, and bottle of medicinal alcohol. She looked about before returning to Anarim. She wondered suddenly where Dumur was and worried for a moment if he was alright before realized she could simply ask Anarim. She turned to the King who was resting against one of the pillars of the hut's canopy.

"Do you know where Dumur is?" Erisha asked as she approached.

"With the men and fast asleep the last time I saw him," Anarim replied. "Don't worry. He was bruised and battered but otherwise unharmed."

Erisha took a breath as she set down the supplies. "Good," she said. "Thank you."

Anarim nodded. He pulled back the sleeve from over his first wound and allowed Erisha to cleanse the area and wash the deep gash out with alcohol.

"How many men did the Lekur lose?" Erisha asked as she worked.

"About a dozen," Anarim replied, "and many of those who are injured or remained behind are still on the beach. There were arguments last night of setting up a guard, but the Lekur were adamant of their peaceability. The men quickly fell asleep once those who were dead or injured were situated and I let the matter go. They were all here still in the morning and with no sign of foul play."

"I suppose, after knowing Mita," Erisha said, "it is quite possible that not all the Lekur feel as strongly against you as Lord Kankal."

"That does not mean they won't still fight for him," Anarim said as Erisha finished wrapping his forearm.

Erisha looked critically at the amount of dried blood that stained Anarim's sleeve. She wondered how light-headed he had felt the night before. "I should have had you drink some of this water before using it," she commented as she moved to look at the wound along his back."

"I'm alright," Anarim replied.

"You are not," Erisha answered. "You've lost a lot of blood." She lifted his shirt, stiff with dried blood, and grimaced at the now-clotted, long cut along his lower back. She began cleaning it with the wet cloth.

"These are not the worst injuries I have sustained," Anarim comforted.

Erisha sighed and continued to work, not wanting to ask and hear about the other more serious wounds. She appreciated Anarim's forbearance as he never gave a cry of protest while she cleared the wound even though she knew the alcohol especially stung. She worked diligently and her mind wandered for a moment to her father and elder brother. Had they made it home to her mother or had their many wounds ended them despite Abkur's best efforts?

"I have heard from Abkur," Anarim said, drawing Erisha's attention.

She looked up at him in shock. "I was just thinking of Abkur and my family," she stated.

Anarim continued: "A raven arrived this morning which means Abkur has returned to Zari. Your father—"

"How does a raven mean that?" Erisha interrupted incredulously.

"Oh, I have trained ravens who will find me and carry me urgent messages," Anarim said. "Then they return to Zari with my responses."

"Oh," Erisha said. "How interesting."

Anarim laughed. "Not expecting that answer?"

"No, not at all."

They smiled at each other.

"Your father and brother are home," Anarim informed. "Your brother has recovered remarkably while your father still struggles. I have sent word of our plans back to Abkur."

"By raven," Erisha teased.

"Yes," Anarim said.

Erisha took a breath and her mind wandered to her family. "I'm glad they made it home," she said, eyes watering before she composed herself. "At least they are with Mother and Mother has an idea that we are alive. Thank you."

"You'll have to thank Abkur," he replied as he helped her bandage around his torso.

"I will," Erisha determined. She stepped back after lowered his shirt again and surveyed him. She nodded, pleased by her success considering the little she had to work with.

"Thank you," Anarim said.

Erisha smiled. She picked up the supplies. "What is our plan?" she asked. "I'm assuming we're not staying here."

Anarim shook his head. "Kankal will desire to face me again," he said. "He knows the Lerisaba have joined me and the last people in question are the Fasur."

"We go to Semusak?" Erisha asked, thrilled.

Anarim nodded slowly. "The more men we have the easier it will be to overwhelm Kankal," he explained, "and the more deaths we can avoid."

Erisha sobered. "Where will you face him?" she asked.

"Furun," Anarim said. "I mean to avenge your people on their land."

Erisha stared at him. She felt pride swell within her but also great fear. "Do you think Lord Kankal will agree to meet you there?"

"He will," Anarim said confidently. "Abkur will send him notice and he will not be able to give up the chance to get revenge. We just must make sure we get to Furun first."

Erisha began to walk back to where the women were busy and Anarim followed. "When do we leave then?" she asked.

Anarim hesitated again and Erisha looked back at him. "As soon as possible," he said.

Erisha took a breath. "Mita…" she said.

"Time cannot be wasted," Anarim said quietly.

Erisha glanced back at him then nodded. They came to the clearing among the huts and Erisha's eyes scanned over the many people. She was alarmed to see Mita sitting up, but she realized Dumur was crouching beside her. He steadied Mita.

"Dumur," Erisha called, and she ran over to him.

Dumur stood and hugged her tightly. She subconsciously noticed that her head rested on his shoulder now and he had somehow grown half a head in height over the past week. She looked up at his face and glanced over him.

"Are you alright?" she demanded.

He nodded as Anarim approached them. "I am well," he said. "Much better than some of the men. I am fortunate. Are you alright?"

"Yes," Erisha said.

Anarim knelt down beside Mita who was looking up at all of them, and siblings turned their attention to her.

"How are you?" Anarim asked.

Mita swallowed. "I'll be well eventually," she promised.

Dumur bent down and handed her water.

Mita smiled at him weakly and drank.

"Mita," Anarim began gravely. "We must move on."

Mita looked over at the King. She studied his expression. "You would leave me behind?" she grieved.

"No," Dumur said before Anarim could respond. "I will be responsible for her."

"Dumur, you don't even know where our journey is taking us," the King replied dryly. "We will be taking Mita even farther from her home."

"That's probably safer for her after what happened last night," Dumur exclaimed.

"The journey will be hard, Dumur," Anarim asserted sternly. "And swiftness is imperative right now."

"Your Majesty," Mita said, struggling to stand.

Erisha helped her and had Mita lean against her.

"Your Majesty," Mita said again, "I'd rather come with you and your company." She looked at him demurely.

Anarim looked at the three young people as they stood together.

Erisha wanted to plead with him, but she knew he didn't deserve that. "It's your decision," she affirmed. "You decide what is wise and we'll do as you say." She looked at Dumur and pinned him with a look.

Dumur paused then nodded. "Yes," he agreed, lowering his head.

Anarim looked to Mita. "Can you walk?" he asked.

Mita breathed deeply then stepped away from Erisha. She walked about Anarim then stood before him again.

Anarim nodded. "Very well," he said. "Gather yourselves. I must give my respects to Lord Tubgal." He left them and greeted women and children with a smile as he passed them by.

Mita faltered as the King disappeared from view and Dumur quickly moved to steady her. She looked up at him then over to Erisha.

"I'm alright now," she told them. "But I'll need your help."

"You have it," Erisha said.

CHAPTER ELEVEN

ERISHA'S CHOICE

A narim gathered his company of friends and they all wished Lord Tubgal and his people farewell. Anarim told the Steward of his plan and Lord Tubgal pledged his allegiance and promised to be with the King on the day he faced Lord Kankal again. Two horses were given to the group for the women. Erisha was relieved for Mita's sake. Provisions and extra weapons were also given to them, being the weapons of the Lekur still among the Lerisaba. The Lekur were closely guarded by warriors but had expressed respect and had acted justly so far. Lord Tubgal was allowing them to stay until their whole group was well.

The small company turned away from the sandy shores and marched back into the tall grasses following the river. The Lerisaba called their goodbyes behind them and the Sadurras waved to the children several times. Mita rode on her horse and breathed slowly as she forced herself to sit straight and lively. Erisha and Dumur exchanged worried glances as they kept their attention on her condition.

Soon into the journey, Erisha dismounted and declared that her horse could be used to carry supplies. The men did not resist the idea and Erisha positioned herself to walk beside Mita's mount. She took the reins after a while as Mita's head began to drop and her eyes began to flutter closed. Erisha led the horse as Dumur watched Mita at the back so that the tired young woman did not fall.

They kept a good pace throughout the day and ate once the sun was high in the sky as they marched along. They crossed the river in the late afternoon. As they crossed over to a shallow bank, Dumur reminded Erisha that the wide river was called the Pisuga.

"How could you have forgotten?" Dumur chided. "All those days looking at maps?"

Erisha rolled her eyes as she slowly guided the horse with the half-conscious Mita atop across. "I did know it," she defended herself. "It simply slipped my mind. Much as happened these past few days for me to remember the name of a river which I never grew up seeing."

Dumur feigned disbelief as he put a hand on the horse to steady it as it splashed out of the water and onto the opposite bank.

Erisha glared at him.

"The Pisuga branches in the North," Girisu chimed in, "a little above Zari, in the hills. One of the two inlets comes down almost directly from the North through the thick of forests and mountains. The other inlet flows from the West through the deeps of the Forests of Tiranna to us. It is said that it is connected to another branch of the river that flows into the Apinu Lake in the Uncharted."

"The Apinu Lake?" Dumur asked.

Girisu nodded. "There are not many maps that attempt to lay out what little can be seen and supposed of Nuzuza from atop the Gisgal Mountains. But the few I've seen in the Palace in Zari depict a huge lake beyond yet surrounded by the trees. It has three inlets that run from it and empty into the sea, but another inlet comes from the North and fills the lake. It is that inlet that the Pisuga also draws from."

Erisha stared ahead of her, imagining the scene of a grand lake banked by forest and untouched land. The image seemed to match what little they had glimpsed from atop the Gisgals. She sighed deeply, wondering what it would be like to wander in such an area.

Dumur was also thinking. "Why hasn't anyone tried to roam through the Uncharted?" he asked.

"They have," Anarim answered somberly. "A few men in the kingdom's past have crossed over the Gisgals and descended to the other side. They never returned." He looked pained as he stared ahead of him, and Erisha wondered at his expression.

The group was silent for a few moments.

"There is a saying in Semusak," Girisu said. "*Some lands remain shrouded in mystery by design.*"

"A double meaning," Erisha heard Anarim mutter darkly.

"But we could inhabit the realm if we really wished to," Dumur declared.

"I have thought the same, man," Sidukur agreed. "And it would be our right to do so, but I've learned that having the ability is not enough to justify the doing."

Dumur looked at him, but he nodded. "I suppose that is true," he assented.

"There is a darkness that covers the Uncharted now," Anarim said firmly. "After knowing that Lord Kankal uses the realm as a sight for execution, it surely is cursed."

Erisha stared at Anarim in startled wonder but no one else spoke.

They marched on then camped near the river as the sun began to set in the evening. The Igi Mountains of the East shouldered their paths closely, only a couple paces from the riverbank. Anarim built a fire while the others prepared food and the blankets around the fire. Kas helped Mita off her horse. She lay down on one of the blankets. Erisha came to her side and Mita started up at her through lidded eyes.

"Erisha," she murmured. Erisha had to bend over her to hear her. "Something isn't right." Weakly, she dragged her hand over to the wounded shoulder.

Erisha frowned and carefully began unwrapping the bandages. She grimaced at the sight of the swollen, bloody wound. After her visceral reaction, Erisha studied the injury. The redness had seemed to spread from the injured area down Mita's arm and close to her neck.

"Will one of you please come look at this?" she announced to the men.

Dumur made his way over first though Erisha had not necessarily been requesting his presence.

Sidukur came over from around the fire and knelt beside Erisha. His brows furrowed as he looked at Mita's wound. Mita watched his face languidly.

"Is there anything we can do to relieve the pain?" Erisha asked.

Sidukur nodded shortly. He stood. "We need Girinda flowers," he declared to the group. "Now. While we have the last light."

Erisha remained with Mita while the men went out in different directions, looking down at the ground. The time seemed to pass slowly as Erisha held Mita's hand and watched the men wander about in search of a specific plant.

Kas bent down near the mountain's slope and called to the others. They all hurried over to him and then they came back to camp. Anarim and Kas joined Erisha while the others took responsibility for dinner. Kas held a small bunch of light purple petalled flowers. Anarim took a small shield given to the group by the Lerisaba and washed some water from the river into it. He took the flowers from Kas. He tore the petals and heads of the flowers from the stems and put them into the water in the shield. He threw the stems into the fire and began to mash the flower heads in the shield with a rock. Sidukur walked by and raised his eyebrows skeptically.

"Not quite how I'd do it," Erisha heard him mutter.

Erisha could not stop a small smile from responding to his dubiousness. Yet, Mita had fallen into a half-consciousness and her skin was hot to the touch. Erisha's smile quickly faded and she watched anxiously as Anarim's flowers mixed into a watery paste.

Anarim squeezed the mixture in his palm to dilute some of the water. He carefully applied the Girinda paste to Mita's shoulder and wound. Mita winced but her eyes remained closed.

Anarim looked to Erisha and up to Kas who stood nearby. "Hopefully this will ebb some pain and stop the swelling," he said. "She needs food then she can sleep."

Erisha nodded. "Alright. Thank you," she said. She stood and hurried over to where Dumur was watching Girisu and Sidukur prepare the fish they had been given. She grabbed a fish that had already been skinned and stabbed it through with one of her arrows.

"Erisha," Anarim said warily, but Erisha stuck the fish over the fire.

"Dumur," Erisha called. "Fill a water flask."

Dumur lept into action.

Anarim and Kas joined Girisu and Sidukur and began roasting fish for everyone else on their swords.

Dumur returned from the river with a full flask. By now, the sun was set and they worked by firelight and starlight. The moon was dark that night and shed no light. Erisha's fish finished cooling and Erisha flopped it onto the shield. Sidukur audibly groaned from the other side of camp. Dumur grinned.

"I'll wash it off," Erisha promised.

Sidukur grumbled to himself but said nothing harsh.

With her hands, Erisha tore the fish's meat into tiny pieces. She lifted Mita up with Dumur's help and they shook the young woman awake. Mita's eyes fluttered and Erisha announced her dinner. Gently, Erisha put a piece of meat into Mita's mouth and, according to her orders, Dumur followed with a gulp of water.

They worked patiently until Mita had swallowed each piece of edible meat. They lay her back down and Erisha was pleased to see the young woman's face look more peaceful.

Erisha and Dumur smiled tiredly at each other. Dumur stood and left for the fire and for food.

"Erisha," Mita breathed before Erisha rose to follow her brother.

"I'm here," Erisha said, bending down.

"Kankal's first arrow is always dipped in poison," Mita whispered, eyes closed. "It's tradition."

Erisha stared down at her friend as Mita fell asleep and her breathing came more deeply.

"Come eat," Sidukur called quietly.

Erisha rose and she moved to take the shield to the river. Sidukur, however, came over to her. He took the shield from her and smiled.

"Eat, my Lady," he said. "You did a well with Mita. Now, rest."

Erisha took the fish offered to her. She sat beside Dumur and they both ate leisurely. Kas and Anarim had the last two fish on their swords roasting over the fire. Erisha took her scorched arrow and threw it into the flames. Erisha debated sharing Mita's comment with the others, but she grew distracted when the fish on Anarim's sword began slipping. The King was busy talking with Kas about the lay of Alland.

The fish continued to slide.

"Anarim," Erisha warned.

"What?" Anarim asked as Erisha pointed towards the fish. He made to lift his sword, but the quick motion tipped the fish off the weapon.

The camp erupted in encouragement and advice as Anarim tried to save the fish from the flames. He eventually got the fish back onto the sword. They were all quiet for a moment.

Erisha giggled first then they all laughed heartily before Erisha remembered Mita and shushed them. She looked over at her friend. Mita, however, seemed to be sleeping soundly.

They all finished their meal in better spirits and drank from the river before bedding down for the night. Erisha lay near Mita, and she looked up at the stars. There were so many of the light, white gems in the sky and Erisha marveled at them. She wondered what it would be like to lay among the stars and look down over Alland. To look down from so high, she could not imagine the experience properly. She fell asleep wondering what their little camp looked like from above.

Erisha awoke to her name being called.

With a gasp, Erisha opened her eyes and sat up, but she was greeted by the cold dark of early morning. She waited for several moments and was about to lie back down when she heard Mita moan. Erisha hurried to the young woman's side. She blinked the sleep from her eyes and knelt beside Mita. When her eyes grew accustomed to the darkness, Erisha felt Mita's forehead — she felt hot again. Erisha went over to the fire which was only embers now and managed to reignite a thick stick. She realized that they had all slept and not assigned a guard. She looked about at all the men who slept and decided that they must have felt safe enough this side of the river.

Erisha brought the small spark of light over to Mita and she looked at the young woman's wound which they had left open to the air the night before. She looked closely, confused by what she saw at first. A yellow liquid oozed from Mita's injury, and the young woman was breathing heavily. One word came into Erisha's mind:

Poison.

Erisha's heart seized as foreboding swept over her. She set her jaw and stood, refusing to accept the likelihood of what lay before her. She stared out into the darkness and a plan quickly formed in her mind. The wind blew about her, and she felt like she heard her name being called again. A feeling of affirmation washed over her. She decided. She would do it — no matter how foolish or impossible it seemed.

She hurried over to where Dumur lay, and she quietly woke him up.

"What?" Dumur said, blinking in the firelight.

"It's Mita," Erisha whispered. "I need your help."

Dumur rose without a word, and they returned to Mita's side.

"She's dying," Erisha whispered. "The wound is infected. I think the arrow may have been poisoned. She will not make it if we keep on like this."

"What should we do?" Dumur hissed.

"Her only chance is to find the Fasur," Erisha said firmly. "Anarim was telling Kas last night that the forest begins not far ahead from here and the Fasur are supposed to be living not far within the forest itself. I will go to them for help."

"Alright," Dumur said. "Let's be off."

"No," Erisha said. "I said I'll go with Mita. You need to be here to explain and tell them to follow our tracks. I will ride on Mita's horse with her. You need to keep the other horse for supplies so you can come after us quickly. Help me get Mita onto the horse."

"How do you know you'll find the Semusakians?" Dumur asked as he lifted Mita up.

Erisha took a water flask and strapped a short knife around her waist before putting her bow and quiver over her shoulders.

"I don't," she admitted, "but I think it's Mita's only chance." She untied the horse and mounted.

Dumur lifted Mita up to her and they arranged the sick girl in front of Erisha.

"Erisha," he said after they were situated. "Are you certain? They could be dangerous, and you don't know where you're headed." He held up the small torch Erisha had made.

Erisha nodded. "I have to try though," she demanded. "Find us."

She urged the horse forward and the creature walked away from the camp. Once Erisha decided they were far enough not to wake the others and she had figured out a way to hold the reins properly around Mita, she urged the creature into a run.

The galloping was uncomfortable as Erisha held Mita in front of her, but she tried to move with the horse and keep her focus on what was ahead. They thundered along with the mountains on their right and the river on their left. The sun rose and the day warmed. Eventually, the mountain foot and the river both arched away on either side and forest appeared on their left instead.

The trees appeared almost instantly with only a few growing on the mountainside to warn Erisha. Even in the broad daylight, she still noticed them too late. She looked at the looming trees nearby as they raced on, the trunks flashing together in slices.

The horse veered toward the forest, but Erisha grabbed the reins and directed away. It was nearing midday now. She wondered how far behind the men were, surely up and chasing after her at this point. Her body ached from riding awkwardly for a long period of time, holding Mita. Mita's breathing had grown shallower and shallower. Yet, the forest seemed forbidding.

She slowed the creature and peered into the darkness under the leafy canopies. The horse whinnied and snorted and cantered towards the trees again. Fear welled in Erisha's heart, a paralyzing fear of the cold, damp unknown that awaited within, yet before she could direct the horse away again Mita coughed loudly and leaned from the saddle. It was all Erisha could do to keep them both from toppling off. The horse had enough sense to halt and when the young women were righted again Erisha realized they were at the very edge of the forest. She heard birds chirping within and a branch bent nearby with the weight of a squirrel on it.

Erisha held the reins tightly and looked about for signs of civilization or encampment. She didn't see clues anywhere. The horse stretched against her slightly and kept its attention towards the Northeast into the forest. It shook its head and whinnied again. Erisha gulped for air, frightened, but she held onto Mita tightly as she loosened the reins.

The horse trotted into the forest briskly and weaved its way through the trees. Erisha had the horrible urge to close her eyes, but she kept alert. The horse shook itself a couple times and Erisha got the sense that it was irritated with her. She was sitting so tensely that she was sure that not only she but the creature was uncomfortable. She tried to calm her body.

"Sorry," Erisha murmured, and her voice sounded loud in the crowd of trees.

The horse snorted gently in response.

Erisha nodded. "Thank you," she said amusedly.

The horse carried them on, and Erisha sensed they were no longer travelling into the forest but to the North through the forest. The sun above the treetops through the leaves. Erisha noticed eventually that the birds' chirping seemed to always be coming from in front of them. She looked up at the trees and watched a few birds perch ahead of them on a branch. Once they reached the birds, the small, feathered creatures took to the air and flew a few branches ahead of them again.

Erisha continued to watch the birds. "It's almost as if they're leading us," she mused.

The horse brought its head up and down a couple times in front of her.

Erisha stared at the horse. She watched as its ears quivered when the birds' song rang out and how its head would turn up every time the birds flew ahead a few paces.

"Are we following the birds?" Erisha asked tentatively.

The horse nodded, having slowed to a walk.

Erisha hesitated, shocked. She opened her mouth then closed it. She waited for a few moments. The birds flew a little deeper into the forest and the horse followed.

"Can you understand me?" Erisha asked the horse.

The horse nodded.

Erisha was, admittedly, speechless for a while. She sat back in the saddle as she held Mita, her hands no longer holding the reins at all. "Have you always been able to understand me?" she finally asked.

The horse shook its head. A negative reply.

"Oh," Erisha managed. "Well, I don't know quite what to say."

The horse whinnied in such a way that Erisha swore it sounded like laughter.

"This is so strange," Erisha breathed.

The horse nodded.

"Oh, you're surprised too?" Erisha asked.

The horse nodded.

"Well, at least it's not just me," Erisha said. "You're handling the shock better though."

The birds' song suddenly sounded suspiciously like musical laughter.

"Well, the birds are obviously used to this," Erisha said.

The horse snorted.

Erisha laughed. "So strange," she said. "It must be the forest. The Forests of Tiranna." She looked about and her surroundings were looking more friendly as the day grew lighter.

Suddenly, there was a rustling in the brush about them and there were several figures surrounding them. Erisha glanced about and decided quickly that they must be the Fasur, the forest dwellers of Semusak. Their clothes covered every inch of their bodies save their heads, necks, and hands. Their feet were covered with hand-made shoes made from thick animal skins that feathered the ground beneath them. The fabric of their clothes looked thin and airy, and some of the Semusakians worn large, furry cloaks over their clothes. Everyone's hair was long, but the men in the group all had their hair pulled back and braided together while the few women still let part of their hair flow down to their waists.

"Please," Erisha said. "Help me." She lifted up Mita. "My friend is dying. She needs your help. She must live."

"Is it up to you whether she lives or dies?" a young male Semusakian asked.

"No," Erisha admitted. "If her time has come, it has come. But I don't think it has."

"You hope it hasn't," the man stated, but he stepped forward and the group all relaxed.

Erisha also relaxed, having not realized how tense everyone had been. The young man who had spoken lifted Mita off the horse and carried her away. Erisha moved to dismount but another warrior stopped her.

"Stay," he said. "You must be blindfolded."

Erisha looked to him, but one of the women stepped forward with a long cloth and smiled gently up at Erisha. Intuitively trusting, Erisha lowered her head and allowed herself to be blindfolded.

After a moment, the horse began to walk forward and even though Erisha could not hear the Semusakians walk around her she knew they were there. She rode silently and tried to sense the direction of the path they were taking. They seemed to be weaving deeper into the forest for a little bit, but the path turned again back to the West. They neither descended nor ascended as far as Erisha could tell.

The horse moved at a slow walk, but Erisha mused that not too much time had passed before they stopped. She heard whispering voices about her and movement nearby. Suddenly, the horse jerked about and snorted angrily. It was all Erisha could do to grip the reins and remain in the saddle as she screamed in surprise.

Several people hushed the horse and spoke calmly to it. The horse relaxed for a moment, but Erisha felt the creature tense again. She clutched the reins. Someone's hands brushed against her arm, but her horse bucked around. It neighed wildly and all at once the wind rose. Erisha thought she heard tree branches creaking above her. She whipped off the blindfold and stared at the Fasur who were all grouped opposite of her on the horse. The horse had situated itself on the edge of a wide glade away from any of the Semusakians. A strong breeze pushed and pulled against everyone, but the trees' branches appeared to be waving about more vigorously than necessary in such a gust.

At the front of the Fasur stood a middle-aged man with a weathered face and dark hair. "You have a very loyal horse," he said, his voice deep and rich. It would have put Erisha at ease if not for its wary, unsettled tone.

Unsure of how to respond, Erisha simply nodded.

The man smiled and took a step toward her and the horse. "Welcome to the Tirannan Forests," he said kindly. "I am Lord Sulzi of Semusak." The winds calmed and the trees stopped creaking.

CHAPTER TWELVE

TIRANNA

E risha looked about warily. Tents and huts were built up and scattered throughout the glade and deeper into the forest in every direction. They had been built up and around trees or between trees. Small firepits burned near each house and lines stretched between trees with clothes and dead animals hanging from them. She looked up and some trees stretched up to the skies above and she marveled at how huge branches touched and intertwined among themselves; she swore she also saw rope stretched up nearer to the leafy tops with the branches so that they became pathways and bridges among the trees.

The Fasur were all watching her. All ages stood and studied her. They all had long hair and light clothing. Erisha noticed how the women's and girls' clothes hung lower like dresses as their hair hung freer than the men's and boys'. She did not see any weapons but that meant nothing.

Erisha met the gaze of Lord Sulzi. She stroked her horse's neck soothingly then dismounted. She bowed to the Steward.

He bowed to her.

"I am Erisha, daughter of Lord Ansira of Furun," Erisha said. "My friend—"

"Is with our healers now in my home," Lord Sulzi said.

Erisha hesitated and her horse came up beside her. She turned and stroked the horse's snout. "Will Mita… be alright?" she finally asked as all the Semusakians watched her.

Lord Sulzi studied her. "I do not know," he said. "She is near death, as you well know. You were right to seek help."

Erisha nodded slowly.

"You were alone?" Lord Sulzi questioned. "Just the two of you?"

Erisha wondered why the crowd did not disperse. They all continued to stare at her horse and herself. "I'm sorry. Are we enemies?" she asked sharply. "Why do I feel hostility in the air?"

Lord Sulzi shook his head. "We are not enemies," he said. "We are strangers. And the hostility is not ours. It is the forest's."

"The forest hates me," Erisha inferred though the sur-rounding sense of antipathy began to fade.

"On the contrary," Lord Sulzi said. "The forest is upset with us. It is being protective of you for some reason."

"Oh," Erisha stammered. "Well."

A few Fasur smiled, amused by her bewilderment. The peo-ple began to wander away back to their business. Lord Sulzi continued to study Erisha.

He stepped neared. "You were alone?" he asked skeptically. "Just the two of you wandering about Alland?"

Erisha shook her head. "No," she said. "My friends are back by the river. They don't know where I am. They'll be worried. I came with—"

Here the horse nudged her, and Erisha turned to the creature. It looked at her and, although Erisha did not understand completely, she knew she needed to say less. She looked back to Lord Sulzi and a hardness had come into his face.

"Are the rest of your companions men?" he asked sternly.

Erisha swallowed. "Yes, sir," she said.

He sighed. "They will be seeking you." He looked up and signaled to a group of young men across the glade. The young men nodded and strode away.

Erisha watched them go then looked to Lord Sulzi. "My friends are not your enemies," she told him.

"There is an uneasiness falling over Alland," Lord Sulzi replied. "Our homes are not open to all, especially not to war bringers."

"You're helping me," Erisha replied, "and Mita."

"You are in need," Lord Sulzi said, nodding toward someone else in the quietly busy community. His face softened. "One of my head warriors made a judgment and I trust his judgment. We do help those in need." He smiled gently and Erisha breathed a little easier.

A woman came to Lord Sulzi's side with two girls. They were all strikingly beautiful and the girls bore a strong resemblance, each in their own way, to Lord Sulzi and the woman.

"This is my wife, Esi," Lord Sulzi introduced, "and my daughters, Zida and Damalia. They will take you to your friend."

Lady Esi and her daughters bowed to Erisha, and she bowed in return. The girls smiled shyly. Lady Esi's manner was welcoming and motherly. Erisha's chest tightened momentarily as she thought of her own mother.

"Come this way," Lady Esi directed, coming up and touching Erisha's elbow.

The Fasur all nodded to Erisha as she passed, and Erisha hoped she looked respectful as she tried to acknowledge most she could. The horse followed close behind them. Zida giggled and Erisha looked to her.

"I'm sorry," Erisha began. "I must be so out of place—"

"Oh no, you're alright," Zida said quickly. "It's amusing how quickly your horse has become attached, that's all."

Erisha looked to Lady Esi and back to Zida and Damalia. "So, I'm not deranged," she said. "The horse is talking to me."

The girls smiled and Lady Esi spoke. "Not talking," she corrected. "The animals do not speak to us in words."

"But why?" Erisha exclaimed excitedly. "This has never happened before."

Lady Esi shook her head. "We do not know," she admitted, "but here in Tiranna the creatures live alongside us and come to our aid often."

"It's so strange," Erisha breathed.

Before Erisha could question them further, they came up to a low expansive house in the forest. Large trees bent and wove together with their strong branches to create a frame. Other dead branches and trunks had been used to create ways under and among the interwoven branches. Windows were open with dark clothes draped to the side and the large door that Erisha could see appeared to be a work of weaving together branches and leaves and tall grass. Two small bonfires were crackling happy on either side of the door a safe distance from the house. The trees' surrounding leady canopies draped over and added extra covering to the roof.

Erisha had stopped to stare and take in the marvel of man's work and nature's work woven together. Lady Esi and her daughters waited by her patiently. Erisha felt like she was in a dream, and she neared the house. She looked up as she approached and saw rope leading from the roof up into the trees which stretched up high above her. An elderly man opened the door for them and after a glance to Lady Esi he welcomed Erisha in.

The young woman stared up as the branches, dead and alive, twisted and turned to make walls and folded into a ceiling. In the main entry way, the room was large and a fire glowed on one side of the room by a window across the way. The smoke and sparks flew out the window and a cut opening in the ceiling. A long, make-shift table sat in the center of the room and Erisha guessed that this large area served not only as a main entrance but also as the kitchen and dining area. She noticed a large pot broiling over the fire and other cooking utensils and ingredients hanging on the wall such as different sized cups and bags of spices and salts and herbs. Plates and other cups and bowls were stacked neatly on the floor made up of many unique flat stones.

The table was surrounded by stumps that served as chairs. There were three different doorways that led from the room.

"Welcome to Nuzua Hall, Lady Erisha," Lady Esi welcomed.

Erisha finally remembered herself and woke from her reverie. "Oh," she cried. "Thank you. This is your home?" she asked.

"It is," Lady Esi replied.

"It's wonderful," Erisha said, taking in the two tapestries that hung on either side of the door to outside.

Lady Esi smiled, and her smile was bright against her olive skin. "Thank you," she said gently. "Have you eaten?"

Erisha realized that she had not eaten and that she felt famished. "No," she said with a shake of her head.

Lady Esi handed her some bread and berries which were centered on the table. "Please," she offered.

"What does your home look like in Furun?" Damalia asked as Erisha ate.

"Oh, nothing like this," Erisha said after shallowing a large bite of bread. "This is so… natural and earthy." She looked over at the girls and realized they were still expecting to hear about the Manor. "Well, my home has a large welcoming room like this we call the Hall. It is a large square and it's also where we have our meals. Beyond the Hall are hallways leading to the kitchen and our council chamber and our armory and our bedrooms and such. It's on a knoll just outside the village. It's situated high up on stone and we can look out either over the village or fields. I miss it," she said, realized how much she truly did.

"Oh, we have all that too," Damalia said. "Would you like to see?"

The girls and Erisha looked to Lady Esi who was with the old man by the fire. She hesitated then gave her consent and the girls gave Erisha a tour of Nuzua Hall. They went through the doorway to their right first and it gave into another open area with a large, unlit firepit in the center of it. A hole was also in the ceiling above it. Four different entry ways led to bedrooms where thick blankets were places upon piles of soft, downy grass and leaves. These were the beds. Wide, carven wooden trucks acted as chests and cloaks hung from knots in the walls. A couple weapons were situated in accessible areas in each bedroom.

From the fourth, large bedroom which was obviously the Lord and Lady's, the girls led Erisha through a different doorway back into the main room. Now, only the old man remained, and they crossed the room to the doorway on the left. They entered a wide space with a thick table centered in the middle. There were no windows in this room and Erisha, unconsciously brushing the breadcrumbs from her hands, missed the sun shining through and lighting up the dusky wooded surroundings. Unlit torches lined the walls but the two torches on the table were lit.

Lady Esi was already in the room which the girls told Erisha was the war room. Lady Esi was kneeling on the ground on the other side of the table and Erisha rounded the table to see Mita lying on a blanket on the ground. Erisha stood in surprise for a moment before rushing to Mita's side.

Lady Esi placed a hand on Erisha's shoulder and shushed her. "She is asleep," she said softly. "Our healers have done what they could for her. They have given her several draughts and replaced her wrappings with more healing herbs. There is nothing more to be done except to let her rest. She must fight off the poison now."

Erisha looked down at Mita's sleeping face. "I knew it was poison," she said. "How could he?" She wondered if all of the Lekur's arrows had been tipped with poison.

Mita breathed shallowly but slowly. Her expression was peaceful, and Erisha admired the expert job of bandaging done to Mita's shoulder. Erisha touched Mita's forehead and although she still felt warm her skin was no longer hot to the touch.

Erisha sat back on her feet then rose. Zida and Damalia were at her side. They quietly pointed out the weapon room then led Erisha excitedly out the other doorway leading from the war room. They ushered Erisha in, and Erisha was astonished by what she saw.

The room was a library. In between dozens of jutting branches sat books and scrolls. There were two firepits about the room which were both flickering pleasantly, and large windows opened out in the walls wherever there were not rows of books and scrolls. The smell of old paper mixed with the smell of the fire and earthiness of the trees made Erisha feel deliciously calm.

"This is the best room in the whole Hall," Zida declared.

"Yes, it is," Erisha agreed.

The girls watched as Erisha looked about and fingered old books, many titles of which she recognized from home. Then all three went back into the war room.

Erisha checked on Mita once more then looked at the table. Much like the table in the Manor's council chamber in Furun, a huge map covered the table. Yet, Erisha was arrested by this map because the Uncharted realm was included and charted almost as well as the five realms were on the map.

"Where did you get this map?" Erisha whispered sharply.

"It's been in the Nuzua family for generations," Zida replied. "Why? What's wrong?"

"How… Is this the Uncharted realm?" Erisha asked.

The girls came over by her and nodded. "Yes, that is Nuzuza."

"How is it charted here?" Erisha questioned, looking down at the Apinu Lake and the forests surrounding it. The rivers connected and flowed from the Lake from the North and into the Numun Sea in the South and West as Girisu had mentioned. "Has someone been?"

"Oh no," Damalia cried. "No one has been from here, of course."

"Then how—"

"Oh, I'm sorry," Damalia said, and Zida quickly shushed her. "The birds drew out for us what they saw across the Gisgal Mountains to the West, pass where the Lekur live," she explained in a whisper. "That's how we know."

"Oh," Erisha said, taken aback. "Of course." She nodded several times, staring at the map, but then she let the girls lead her back into the main entrance room.

Lady Esi was helping the old man with what was cooking in the pot. She was arranging several bowls and placing cups on the table.

"Zida, please go for water," her mother said.

Zida grabbed a large bucket from near the main doorway and she left the Hall.

Lady Esi looked to Erisha and was about to speak when they all heard a loud whinny outside.

Erisha rushed outside and the horse was right there, waiting for her. It whipped its head about back towards the glade.

"What's wrong?" Erisha asked, sensing the urgency. "What is it?"

The horse pushed her hand towards its back with its head. Erisha saddled up and the horse took off through the forest past the different huts even though Lady Esi and the other Semusakians called after Erisha. The trees and leaves and huts and people blurred in Erisha's peripheral vision as the horse sprinted by. The creature pulled up abruptly in the glade and Erisha looked about frantically.

The Semusakian warriors were dragging struggling figures into the glade. Each captive was blindfolded, gagged, and tied at the wrists. There were five captives, all were men, and Erisha recognized them instantly. She slid from the saddle and raced over to Anarim.

"What are you doing?" she demanded of the warriors.

Anarim and the others all turned at the sound of her voice but there were two warriors for each of them. Her friends struggled against their bonds, and they were so persistent that they were forced to their knees. Each warrior on either side of them lay a heavy, strong hand on either shoulder.

Erisha stood beside Anarim and touched his arm. "I'm alright," she told him.

He quieted and then nodded.

Dumur still struggled where he was being held.

Erisha turned to the warriors. "Let them go," she demanded. "You have no idea who you hold here."

"It does not matter who they are," came Lord Sulzi's voice behind her.

Erisha turned to face him.

"They are not welcome here," Lord Sulzi continued.

"They are also in need of your help," Erisha said, but Lord Sulzi interrupted her.

"Then they must look elsewhere," Lord Sulzi said, but Erisha interrupted him.

"Hypocrite!" she exclaimed angrily, and a strong gust flowed through the glade, leaves flapping noisily in the wind. "I am tired of each realm's lack of loyalty. This kingdom is under attack, and you have a responsibility to help." The trees' branches arched down near Erisha and her friends. Erisha was afraid they would curl themselves around her and trap her, but they pointed out threateningly towards the Fasur.

The Semusakians looked about at the trees in shock. Lord Sulzi eyed the nature around him before looking back to Erisha. He stood back.

"Who are you?" he demanded, thoroughly baffled.

Erisha stood tall, feeling the weight of the power of the Tiranna behind her although she did not know why it was. "I am Erisha of Furun," she said. "My realm has always been loyal, not just to the Askattes, but to the good of Alland. I am here because something horrible has happened to my people which may happen to yours. We are here to warn you and to ask for your help. There men are here for your help, and you must listen to them. Lord Sulzi, you seem to be a man of honor who wishes to protect what is rightfully his to protect. But you have no right to treat these men as they are being treated now. No matter who they are. And you have a duty to help them."

The forest had grown perfectly quiet. The birds and squirrels who had been chattering moments before were all silent now. There was not a breeze blowing by. Everything stood, waiting.

"And who are they, my Lady?" Lord Sulzi asked carefully.

"He is your king," Erisha said, gesturing to Anarim. Her voice seemed to reverberate around the glade, but she started as she spoke because a nearby tree's limbs stretched down to Anarim.

The warriors guarding him fled as the crowd erupted with startled cries. The tips of the branches stretched under Anarim's arms and lifted him up to stand. His bonds were snapped with the strong tug of the tree, as was his gag.

A gentle breeze blew by. Anarim looked over the Fasur, his expression stern. He exchanged a glance with Erisha but remained silent. He directed his gaze towards Lord Sulzi and pinned the Steward with a hard look.

"Release them all," Lord Sulzi ordered.

Dumur stood impatiently as the trees all bent back into their normal shapes and the birds began to sing again and the squirrels appeared in the treetops. Dumur rushed over to Erisha's side after he was untied. "Are you alright?" he asked swiftly.

"I'm well," she told him.

He nodded and gave her a small smile before Sidukur, Girisu, and Kas came up to them. All eyes were on the King and Lord Sulzi. All save Kas, however, who looked curiously from the forest to Erisha and back again.

"My Lord," Lord Sulzi said, and he knelt before Anarim. "I'm sorry."

The Fasur, the entire community that appeared to understand why the forest had been upset, all followed suit.

Anarim walked over to Lord Sulzi and placed a hand on his shoulder. "Rise, Lord of the Forests," he said.

Lord Sulzi stood. A tall man, he was the first man who Erisha had seen stand taller than Anarim. "I am here to aid you, my Lord," he told his King. He glanced at Erisha for a moment.

Anarim looked back at Erisha and she could not understand his expression. "I hear it took some time to convince you of such a position," Anarim said, looking from Erisha and turning back to Lord Sulzi with a challenging raise of an eyebrow.

"That is true," Lord Sulzi said with a smile and the genuine, friendly expression relaxed his face. "I have played the fool today though both the young Lady of the Fields as well as the Forest tried to warn me." He looked up at the trees' canopies.

Anarim also looked up but Erisha, having come to stand beside him, saw that he did not completely understand.

Lord Sulzi smiled down at Erisha. "My Lady," he said with a bow. "From now on, you and anyone else who invokes your friendship will be welcome in the Tiranna."

Erisha smiled graciously. "Thank you," she said.

Anarim watched the exchange with veiled confusion. "Is there a place we can talk privately?" he asked a moment later.

Lord Sulzi nodded. "If you would follow me," he said.

He offered Erisha his arm and Erisha hooked hers through his and walked by the Steward's side. They led the group toward Nuzua Hall. The crowd parted before them. The Fasur watched the King, but they all inclined their heads to Erisha as she passed with Lord Sulzi.

"What did I do?" Erisha asked Lord Sulzi quietly.

He smiled down at her. "You've befriended the Forest," he said. "Or the Forest has befriended you. Obviously, the Forest knows something about you or your future that you do not know yourself."

"You do not... revere the Forest, do you?" Erisha asked suddenly.

But Lord Sulzi shook his head. "We respect the Forest," he said. "But the Forest knows that, if we wanted to, we would be allowed to overcome it."

Erisha looked back at Kas. He inclined his head to her. Then he winked. Erisha relaxed.

Erisha's horse came up to Erisha and walked beside her. They arrived at Nuzua Hall and Erisha remained with the horse as Lord Sulzi walked into his home. Anarim looked curiously at Erisha as he passed. He did not speak but reached out a hand and put it briefly on her arm. Erisha put one of her hands over it comfortingly before he continued into the Hall. Girisu and Sidukur nodded to Erisha as they passed. Kas walked by, looking around at the Hall and the trees. Dumur remained with Erisha outside.

He smiled at the horse as it nuzzled him. Suddenly, his eyes widened. "Mita?" he breathed, looking to Erisha with wide eyes.

Erisha grimaced at him. "I don't know," she admitted. "Their healers have done all they can."

"Well, I'm glad at least she could be helped some," Dumur finally replied. "I'm glad you're alright." He glanced at the Hall. "They were not happy when they woke up and found out."

Erisha smiled. "I can imagine. But I think we did the right thing," she comforted.

Dumur grinned at her and nodded. "So," he said, looking at the trees. "This is Tiranna."

CHAPTER THIRTEEN

PREPARATIONS AND FAREWELLS

M ita was being moved as carefully as possible into the library when Erisha and Dumur entered the war room. Both Anarim and Kas checked on her condition before rejoining the others. Erisha watched as Dumur struggled internally between his care for Mita and his desire to hear the proceedings between Lord Sulzi and the King. Erisha was impressed when he settled on Mita and left to go to the sick woman in the library.

Anarim explained the threat of Lord Kankal as succinctly as possible to Lord Sulzi. The Steward of Semusak became more subtly indignant as the King continued to explain. Yet, when it was his turn to speak the Steward hesitated.

"Please don't interpret my silence as disloyalty, my Lord," he eventually said. "Firstly, I want to apologize again for how you were treated. Most of my people also do not recognize you since we always meet you outside the forest—"

"Outside the forest," Anarim said with him.

"Yes, whenever you declare a visit. We are a quiet people who stick to ourselves as you well know. We are happy in the forest and the Forest treats us well. I do not like to rush into conflict. Anyone here would tell you I work hard to keep strife almost nonexistent. I do, however," and here he paused and smiled to himself, "pride myself on knowing when an issue must be worked out more viscerally." He looked to Anarim. "And, here, they are your people too."

He paused and bowed his head. "They are my family, my Lord. I have my wife and children, my sons and daughters, but also my people. Our circumstances here demand that we work together in a way that I believe is different from every other realm. I think it has to do with the animals and the trees, but I cannot explain it. Just losing one man grieves us deeply. But we will help you. My men and I will fight by your side against such disturbance of the peace."

Anarim inclined his head, and his friends relaxed. "Thank you, Lord Sulzi," the King replied.

Erisha sat in a corner and listened to Anarim's plan. Yet, she did not hear much before Dumur came into the room. He looked to her and gestured into the library. Erisha rose and joined him.

Mita was moaning and tossing when she entered, and Erisha hastened to her. She checked her temperature, but she did not seem too warm. She held Mita's hand, and the young woman calmed. Her breathing slowed again and she blinked several times before falling back asleep.

"Only a nightmare," Erisha guessed, and she looked across at Dumur who sat on Mita's other side.

Dumur nodded and let out a breath. He sat back and gazed at Mita, concern written across his face. He suddenly rose and went over to a window.

Erisha also rose and joined him.

"I can't say she'll be well because I don't know," she told her brother, "but she does seem to be doing better."

He nodded again and moved about irritably.

They stood in silence for a couple moments.

"Were they that angry?" Erisha finally asked.

Dumur smiled to himself, and Erisha relaxed. "They were angry," he affirmed then he laughed, "and confused. They didn't say much, but I told them what had happened and we started after you. It was easy enough to follow your trail."

"Even in the forest?" Erisha asked.

Dumur hesitated. "No, we lost track of you in the forest," he admitted.

"I didn't even know where I was going," Erisha said. "The horse was deciding the path."

Dumur laughed quietly.

Erisha smiled. "I'm serious," she said. Her smile faded. "It understood me. It understands me."

"The horse?"

"The horse."

They were quiet again as they looked at each other.

"I'm serious," Erisha said again. "It was following the birds who knew the way."

Dumur nodded. "We were warned by the birds and squir-rels," he said thoughtfully.

"Really?" Erisha asked, elated.

"It was the strangest thing. It sounds ridiculous," Dumur explained. "We lost your tracks and were discussing what to do when three birds came and sat on a nearby branch. They watched us for a while then got really flustered and started squawking like mad. It was ridiculous. Squirrels appeared and screamed at us. We were all confused. One squirrel actually threw a nut at Anarim."

"It did?" Erisha exclaimed with a laugh.

Mita groaned and the siblings urgently shushed each other.

Dumur grinned. "It did," he whispered. "It was the strang-est thing. Then the Fasur showed up and attacked us and I un-derstood—"

"They were warning you," Erisha mused.

"Yes," Dumur said.

Erisha shook her head and neither spoke. Erisha looked out the window and breathed in the fresh morning air. There was a quiet peace in the forests that was different from the calm of the fields. Erisha did not know what to think of it. She felt both trapped and protected by the surrounding trees. It was such a different way of life here, she could sense it.

Girisu came into the library and gestured to the Sadurras. They came quietly and approached the table in the war room where Anarim was waiting for them. There was a hardness in his face that perplexed Erisha.

"We ride to Zari," Anarim told them. "I must organize the troops and bring them to Furun to meet Lord Kankal. Lord Sulzi has agreed to meet and join us in three days' time."

Erisha and Dumur nodded in understanding.

"Lord Sulzi has graciously offered to send two Semuskian warriors along with you two and Girisu. You all ride for Furun while Sidukur and Kas ride with me to Zari."

Both the siblings looked to Anarim.

"We don't come with you?" Dumur asked.

Anarim shook his head slowly. "I'm afraid this is where our paths must part," he said. "At least for a little while."

Erisha stared at Anarim. "But we have journeyed with you this far," she said.

"You must get home," Anarim said. "You must go to your parents and your brother."

Erisha felt her emotions rising but a soft breeze flew up and calmed her anger. She decided not to respond. There was nothing to say. Dumur seemed to feel the same and both looked away from the King. Erisha acknowledged that Anarim was right, but his refusal to allow them to come with him hurt in ways she could not have imagined. Admittedly, they had only encountered the King and his men about nine days ago, but they had experienced so much together since. Now, they were to be sent home.

"We leave…" Erisha asked.

"Immediately," Anarim answered.

"Mita's in no state to travel," Dumur replied.

"Mita will remain here," the King said. "Lord Sulzi and his people will care for her and... if she improves, she will come to Furun with the Semusakians."

"If... You leave her to die among strangers?" Dumur asked, not so much accusingly but in grief.

"Dumur," Anarim said softly.

Lord Sulzi come to the King's aid. "We will do all we can for your friend," he promised. "The gods willing, you will see her in three days."

"Let it go, young ones," Sidukur said quietly. "The King's way is best."

Neither Erisha nor Dumur spoke but they left the room to go to the main entry way. Girisu and Kas followed them.

Erisha spoke to Lady Esi. "Thank you for your kindness," she said to the woman as she was setting the table. "We are off."

Lady Esi raised her eyebrows. "So soon?" she asked in surprise.

"According to the King's wishes," Kas replied, and he gave Erisha a pointed look.

"Oh, very well," Lady Esi said. "I suppose you'll need horses and supplies. Give me a moment." The elegant woman swept from the room into the war room.

Girisu led the group out of doors, and they were greeted by many of the Semusakians' faces waiting outside Nuzua Hall. Erisha's horse trotted up to her. Erisha grabbed the reins and fought the urge to hide her face in the creature's mane.

Kas whistled lowly and the Fasur around them gasped in surprise. Four unsaddled horses appeared after a moment coming from several different directions through the forest. The other Abakiti horse trailed behind one.

"How did you know how to do that?" Girisu asked in amazement and admiration.

Kas smiled but did not answer.

Lady Esi and the old man came out of the Hall and both carried a saddle and a satchel. Girisu and Kas rushed to help them. The two men saddled two horses as the Stewardess of the Forests and her cook reentered the Hall to get more saddles. Girisu followed them.

Kas gave a satchel to each Sadurra to strap to their mount. The Fasur watched him closely and Zida and Damalia approached him. Three young men and a young boy stepped behind them and Erisha guessed that were the girls' brothers, the Steward's sons.

Kas allowed himself to be scrutinized.

"Who are you?" one of the young men asked.

Kas shook his head and smiled gently. "It is not for you to know," he replied.

The young man stared at Kas then he knelt before him. The Sadurras watched in awe as all the surrounding Semusakians followed suit.

"Rise," Kas ordered lowly, but his voice echoed through the Forest.

The people all looked up in confusion and obeyed.

"You should be ashamed," Kas berated firmly. "You know not to bow to me."

The Sulzi children looked sheepish, and, with that, the crowd dissipated. The Sadurras, Kas, and the horses were left alone in front of the Hall.

Erisha stared at Kas, mouth open, but Girisu returned with Lord Sulzi, his wife, and their cook all carrying saddles. The cook also carried more supplies and weapons. The rest of the horses were saddled, and all the horses were supplied generously. Girisu thanked Lord Sulzi and his wife and he nodded respectfully to the cook. He mounted his horse. Erisha and Dumur followed his lead.

Sidukur came out of the Hall and looked to them.

He came up to Erisha. "You must trust Anarim," he said, looking up at her. "He is a good man and a great King. He is trying his best."

Erisha nodded. "Goodbye, Sidukur," she said.

"This is not goodbye," he replied.

Feeling tears in her eyes, Erisha pulled her horse about after lowering her head respectfully to the Steward and Stewardess. She saw Kas speak to Dumur, but she did not hear what was said.

Girisu began leading the way out the forest. Or he began leading the way. Without warning, two Semusakian warriors on foot appeared on each flank. They walked up by Girisu as Erisha followed and Dumur brought up the rear. They seemed to interact with Girisu's horse from time to time and directed the group in a slightly new direction.

Unknown but maybe sensed by Erisha, Anarim sat in the library having gone in to check on Mita. He sat on a log seat against the wall and sat back after having satisfied himself with his knowledge of Mita's health. He was unsettled. His fists clenched and unclenched repeatedly before he rose suddenly and left the library, ready to give his farewell to Lord Sulzi.

As Erisha rode, the only signs of her distress were the few tears that rolled down her cheeks. She bowed her head, willing no one see her discontentment, but her horse whinnied several times before Erisha stroked its neck to calm it. The smoothness of the silky horsehair quieted Erisha and the tears stopped. The horse quickened to a trot and Erisha laughed softly. The horse neighed in a happy way.

Erisha watched as Girisu looked about the forest and allowed the Semusakians and his horse to lead the way. She wondered at him. She waited a few moments but decided it was best if she broke the silence.

"You seem quite at home here, Girisu," she commented.

He turned to look back at her and Erisha urged her horse forward to be closer. "I have always loved the forests," Girisu said.

"You could come back," Erisha mused. "Marry a Semusakian woman. Join them here and become a Fasur."

Girisu smiled. "I could," he said, "if they'd have me."

"Why haven't you married?" Erisha asked, suddenly curious.

Girisu paused and thought. "I don't know," he admitted. "I just haven't. Hopefully I will one day. I've time still. I am a good few years younger than Anarim and Sidukur."

Erisha nodded. "I'm sorry you had to come with us and not go with the others to Zari."

"I am not sorry," Girisu replied. "I offered to go back with you. Dumur and you have proven yourselves as members of our company. We do not abandon our friends."

Erisha's throat tightened but she smiled. "Thank you," she managed.

They rode on until they saw the sunlight on grass ahead of them between the trees. They left the forest behind and walked out into the afternoon sunlight. A cool autumn breeze tugged at Erisha's skirt, but the sun's rays warmed her skin. She saw the river glistening a ways ahead and she smiled. She closed her eyes and allowed the sunlight to wash over her. Her patted her horses's neck and a thought struck her that dampen her spirits. She spoke in the horse's ear, and it did not respond to her. She suddenly felt like sobbing and she turned back to the forest. She wanted to go back. The trees grew into a line of trees as they rode away. She had discovered something outside of and within herself in the Forests of Tiranna that she knew she would struggle to regain. And she sensed that the special communication with animals was something that would not be regained at all.

Her lips quivered but she signed deeply instead. There was a long journey ahead and it would not be useful to exhaust herself with crying now.

They rode faster across the field towards the Pisuga River. The Fasur kept up beside the horses, running with short quick strides. Erisha saw the open fields across the river and she felt her heart lighten despite herself: they were going home.

CHAPTER FOURTEEN

HOMECOMING

T hey splashed across a shallow part of the river. The horses cantered at a consistent pace, and Erisha and Dumur marveled at how the two warriors kept up with ease. Dumur attempted to run with them for a while, but he tired eventually and had to swing himself back up into the saddle.

Girisu kept a cautious eye on their surroundings and horizons. They stopped for a couple moments at one point to snack and to let the warriors rest. Then they continued until dusk. As the sun began to set, they set up camp and a guard. Girisu took the first shift after they had supped, and the others fell asleep.

Erisha awoke the next morning and saw Dumur standing guard. He was pleased that Girisu had included him along with the Semusakian warriors to help watch during the night. He had received the last shift in the early morning. Erisha smiled at his enthusiasm as he stretched.

They rode on and, as they crossed wide fields of grass with spare trees and brush dotted about, a feeling of familiarity grew in Erisha. Her heart was glad to be returning to Furun no matter how hurt it was by Anarim's departure. She allowed the cool wind to tug at her hair and cause her to smile.

The horses traveled at a steady pace and the group only stopped once at midday again to eat. As the sun began to set and the light shifted from a bright gold to a warm bronze, Erisha and Dumur cried out with joy when they saw the village and the Manor in the distance. As they drew closer and Girisu and the warriors were satisfied that they did not see any signs of an ambush or nearby hostility, Girisu had Erisha and Dumur lead the way. The siblings debated for a moment whether to ride through the village up to the Manor or to ride around to the Manor.

"It is almost dusk," Erisha said. "I don't think we should disturb the people."

"I suppose you're right," Dumur admitted.

So, they led the way around the village and pass the backsides of houses and stables and barns. They rode up the knoll to the Manor and left their horses with the startled stable hands. Dumur, who often spent time with the horses and thus also with the stable hands, was hugged fiercely by one and clapped on the back by the others. Erisha was bowed to and smiled at several times, and the others foreign warriors were forgotten by the happy bunch.

"We feared the worst," the head stable hand explained. "You two disappeared and Lady Semirra fell ill—"

"Mother is ill?" Erisha exclaimed.

"Not anymore," another stable hand said quickly.

"She grew better when you father and brother were brought home by the King's man," the head stable hand continued.

"They brought word that you both were alive. But it has been days since then. Our assurance wavered."

"Thank you," Dumur said as Erisha tugged at his arm. "We'll go present ourselves to our parents."

Erisha practically ran up to the Manor's steps. Dumur was on her heels while Girisu and the warriors followed. The siblings flew up the steps and pulled one of the heavy doors opened, and they walked in.

They looked into the Hall and a figure was sitting on the throne on the dais across the room. The dejected-looking young man lifted his gaze as they entered. The two soldiers on either side of the Hall also stared incredulously.

"Esirim!" Erisha cried.

The eldest Sadurra sibling sat up straight and continued to stare. Erisha and Dumur shared a look and walked into and across the Hall.

"It's us, Esirim," Dumur said when they stood before him.

Their older brother stood slowly, keeping a steadying hand on the throne.

There was noise to their right and a servant and Lady Semirra walked in aiding the Steward of Furun. Before either Erisha or Dumur could call out, however, Esirim suddenly moved and hugged them close. Tears wet everyone's face as realization dawned, and laughter and questions echoed throughout the Hall.

Lady Semirra steadied her husband with the servant then rushed over to her children. She cried and kissed all of them as

Esirim tried to gain answers to all his questions. Erisha watched as he quickly remembered their father and helped the servant bring Lord Ansira over to the throne. They helped Lord Ansira sit and Erisha and Dumur were instantly by his side.

Erisha noticed how Esirim appeared fully healed save new scars and purple marks from bruises on his face. Her father, on the other hand, still looked weak. His left arm was in a splint and his forehead was bandaged. Yet, his eyes were bright and aware and they glistened with tears.

Lord Ansira lifted a hand and touched Erisha's cheek then Dumur's. "You are here," he croaked.

Erisha began crying and she fell into her father's arms. Dumur knelt beside the throne and lay his head on his father's arm to hide his tears. Lord Ansira cried openly over his children and held them close. He gestured to his wife and Esirim and the whole family stood together as Erisha and Dumur rose, sniffling. Lord Ansira smiled up at each of them, and he held his wife's hand as she continued to cry. The Steward looked to Girisu and the two Fasur who had entered after Erisha and Dumur. The two Furunian guards flanked them and eyed them warily.

"You are welcome," Lord Ansira told them. "You have helped to make my family whole again. I am in your debt."

The guards slowly returned to their posts.

"My lord," Girisu said with a bow. The Semuskians also bowed. "It was my pleasure to help your children," Girisu continued. "I am here on behalf of your Lord and mine, the King. He is in need."

Lord Ansira's brows furrowed. He waved to them. "Come forward." Although he was temporarily crippled, Erisha was overjoyed to see the familiar firmness around his mouth and the bright, intelligent glint in his eye.

Girisu came near while the Fasur remained where they were. "Lord Kankal means to overthrow the King. His Majesty has challenged Lord Kankal to face him in your realm to avenge the deaths of your men. He requests your aid to subdue Lord Kankal."

Lord Ansira moved to push himself up. "Esirim, help me," he required. "How much do you know of his Majesty's plan?" he asked Girisu as Esirim helped pull him up and Dumur supported him on the other side.

"I know some," Girisu admitted.

"Show me," Lord Ansira replied, inclining his head out of the Hall.

Erisha knew they were headed to the council chamber and she longed to follow them, but her mother hooked her arm through Erisha's. Erisha smiled up at her. Lady Semirra smiled back, tears still in her eyes.

"Are you well?" Erisha asked.

"I am now," her mother replied.

The men talked in the council chamber for an hour or so. Lord Ansira tried afterwards to convince Girisu to at least stay the night but neither Girisu nor the Semusakian warriors would be persuaded. The warriors took their leave and left swiftly from the stair top outside the Manor. Erisha watched them disappeared into the darkness of the night.

"I fly to the King," Girisu was telling Lord Ansira as they all stood outside the Manor's doors. "He will be very happy to know he has your aid."

Lord Ansira shook Girisu's hand. "He will always have Furun," the Steward replied. "I wish safe travel upon you. I will expect you in two days' time."

Girisu nodded. He bowed to Lady Semirra and shook Esirim's hand. Then he turned to Erisha and Dumur.

"Please," Dumur said, "say hello for us."

Girisu smiled. "I will," he promised, shaking Dumur's hand. He looked to Erisha.

Erisha held his gaze, hoping that he would somehow read her mind and stay. She needed him to stay. Everyone else had left her. She was terrified that after he had gone that she would forget any of it had happened.

Girisu bowed to her, breaking the connection though his smile faded.

"Are we not friends?" Erisha asked gently.

Girisu looked to her and a small smile appeared on his face.

Erisha put out her hand, ignoring custom, and he shook it.

"Two days' time," he said, looking from Erisha to Lord Ansira.

Then he was gone. He hurried down the steps and lept onto his horse. It thundered away to the North and the Manor's doors began to be closed by the two guards.

Erisha turned back into the Hall.

Lady Semirra looked to her. "My dear?" she asked curiously.

Erisha realized her family was studying her. Dumur came over and stood at her side. He offered her his arm.

Erisha met her parents' gaze and shook her head. She smiled and looked to Dumur.

"How about we scrounge around for some food then go to sleep?" Dumur suggested.

Erisha laughed. "That is a perfect plan."

"Oh, of course!" Lady Semirra exclaimed. "We must tell Cook and the rest of the household."

Erisha and Dumur followed their mother and exchanged a smile. Erisha stifled a yawn and Dumur stood straighter. Erisha snorted softly and Dumur grinned.

Cook was still cleaning up in the kitchen with her two apprentices. One of the apprentices nearly dropped a stack of dishes when she saw Erisha and Dumur. Dumur rushed forward and took the dishes from her and placed them on a nearby counter. Cook began to cry and she hugged Erisha. The second apprentice rushed out of the room without a word and a few moments later, as Cook was demanding details, the whole household stuffed themselves into the kitchen. Erisha and Dumur were showered with love, and many different servants offered to help prepare them a small feast. This, of course, was not what Erisha and Dumur were interested in, but it was too late and would be too heartless to refuse. They waited patiently as their meal was prepared and answered as many questions as they could.

Lord Ansira and Esirim joined the party in the kitchen and sat back with Lady Semirra. They watched the unfolding event with pride and joy. Erisha looked over at one point and exchanged grins with Esirim. He stood and made his way through the chaos to her side. Dumur was busy telling about his encounter with the Usuma, practically standing on a counter and dramatically waving his arms about as he spoke.

Esirim stood behind Erisha's chair.

"You'll want to pay attention to this story," Erisha encouraged him.

Esirim leaned against the counter. "I'm sure I'll hear it again," he said, "and the fuller story at that. How are you holding up?"

Erisha turned about and looked up at him. "I'm exhausted," she whispered with a small smile.

Esirim nodded. "I'm sorry," he said.

Erisha shook her head. "It's fine," she replied. "It's all for the best."

Her elder brother placed a comforting hand on her shoulder. Erisha smiled up at him then turned to receive her meal. Dumur and she thanked Cook and her apprentices profusely before eating. They ate quickly at first, feeling starved, then slowed as the food began to settle.

As neither of them could speak now, many servants said their goodnights and left the kitchen. Lord Ansira sent one young man to go find Turin. Esirim told his younger siblings the news of the village and the Manor while they ate. All was as it should be at this time of the year, but work had been delayed for a few days by the return of the Steward and his heir. With the Stewardess being ill and Erisha and Dumur gone, the people had been in a state of disarray. As Esirim had healed and improved, he had dealt with issues about the village for his father and informed the people of what had happened at the border. Many families were directly affected and the whole village had dived into a period of mourning. A funeral ceremony had been held a couple days ago and now the men were becoming angry.

"I pacified them as best as I could," Esirim explained, "but their sense of justice is rightfully enflamed."

"That energy and courage will be put to good use soon," Lord Ansira said, sitting by them at the table.

"My dear, you are exhausted," Lady Semirra said, coming to his side. "You all are," she added, looking to Erisha and Dumur. "We should sleep."

"A moment," Lord Ansira said. "I must speak to Turin."

They waited in silence now, except for the clink and splash of Cook washing the last dishes. Erisha had just finished eating when Turin appeared with the servant. Turin stopped abruptly at the sight of Erisha and Dumur. He hailed them happily and bowed to Erisha before giving Dumur a hug.

Lord Ansira thanked the young servant and sent him off. "Turin," he said. "I'm sorry to steal you from your family. A guard must be established around the village and the Manor from all directions."

"Of course, my lord," Turin said in surprise. "What has--"

"The King has declared war against Lord Kankal," Lord Ansira explained.

A look of understanding alighted in Turin's eyes. He nodded and his jaw clenched. "I will see to it," he said, already turning away in his excitement.

"The King will face Kankal here," Lord Ansira added, and Turin stopped. "We will stand with him. Prepare the men."

"Of course, my lord," Turin replied, and Erisha noticed a small grim smile appear on Turin's face as he bowed and left them.

Lord Ansira laughed humorlessly. "The men will not need persuading," he said gravely. "I will have to speak to them. This is not a battle for vengeance."

Lady Semirra helped her husband up and Esirim was at his other side. They all thanked Cook and left the kitchen. Soberly, they then wished each other goodnight and went to their respective bedrooms to sleep.

The Manor and the village were in a flurry of activity the following two days. Esirim and Turin organized the men and rotated the guard. Battle ideas were mapped out with Lord Ansira, but nothing definite could be decided without the King. The Manor household was busy cleaning armor and sharpening weapons. The village wives and mothers and daughters cooked and baked furiously to make enough food for the warriors for a couple of days. The one thing Lord Ansira already decided on was that the battle was going to happen far from the village and a troop of men would remain behind as protection. So, the men needed supplies to last them for many days in order for the villagers to not be endangered.

Also, regular life on top of all the bustle had to continue. Winter preparation for buildings and animals had to be made. Warmer clothes were still being knitted and sewn so they could be distributed.

Erisha helped wherever she could, but she began the first morning home by sleeping until the sun was nearly overhead. When she awoke and went in search for food, wistfully wandering through the Hall then to the kitchen, Cook informed her that Dumur was still asleep himself but the rest of the household had been up since dawn. Erisha ate quickly then went to find her father to see where she could help. She passed one of her favorite wide windows in the hallway leading to the council chamber. She stared out over the rolling fields and saw wisps of the mountains in the blue sky far away. She had been *in* those mountains. She laughed softly to herself.

Lord Ansira was initially determined to send Erisha to rest for the day, but Erisha would do no such.

"I've been on the move for so many days," she explained. "I need to do something."

Lord Ansira sat back in his chair at the table in the council chambers. "Well, first you can tell me how you're doing," her father said.

"I am well," Erisha replied. "I am very rested."

Lord Ansira shook his head. "There is something different about you," he announced. "You are ill at ease."

Erisha paused. "I am readjusting," she said. "I have been out over the country. I've seen beautiful places and terrifying sites. I've been with companions who quickly became friends who are now gone. I am happy to be home — I was so excited to see the Manor yesterday but…"

"You are not the same," her father said.

"I was going to say that it seems like it's not the same here," Erisha said, "but you're probably right."

Lord Ansira smiled. "The fate of an adventurer is an exciting one, Erisha," he said, "but it is not stable, not enduring."

Erisha nodded. "Yes, I understand," she said.

"But it is still hard to come back," her father added.

"It sounds terrible," Erisha said. "But I want more…"

Lord Ansira smiled sadly. "You want something of your own. You are too big for your childhood home now."

"That sounds awful," Erisha lamented.

"It is inevitable," Lord Ansira replied.

Erisha shook her head and hurried over to him. "There is nothing more I could want that you and Mother and Esirim and Dumur," she said, hugging him.

Lord Ansira hugged her tightly with his uninjured arm then pulled her away to look into her eyes. "Nothing more?" he probed.

Erisha hated how she instantly thought of Anarim in Zari. Her throat tightened and she stared in front of her.

He smiled at her gently, knowing her pain but not knowing the source. "Why don't you go into the village and find your mother," he said, patting her hand encouragingly. "I'm sure she'll find something for you to do."

Erisha obeyed.

The day passed and Erisha helped to bake and sew where she could. She also spent time with the village children, and Dumur, who eventually joined her, told the children of their journey. The children listened with wide eyes, especially to Dumur's story of the Usuma and Erisha's story of battling Mita.

"I wonder if she's better," Erisha mused with Dumur by her side.

Dumur nodded but said nothing. His eyebrows remained furrowed against the sunlight. His mouth was set grimly.

Lord Ansira had insisted that Dumur also take the first day calmly. They were all exhausted, however, by the time night came again. The Steward was pleased with the progress of the day and a rider from Zari arrived after dinner. It was a message from the King announcing that they would be in Furun the following day's afternoon. Erisha stared at the letter in her father's hand before she turned away and stared into the fire burning in their private sitting room.

"Good," Lord Ansira said, folding up the letter and putting it in a drawer of his writing desk in the room. "So far, things are going well. We should sleep." He stood himself and Erisha was gladdened by his appearance and stature compared to its state the previous day. He had been improving rapidly since the morning yet now he nearly seemed to be like his old self if he did not look a bit older. He walked with a limp as he led his wife from the room, but he walked by himself.

"It is because you both are here," Esirim said, rising from his chair after their parents had left. "The family is whole."

"How weak we are if the loss of a person or two can destroy us," Erisha murmured absently to herself.

Dumur, however, heard and turned to her. He frowned. "How brave we are if we can grow to care so much," he countered, "that it destroys us. Though, agreed, we should not wallow forever."

Erisha looked at him sharply, but Dumur irritatingly held her gaze.

Esirim, having watched the interaction, came over and sat by Erisha. "Who has hurt you?" he asked her, searching her face.

Erisha shook her head vigorously. "No one," she assured. "I was being cynical, I'm sorry." She smiled up at him.

Esirim cocked his head to the side, obviously not convinced. Yet, he stood and wished them a goodnight. Dumur rose and looked down at Erisha. He offered his hand to her, and she allowed him to help her up. He was definitely a good bit taller than her now and he looked down at her still.

"You didn't do anything wrong," he said. "It is no use wondering what we could have done differently. We must face tomorrow."

Erisha nodded.

Dumur squeezed her hand then left her in the room alone.

Erisha looked to her father's desk. She slowly went over to it and opened the drawer with the letter inside. She took out Anarim's letter and read it for herself. It was brief and to the point.

Lord Ansira reentered the room and startled her. He saw the letter in her hands.

"I'm sorry," Erisha said quickly. "I just wanted to see it."

Her father nodded. "That's alright," he said. "I realized that I wanted to ask the King to camp in a specific area. I need to write him and send a messenger. I'm glad you're here actually. My hand is still stiff. Could you write for me?"

"Of course," Erisha agreed, and she penned the response for her father.

"Write your name at the end," her father instructed.

"My name?" Erisha exclaimed in surprise.

"I can't very well sign it as if it was from me when our writing is so different," he replied with a laugh. "That would be odd. Just sign it and write that you scribed it for me. The King will accept that. He knows you, does he not? He will trust it."

Erisha licked her lips and nodded. She signed the note, explained herself in a script at the bottom, then handed the letter to her father.

"Thank you," Lord Ansira said. He offered her his arm and Erisha took it. They left the sitting room and wished each other goodnight. Erisha watched as her father walked away with the letter in hand. She shook her head abruptly and went to her bedroom.

CHAPTER FIFTEEN

WAR

Erisha woke earlier the next morning and went outside to greet the day. She found Dumur sitting at the back of the Manor on the stone foundation that protruded from under the Manor. She joined him and breathed in the morning air.

"You keep looking East," she pointed out.

"You keep watching the North," he countered.

There was silence.

"Everyone should be arriving today," Erisha said.

"Including Kankal," Dumur added. "The battle could begin today, this afternoon. Peace yesterday, war today."

"Maybe even before this afternoon," Erisha said suddenly, the thought filling her with anxious dread. "How do we know Lord Kankal will respect the King's wishes? He probably won't." She stood and rushed back indoors. Dumur followed her.

They found their father breakfasting in the Hall with their mother.

"Good morning," their parents greeted.

"Father, Lord Kankal may attack before the King even arrives," Erisha said urgently.

The Steward, however, nodded calmly. "I would be surprised if he waited," he replied. "Esirim is already with the men. We ride onto the fields soon."

"I shall head out immediately then," Dumur announced.

"Have you eaten?" his mother asked.

"No, but—"

"Go eat. You will be no help if you are without sustenance," Lady Semirra said. She turned to her husband as their youngest left the Hall. "Must he join you?" she asked.

"Would you destroy his honor and esteem?" Lord Ansira replied. "He will not be on the field, don't worry. I'll keep him with the archers. I'd rather have him in the tents, but he'll demand to do something."

Lady Semirra nodded but was unhappy.

"And we will stay here?" Erisha asked.

Her father looked over at her. "You will ride out with us," he said. "Then you will ride back here and stay here. Our home must be looked after and fortified. Your mother knows how this works. You are to help her if the Manor must become a barricade."

"Do you think that will happen?" Erisha asked in alarm.

Her father sighed. "I do not know," he said. "Go breakfast with your brother. We do not know what this day holds."

Erisha left for the kitchen and found that Cook had already laid out a meal for her. She sat beside Dumur in the kitchen. Cook and her apprentices were quiet as the two siblings ate.

Erisha told her brother that their mother and she were to ride with the men, and Dumur waited for her to finish her meal.

Once they were both done, they rose and brought their dishes over to the large, deep washing basin. They thanked Cook and her apprentices. Cook nodded and the young man, Segi, and the young women, Endua, smiled.

"You both come back now, you hear," Cook said as they were leaving the kitchen.

They turned back to her.

"The Manor was lonely and empty without you. We'll not stand for such again, you understand?" the older woman stood tall and spoke sternly, but she could not hide the tears in her eyes.

Erisha and Dumur nodded.

"We'll be back," Erisha said.

"We made our way back once already," Dumur said. "We can do it again." He grinned and Erisha smiled.

The kitchen workers all smiled and Cook sniffed.

"May Lord Kankal rue the day he disrespected the King and attacked Furun!" Cook declared.

"Hear! Hear!" Dumur agreed.

With such encouragement on either side, Erisha and Dumur joined their parents in the Hall. The Manor's front doors were pulled open, and the family walked out to look over the village. Two stable boys were waiting for them at the bottom of the steps with their horses.

Erisha saw the warriors being organized by Turin and Esirim on the West side of the village. She heard Dumur exclaim beside her, however, and she turned to see Dumur rushing down the steps to the horses.

"Kuranga!" she cried, and she also hurried down the steps to her horse.

Dumur was already looking over Sisi and talking to his horse affectionately.

Erisha hugged Kuranga's neck, and the horse lowered her head to nuzzle her. Erisha laughed. "So, you made it home," she murmured, feeling her heart lighten.

Dumur lept up into Sisi's saddle and he raced the creature around the Manor. Lord Ansira and Lady Semirra were laughing at they joined them. Lord Ansira gestured to Dumur as he came back around and Dumur joined them, grinning widely.

Erisha mounted with her parents, and they all followed Lord Ansira down to the army. Turin and Esirim were armored, and they mounted when the Steward and Stewardess arrived. The men were all set, and the cavalry was waiting on the side. Lord Ansira looked to Turin. The military captain nodded.

"Chins up," Lord Ansira said to Turin. "Many are watching."

Erisha looked back into the village and saw many of the people gazing at the warriors from doorsteps, windows, the streets. Lord Ansira raised his hand in salute and the people cheered.

"Off we go," Lord Ansira said quietly. He turned his steed around and led the way. Turin, Esirim, and Dumur fell in behind him, and Lady Semirra and Erisha behind them. The men followed and the archers and cavalry brought up the rear.

They marched out from the village and aimed slightly towards the South where tents, fire pits, and extra weapons were laid out. It took at least a quarter of an hour to march out to the camp. When they arrived, Turin began barking orders and scouts were sent out to relieve the ones who had been already out since early morning. Lord Ansira brought his family into the largest tent. Inside, tables and chairs were set up. Lord Ansira's armor hung in a corner. Torches were stuck in corners for the evening. A bed lay in another corner. Maps and battle plans were organized on the largest table in the center of the space.

Lord Ansira turned to his sons. "Would you help me?" he asked, gesturing to his armor.

"Already?" Lady Semirra asked in surprise.

"I doubt the wait will be long," her husband replied.

While Esirim and Dumur proudly helped their father, Erisha went back to the tent opening. She looked to the North but saw no sign of movement in the distance. She looked about at the men, young, old, middle-aged; all ready to sacrifice their lives for their families and their realm. Although the day was sunny and breezy and crisp, Erisha felt the heavy somber atmosphere close in.

An alarm suddenly went through the camp and men rushed about. Turin ran to the Steward's tent and pushed past Erisha.

"Two scouts have returned just now," Turin told Lord Ansira who was just finishing being armed. "They return with one scout dead and the other mortally wounded. They were attacked by Felrisan scouts. Kankal is near."

Lord Ansira tightened a couple straps himself and stepped forward. He glanced at his wife and his look was one of foreboding. "Find out where they are," he ordered, looking to Turin.

Turin hurried from the tent and Esirim raced after him. Erisha jumped out of their way and went over to her mother.

"You two should head back to the Manor," Lord Ansira demanded.

"The King—" Erisha began.

"We must handle Kankal until the King arrives. And you must go. Now," her father said.

Lady Semirra grabbed Erisha's arm and Dumur came to his mother's other side. Lord Ansira walked out of the tent, and they followed. The Steward of Furun turned to his wife and daughter.

"I love you both," he said, "very much. No matter how this day ends, you must know that."

Erisha nodded, supporting her mother.

Lady Semirra looked like she was about to cry, but then she stiffened and stood straighter. She walked away from Erisha and hugged her husband. Erisha and Dumur watched as their parents exchanged a few words quietly then kissed each other goodbye.

Lady Semirra came over to Erisha and they went over to the horses. Erisha looked back once her mother was in her saddle and saw her father bellowing orders to men nearby. Dumur stood at his side, a hand on his sword hilt and holding his bow in the other hand. Erisha paused then raced back and hugged her father tightly. He gave her a crushing hug then told her to be off. Erisha hugged Dumur quickly and they looked at each other for a moment before Erisha hurried to Kuranga. She lept up onto her horse, but her mother and she had hardly moved a couple steps before more cries went up.

"The Felrisans head for the village!" came the shouts.

The announcement echoed throughout the camp. Everyone seemed to stand frozen in shock.

Lord Ansira spoke first. He pointed at Lady Semirra and Erisha. He looked furious. "Into the tent," he ordered. He turned about. "Cut them off," he yelled. "Protect the people!"

It was an eruption of movement around Erisha and her mother as they jumped off their horses and fled to the tent. Erisha glimpsed Dumur disappear among the men, and she stifled a cry for him. Soon, Erisha and Lady Semirra stood in the tent, gasping for breath.

Lord Ansira appeared in the opening. "Do not leave," he ordered them sternly.

They nodded and he left, hand on his sword hilt.

"My horse," they heard him call.

Erisha and Lady Semirra stood standing and staring at each other as they listened to the fast steps and thundering hoof beats of men and their mounts outside the tent. Then the noise faded away to the South. They continued to stand for a few long moments.

"How are we to know what's happening?" Erisha exclaimed anxiously. She rushed about the tent and found a flap that pointed South. She carefully folded it back and peered through the opening. Her mother came up behind her.

The cavalry was racing to the South around the village to cut off a large segment of Felrisan warriors heading towards the village. Erisha watched, tense, as the two groups made for their targets. She heard her mother breathing heavily behind her as they both stared.

The Furunian cavalry flew across the fields and cut off the Lekur before they made it to the village. The clash of swords and spears meeting greeted Erisha's ears and she winced. Yet, the noise suddenly seemed to be coming from two directions.

Erisha turned and stared across the tent back to the opening. She crept over, leaving her mesmerized mother to watch the South. She peeked out the opening and horror stuck her as she saw Furunian forces meeting Felrisan forces coming from the West. Erisha watched as armour and weapons glinted and flashed in the sunlight. The drum and clang of battle rang in Erisha's head as she watched intently. She quickly gave up trying to distinguish warriors. She grimaced every time that it appeared a warrior fell. After a few moments, she tore herself away and stared into the tent. Her mother was still watching from the flap in the tent.

Erisha walked over towards the table to look at one of the maps but the reality that she and her mother were in the middle of a desperate battle where people would die and never be seen walking in this world again stuck her heavily. She sank into a nearby chair and gazed in front of her.

She was startled from her reverie by the sound of horns being blown. She did not know how long she had been sitting, staring before her and imagining all the horrors that must be happening around her outside the tent. Yet, now, there was clearly the sound of horns — loud, hope-bringing horns. Erisha stood and hurried to the tent opening. She peered outside but saw nothing new. The battle before her seemed to have spread out farther and dark masses of fallen bodies colored the ground. The Esasag appeared to be losing to the Lekur. Thunder rumbled as Erisha watched their group of archers send arrows into the farther half of the battle before her. This time hope filled Erisha.

The sky was clear and blue, and Erisha looked to the North. A huge host of men on horseback became distinct. Their colors of crimson and grey streaked behind them as they sped across the grass. She thought she had never seen horses run so fast.

Erisha laughed out joyously.

The Hursaga came upon the battle, and they plowed through, weapons blazing. Hearty cheers went up from the battlefield. Yells roared from the North and Erisha looked back to see men on foot charging along the same path behind the horse-men.

This new cavalry worked its way through the battle in front of Erisha before suddenly heading towards the South. Erisha watched as a large group of crimson-decorated warriors broke from the rest and moved to follow their horsemen. Three horse-men came out from within the battle and headed towards the camp as the rest of the Zarian warriors joined the battle before her.

Erisha backed away into the tent unable to determine the three horsemen's colors. She turned to her mother who was now sitting, stunned, in a chair.

"Mother," Erisha said urgently. "Someone is coming."

Her mother's attention snapped to her. "Who?" she asked.

Erisha shook her head. "I don't know," she said. "What do we do?"

Not waiting for an answer, Erisha looked about the tent and her eyes found a bow and quiver laying alongside a chair. She grabbed it while Lady Semirra rose and found a bow of her own by the bed. Erisha threw her a couple arrows and they both notched one in place. They heard the horses approaching and they stood back and raised their weapons.

The King strode into the tent.

Erisha felt her mouth open, and she instantly lowered her bow as Anarim's eyes swept the area and landed on them.

Lady Semirra, however, was so startled that she let her arrow fly. Erisha cried out and Anarim moved and brought up his sword just in time to deflect the arrow.

"Your Majesty," Lady Semirra breathed, falling into a chair. She put a hand over her mouth.

"I am unharmed," Anarim told her, holding out an assuring hand. Lord Ansira and Dumur entered. Anarim glanced at Erisha before looking to the Steward. "Why are your wife and daughter here?" he demanded incredulously.

Lord Ansira shook his head. "They could not return," he said.

"Why would you bring them out here into harm's way?" Anarim exclaimed. "This is no place—"

"Now is not the time to berate me, my Lord," Lord Ansira replied. "You may do that later. Now, we need to decide what to do with the men."

Anarim looked to Erisha. "Send them away," he told Lord Asnira, gesturing to Lady Semirra and Erisha.

"I'll not put them anywhere else in this camp!" Lord Ansira replied. "They may hear—"

"Send them home," Anarim clarified firmly. "My men are there now to aid your men and protect the village. They will be safe there. Send them home."

Lord Ansira studied the King then nodded. He looked to his wife and daughter. He gestured to them.

Erisha shouldered the quiver of arrows and the bow as her mother stood. She walked past Dumur and her father before approaching Anarim. He was watching her, and she held his gaze for a moment before he ushered her out of the tent.

The sounds of battle were precariously close. Erisha tried to look towards the South, but Anarim was by her side and put a hand on her arm to hurry her. She looked West and was shocked to see the warriors closing in on the camp. Her attention was torn away from the approaching battle when Anarim lifted her up into the saddle of Kuranga. She glimpsed Dumur helping his mother onto her horse while Turin, smattered with blood, thundered up to her father on his steed. Erisha looked back to the battle and watched with growing alarm as the view of men locked in combat and being wounded or killed grew clearer and clearer as they drew closer. The Felrisans were pushing them back towards the village, at least here on the western side. Erisha realized the majority of Anarim's men must have hurried to aid the attack on the southern side.

"Erisha!" Anarim called, demanding her attention.

Erisha looked down at him as she grasped Kuranga's reins.

"Go," he ordered, and she could hardly hear his voice above the horrible din. "And don't look back."

Erisha nodded and held his gaze as she guided Kuranga about. She paused. She knew there was something she wanted to tell him. It certainly was not goodbye. Yet, before she could say anything, Anarim urged Kuranga forward.

"Wait!" she cried, pulling on the reins.

"Erisha!" Anarim declared angrily.

"Don't die," she ordered.

Anarim stared up at her then a small smile appeared on his face momentarily. He smacked the backside of Kuranga, and the horse took off. Erisha glimpsed the King raise his sword and yell something to the men before she looked ahead.

She saw the village in the distance. Lady Semirra was already a good bit in front of Erisha, her mount sprinting for the Manor. Erisha urged Kuranga into a sprint, but something caught her eye and made her heart skip a beat. She pulled up on Kuranga's reins. She turned the creature about and galloped back to the figure lying in the grass. Once she was close enough, Erisha's fears were confirmed, and she slid from her saddle onto the ground.

"Sidukur!" she cried, falling onto her knees beside her friend.

Sidukur turned his head slowly to look at her. There was a long bloody gash down the side of his face and, by now, the ground where he lay was damp with his blood that had spilt from a large wound in his side.

"Hello, lass," he said tightly. He raised a worn hand slowly up to her.

"Oh, Sidukur," Erisha sobbed, grabbing his hand in both of hers.

"It's my time," Sidukur said, smiling. "I was wounded and worked my way over here on my horse before I fell off. Now I journey onwards to lands unknown by any living soul."

Erisha sniffed. "If anyone is brave enough to travel through those lands," she said through her tears, "it's you."

Sidukur's eyes shone. "Thank you," he said with a cough and blood appeared on his lips.

"Oh, but what about your family?" Erisha lamented. "Your wife and child."

Sidukur's face fell and lost much of its color. "Aye, I know," he said. "I will miss them."

"They will miss you," Erisha said, almost frantically, and she took a few, slow breaths.

Tears fell down Sidukur's face. "Yes," he choked. He looked from the blue sky above back to Erisha as the battle waged nearby. "You must visit them. Make sure they are well. Every day, you hear?" He gripped her hands tightly.

Erisha's tears stopped as she stared down at him. "How—" she began.

"Promise me," Sidukur said before groaning in pain.

"I promise," Erisha said, and she knew she would find a way to fulfill the promise. "Of course, I promise."

Sidukur relaxed and his hand grew limp in her hands. "Thank you, Erisha," he said with a smile. He looked up again at the sky and breathed heavily for a few moments before he breathed no more.

Erisha still held his hand in one of hers and with the other she covered her mouth to stifle her sobs. Tears wet her cheeks but after a moment of despair the cries and yells of men rallied her. She looked up and discovered that the battle was now raging in the camp and Kuranga had walked away a couple steps. She looked to her horse and Kuranga neighed nervously.

Erisha looked back down at Sidukur's lifeless form then she let go of his hand and scrambled up and over to Kuranga. Suddenly, loud strange yells filled the air and Erisha spun around to face the East. Semusakian warriors came running across the fields, continuing to yell shrilly. Only a few warriors rode on horses, and most raced with long strides towards the battle. Their yellow and bronze cloaks rippled in the sunlight, and the large group streamed with fluid movements into battle. Their swords slashed at the enemy and a collective Felrisan cry arose as the other realms cheered. The last tents standing were knocked down and the different colors of Alland's warriors melded together.

Erisha looked over at the battle as she grabbed onto the saddle, and she saw Dumur ride across the edge of the field on Sisi. Her eyes followed him as Kuranga waited patiently for her to mount. Dumur was hunched over on Sisi, riding fast around the battle to the South end. Suddenly, something whistled in the wind past Erisha's head and Dumur jerked up as Erisha watched an arrow strike him in the back. The air caught in her lungs.

Another arrow shot past Erisha and pierced Dumur. Time seemed to slow for Erisha as Dumur fell from Sisi's saddle. He crumbled on the ground, and Erisha's hands slipped off the saddle. Her hands grasped for the bow and an arrow. She whipped around to find the archer.

Lord Kankal sat tall on his horse only a few paces behind her. He loosed another arrow, and Erisha's gaze followed the thin shaft. Dumur was struck again.

Erisha's vision blurred. A dangerous, uncontrollable rage filled her from tip to toe. Her grip clenched rigidly around her bow as she turned back to Kankal. "How dare you," she seethed.

The Steward smiled. "Just some petty revenge," he replied coolly, "since you kidnapped and exploited my daughter."

"Mita is not your daughter!" Erisha yelled furiously. The wind roared to life around them. "You disgrace her by claiming her as such. She has parents who you have unjustly imprisoned in the Mountain."

Lord Kankal looked up at the skies in alarm as they swiftly turned grey.

"You... you nearly killed my father and my older brother," Erisha continued, unable to think as the rage threatened to over-whelm her, "and now you've killed my younger brother." She approached the mounted old man.

The wind was rushing around them menacingly. Lord Kankal's stare flickered uncertainly back and forth between Er-isha and the ominous weather gathering above. His horse backed away from Erisha as she strode towards Lord Kankal.

"You are here alone," Erisha yelled. "Away from the battle. You have abandoned your men and are keeping yourself safe. You watch from afar and have shot down a youth in cold blood. You are a tyrant, a monster, and a coward."

Kankal's eyes narrowed as he returned his attention to Erisha and registered her words. He raised his bow and yelled wrathfully while his other hand grasped for an arrow. Yet, Erisha was ready before him. Body tingling with wild emotion and energy, she loosed her arrow and it thudded into Kankal's chest.

Kankal froze in the saddle and looked down at the arrow lodged in his chest. He looked up at Erisha. He moved quickly, anger fueling him. He notched an arrow, but, again, Erisha was quicker. Another shaft pierced Kankal.

Kankal roared in pain and tensed his whole body in the saddle. He glared at Erisha. He threw his bow and grabbed the reins with one hand as his other hand drew his sword. Erisha stiffed, preparing to raise another arrow then run.

Lightning stuck from the dark sky above. White light flashed and crackled and dove forcefully into the ground between Erisha and Lord Kankal. Both Erisha and Lord Kankal were thrown back.

Erisha rolled over, gasping. A piercing buzz filled her ears, and her left leg felt numb. She struggled to her feet. Her head spun as she stood and steadied herself. She stared at the black mark on the ground in front of her. The grass sizzled and smoked, and small flames flickered on the edges of the mark. The dirt was sooty and fine. A horse neighed nearby. Erisha saw Kankal's horse, riderless, skittering away. Kankal lay on the ground on the other side of the ashen mark. She glanced up at the sky and it remained brooding and black. She looked back over at Kankal and the old man was struggling to roll over.

Ears ringing but blood pumping angrily in her head, Erisha approached Kankal's side. She notched another arrow. She looked down at Kankal as he gazed up at her, panting. She pulled back the string of her bow. Kankal watched her as he began to bleed out, his eyes void of any fear.

The air was heavy and quiet. Slowly, the sound of battle entered back into Erisha's ears. She gulped for breath and her head cleared. She lowered her bow and eased back the string.

"Scared to kill a man?" Kankal taunted.

Erisha looked down at him. "Yes," she admitted softly. She clenched her jaw. "Surrender, you coward," she ordered, "and leave. Go hide in your mountain."

Kankal began to laugh but it turned into a cough and then into a groan. He closed his eyes and lay back. Erisha backed away, suddenly terrified that she had killed him. She stared down at him as the sky cleared and the sun shone down. A cool breeze blew past her, and she remembered Dumur. She looked back toward the battlefield. She saw the outline of Dumur on the ground, laying against the grass. She ran, limping, across the field. She heaved for breath as her leg regained feeling, but she eventually reached Dumur. She fell beside him and looked over him, panic-stricken, while he struggled to draw breath.

His eyes latched onto her as she fell beside him. "Erisha," he croaked.

"I'm here, I'm here," Erisha said, looking from his face to his many punctures. If she removed the arrows, he would only lose more blood. Yet, she was afraid blood loss was inevitable. She looked back into Dumur's face, tears welling in her eyes. "Dumur—"

He braved a smile. "Tell them," he gasped. "Tell them I love them."

"I will," she swore as emotion threatened to choke her.

Dumur closed his eyes, and his breaths came in short, rapid succession. Then, he suddenly became very still. Erisha stared numbly at him for a moment. She could not stop the scream from escaping from between her lips. She felt the ground rumble beneath her as she cried over her brother. There were yells and shouts, and she paused and thought she heard the word *earthquake* passed around. She took a shaky breath as the shaking beneath her calmed.

Without warning, there was a sharp, immense pain in her lower back. She felt the slick, brittle blade slide out. The pain spread everywhere, and it was followed by a liquid warmth. A rough hand gripped her shoulder.

"My revenge against Furun is nearly complete," came Kankal's voice in a sneer as the old man's mouth pressed near her ear. "I will kill your father and his heir, and the King's most devoted realm will fall into ruin."

Erisha tried to breath evenly, but everything everywhere hurt and she soon found herself lying on the ground. Kankal stood above her then his figure, dark against the sunlight glowing down, disappeared from view. She heard him call for his horse. A beast thundered passed her in the direction of the battle soon after. Strangely, Erisha felt a wave of relief wash over her—she had not killed Kankal.

Staring up at the sky and still grasping Dumur with her fingertips, Erisha looked around for someone, anyone, to help. Her vision wavered so she focused on the blueness and openness of the sky above her and the elegant lightness of the few clouds passing overhead. She focused on breathing and tried to ignore the throbbing pain.

There was loud cry from nearby and Erisha was startled by the utter misery conveyed in the sound. There was noise of clashing metal and grunts near her and then she saw Esirim's face over her, backed by the blueness. She tried to call out to him, but the gasps that pained her body would not allow it.

Esirim, however, dropped down beside her and hugged her to him. She cried out in anguish, her body feeling as if it was on fire, and Esirim adjusted his hold.

"Erisha? Erisha?" he called over and over.

Erisha tried to speak but she eventually gave up and used what felt like the last sap of her strength to reach up and touch her brother's face before her hand dropped back down protectively on Dumur's shoulder. As soon as she touched his face, Esirim quieted and began to cry while Erisha's vision began to fade again. The pain — it had spread all over. She hurt so much, and she closed her eyes to try to focus on anything else.

Her mind rested on her fingers gripping Dumur's cloak. Her eyes flew open and struggled to get Esirim's attention.

She stopped and took a slow, deep breath. "Dumur," she finally said hoarsely.

"What?" Esirim questioned, focusing on her again.

Erisha grimaced and marveled at how he had not yet been cut down sitting here with her. She tried to pull Dumur closer and failed, but the action was enough. Esirim's attention flickered down to where Dumur's body lay beside Erisha's skirt.

Erisha felt Esirim's hold stiffen and, one last time, she reached up and placed a hand on his chest. But the world around her was fading. Her vision blurred and she realized her face was wet with tears as she failed to see Esirim clearly. Her body relaxed in his arms and, as the darkness closed in, she knew Anarim would be angry with her.

CHAPTER SIXTEEN

THE AFTERMATH

T he pain was overwhelming. She felt as if she was burning on a pyre then as if she had fallen asleep in the snow outside on one of the coldest days of the winter. Images, blurred, flashed before her eyes between extended times of complete darkness. Then, finally, there was nothing. Or, at least, she felt nothing. In her mind, she saw someone sitting in a chair. He had his head in his hands. He looked so sad. She wanted to go to him, comfort him.

Erisha stretched and she realized she was laying on something soft. The darkness began to give way into a warm, golden light outside her closed eyes. She tried to open her eyes, but she had to blink several times before she could focus on anything. She was in her bedroom in the Manor, lying up against many pillows in her bed and her covers were pulled almost all the way up to her chin. The sun was shining happily through the windows. She breathed deeply and sensed the thick, heavy fabric wrapped around her torso underneath her nightgown. She slowly brought her arms out from under the covers and her body began to throb because of injury and the lack of use.

Someone stirred near her bedside on her right. Erisha looked and took in Anarim seated in a large chair where he sat on the edge of the seat with his head in his hands. Using her arms, Erisha sat up straighter against her pillows, easing back carefully and feeling her abdomen. Other than feeling lethargic and sore, nothing else seemed amiss. She wondered how long she had been asleep. A fire was crackling in her small fireplace in her room to help warm the room along with the sunlight, but Erisha felt cold now that part of her was not under the blankets. Telling by how Anarim was dressed more warmly with several layers, she supposed it was much colder outside now. She dragged a smaller blanket up and carefully and slowly draped it around her shoulder. Then she achingly sat back again, and her movements finally stirred Anarim. He looked up and their eyes met.

Erisha smiled softly after he did not initially react but continued to stare at her. "Hello," she said.

Anarim sighed deeply in relief and sat back in the chair. "Hello," he said. His face was worn and very tired looking.

"How long—" Erisha began.

"Four nights," Anarim answered, "but your recovery was remarkable. The blade that cut you missed your spine and organs. Many were afraid for your life, including me. Although… I shouldn't have been."

Erisha studied him, puzzled. She tried to think back over what she knew had happened, but she remembered something more pressing. Her heart squeezed in her chest and her wound tensed. "Dumur," she cried before grimacing in pain.

"Relax," Anarim said, sitting forward and putting a hand out.

Erisha sank into the pillows. "Have they already performed the lamentations? Has the mourning period started?" she asked quickly.

Anarim took one of her hands in his. "Erisha, Dumur lives," he said.

Erisha stared at him. "He's alive?" she breathed, tears halting. "But I watched him die. He died in my arms."

Anarim nodded. "He was dead," he admitted. "Yet now he is alive."

Erisha shook her head in disbelief, but Anarim continued:

"Erisha, Kas is gone. It all began, apparently, with Esirim. After he found you, with Dumur dead and you dying, he took on a kind of madness. He lost himself and began slaughtering the Lekur with a renewed vigor. An unmatched, dangerous vigor." Anarim eyes her, his hand still encompassing hers.

Erisha looked down. "I'm sorry," she said. She pressed on as Anarim began to shake his head. "But I wasn't looking back, I swear. I just... I saw Sidukur—"

"Sidukur!" Anarim said in surprise.

Erisha nodded. "I went to him instead and..." She looked away. "I was with him when he died. He made me promise I'd visit his family every day. I don't know how I'll do that but that's what I promised."

Anarim also had tears in his eyes, but at this point a small smile appeared on his face and he shook his head.

"Then the Semusakians arrived, and I saw Dumur take an arrow," Erisha continued.

Anarim nodded, interrupting. "I understand," he said, squeezing her hand compassionately.

"It was Kankal," Erisha said, and as soon as she spoke the words she was transported back to the moment when she had spun around and seen Kankal shoot around arrow at her brother.

"Kankal?" Anarim exclaimed.

"He shot Dumur down," Erisha continued, gaze unfocused as she remembered loosing her own shafts. She heard the thuds of the arrows piercing Kankal's chest. She shuddered and her voice sounded far away. "I shot at him."

"Twice?"

The sound of Anarim's voice broke into Erisha's consciousness. She looked over at him, eyes focusing. "Yes," she said. "How did you know?"

"What happened?" he asked.

"A storm suddenly appeared, and lightning struck the ground between us, saving me from his attack," Erisha said. "I recovered and found him on the ground. I almost shot, face to face." She put her hands over her eyes and took a breath. She had almost decided to kill Kankal. She had almost taken his life herself.

Anarim's hands pulled her down away from her face. "But you didn't," he said.

"No, I didn't," Erisha said again. "But I almost did. I could have killed him—"

"But you didn't," Anarim said again, firmly. "You chose not to."

"He asked me if I was afraid to kill a man," Erisha said, looking away again and remembering. "I said I was afraid."

Anarim sighed, letting go of her hands. He sat back and Erisha looked to him. He gazed at her. "You ended it," he said softly.

"What do you mean?" Erisha asked.

"I will explain, but what happened after you let Kankal live?" he asked.

"I went to Dumur," Erisha said. "Kankal must have rallied his strength because he followed me and stabbed me."

"He was the one who wounded you?" Anarim cried.

Erisha nodded. "Dumur had already died," she said. "Then Esirim found us."

"And you fainted and he went mad," Anarim mused, putting it all together.

Erisha nodded again. "Poor Esirim," she said. "Is he well?"

"He is now, but we were all disturbed on the field," Anarim continued. "News of your injury spread and the reality of what happened rested on everyone's hearts. There was outrage that a Lekur had struck down a woman.

I had not known what had happened right away, but I took the lull and the arrival of the Semusakians as an opportunity. I mounted a nearby horse and called for Kankal. Eventually, he appeared. He was already pierced by many arrows, and he looked weak. I demanded his surrender, but he stubbornly refused. I addressed the Felrisans then and rebuked them. I called them to renounce such a man as their Steward and Mita's brother, Lu — you remember him — came forward with his band of warriors and announced his loyalty to me. He looked terrible and I don't doubt that Kankal abused him after finding Mita with us. Many Felrisans followed Lu's example, but there was still a decent number who remained with Kankal. He had also brought women warriors with him as a last resort, and he began ordering them into an attack line. I was at a loss for what to do.

Then, however, an Abakiti woman rode right into battle, carrying a make-shift flag showing the white and purple of Abaki. She came up to me and shouted for all to hear that Kankal had come first to Abaki with a small band and destroyed their village and murdered every man in sight. The Lerisaba were devastated. More Felrisans, once they heard the woman, were so disgusted that they abandoned Kankal until only those blindly devoted were left. We directed the women all off the battlefield and they left, taking some of their wounded with them.

I urged Kankal to surrender again but he refused. The battle continued and the Felrisans now under Lu's command ripped off their colors and fought with us. Girisu found me soon after and told me of you. I would have fallen into Esirim's madness if it weren't for Kas. He was at my side when Girisu found us, and he turned to me and simply said: *We should go to her.* We fought our way to where Girisu had seen Esirim last. We found you moments later and I examined you both while Kas stood guard and Girisu went to find Lord Ansira. No one reared us while Kas was there."

Anarim held Erisha's gaze before he continued, and Erisha wondered what he knew.

"Dumur was indeed dead," Anarim said, "and you were fading fast. I told Kas I didn't know what to do and he looked at the two of you. It seemed a long time before he spoke and all I could do was wait. Eventually he spoke and, in the middle of a battle, he said, *The boy may live, but you may no longer receive my assistance.* His gaze would not waver from mine as he said these words and I almost instantly understood his meaning. It struck me hard."

"So, you knew?" Erisha asked.

Anarim shook his head. "Not until that moment," he said, "but I had had suspicions for a while. I hesitated to make a choice, admittedly, but then I looked down at you and I knew you'd rather your brother live. I'd rather you live, but I wasn't given that choice. So, I agreed to the trade. Almost immediately, the arrows in Dumur dissolved. His wounds disappeared and he began to breath. I was shocked, but I looked up at Kas and he was watching me with an expression I couldn't read. It seemed like sadness but also admiration.

He told me then that I had chosen well in many cases. His whole form seemed to be fading from view right before my eyes. I meant to bow to him, but he put up a hand to stop me. *Tell her that these were the only options I was given,* he said. *Tell her goodbye for me.* We watched each other then he bowed to me and disappeared from view. He was gone and I haven't seen him since."

Erisha was crying quietly and Anarim held her hand in both of his. She stopped crying and breathed evenly. He reached forward with one of his hands and gently cupped her face, smiling sadly. Erisha touched her free hand to his against her head. They gazed at each other, oddly content for a few moments.

"It was not until later that I realized that Kas' words meant you would live," Anarim said, brushing her hair behind her ear. "I remained guarding both of you, now knowing that Dumur lived but thinking you were dying or had died already. I fought off all who came near until the battle was finally won that evening. Kankal soon fainted because of his loss of blood and he was easily captured. Two arrows were stuck *through* him, and I knew they had to have been shot at close range. Now, I know they were from you. You had weakened Kankal and brought about the end the battle." He studied her, a mix of admiration and sadness in his eyes. "I went to face him once Girisu came back with your father. Your father and brother were livid and would have executed Kankal there and then, but I brought Lu forth to decide his Steward's fate." Anarim sighed and rubbed his face with his hands, sitting back and letting go of Erisha' hands. He sat back in the chair by the bedside. "I meant to make Lu the new Steward. But Kankal killed him."

"What?" Erisha exclaimed.

"Yes," Anarim said, staring out a nearby window with a pained expression on his face. "We should have tied Kankal up, but he was dying, Erisha. Yet, he still pulled out a hidden knife, and he lunged forward at Lu and stabbed the poor young man in the heart. I could not stop myself after such an action. Instantly, I raised my blade and I... I executed Kankal."

Erisha realized she was covering her mouth with both her hands.

Anarim looked at her. "It's over," he said. "Whether I've done well enough is for the gods to judge. What's important is that it's done. And you will be well."

Erisha nodded. "Yes, I will be well," she said. "Thank you for all you've done. You didn't need to stay. We could have sent word—"

"I had to stay," Anarim interrupted, leaning forward again.

He was about to say more when Erisha's bedroom door opened and Esirim appeared in the doorway.

"Erisha!" he exclaimed after having gotten over his surprise. He strode over to the bed quickly. "How are you?" He kneeled by her bedside.

Erisha smiled and held out a hand to him. "I am well," she replied. "And you?"

"Never mind me," Esirim declared with a joyful laugh. "All will be well now that you are awake!" He stood and moved to pick Erisha up out of bed. "Come, everyone should know."

Erisha was not as keen on the idea. As Esirim pulled her up and she was struggling to come up with an excuse to remain in bed, she glimpsed an extra bed in the corner of the room.

"Whose is that?" she asked.

Esirim paused and looked in the direction she was facing. Erisha was able to sit back down against her pillows. She hoped she had bought time and would somehow dissuade Esirim was carrying throughout the whole Manor and village.

"That is where Mita sleeps," Esirim said, and he continued to succeed in obtaining Erisha from her bed against her protests.

"Mita?" she exclaimed as Esirim adjusted her in his arms.

"Yes, she has slept in here at night to look after you," Anarim explained.

"What?" Erisha cried, looking back at him awkwardly around Esirim's shoulder. "Then she is alright?"

Anarim smiled as he stood. "She is," he said.

"Esirim, please stop," Erisha demanded. "I'm sure I'm not presentable and—"

"You look fine," Esirim said courteously. "Doesn't she, my Lord?"

"You look lovely," Anarim told her.

Erisha stared after him as Esirim swept her from the room. She would have rather stayed in her bed where it was warm and remained talking to Anarim for the rest of the day. Yet, Anarim was left behind in the room and Esirim carried her down the hallway calling for their parents.

Lady Semirra appeared first from the private sitting room. She gasped when she saw Erisha and rushed over. She cupped Erisha's face in her hands and smiled brightly, eyes glistening.

"Oh, my dear," her mother cried, hugging her tightly. Erisha noticed, however, that her mother's right arm was in a large sling and her arm and shoulder were both heavily wrapped.

"I'm here, Mother," Erisha said. "What happened to you?

Lady Semirra grimaced. "As I was riding back to the Manor, I was struck by an arrow," she explained. "It caught me completely unawares. I fell from the saddle and broke the arrow into my back near my shoulder. I also hit my head when I fell and was knocked unconscious. Fortunately, my horse remained with me and, when I came to, I still made my way back to the Manor. The physician had to extract the arrow and here I am."

My revenge against Furun is nearly complete... Kankal's words floated through Erisha's mind. She knew in her heart that Kankal had shot down her mother in the same way he had killed Dumur. Kankal must have thought her mother was dead when she fell from her horse and did not rise since she was unconscious. Then he went after Dumur. She shuddered as the reality that Lord Kankal had truly tried to extinguish her family dawned on her.

Lady Semirra looked to Esirim as Erisha put an arm back around his shoulders. "Why is she out of her bed?" she questioned. "She'll grow ill in this cold."

"She has a blanket," Esirim replied, continuing down the hallway.

"Her feet are bare!" Lady Semirra said indignantly.

"The only part uncovered," Esirim said with a grin.

They entered the Hall and Lord Ansira was seated on his throne while he was speaking to Girisu, Abkur, and a woman Erisha had never seen before. Lord Ansira stood and hurried over as soon as he saw Erisha.

"My daughter," he said, his voice thick with emotion.

Erisha smiled and blinked away tears. "Hello, Father."

"Come," Lord Ansira said, gesturing towards his throne.

Esirim carefully set Erisha into the large chair. Out of the corner of her eye, Erisha saw Anarim enter with a blanket which he handed to Lady Semirra. Lady Semirra, then, came forward and wrapped the blanket about Erisha's waist and down over her feet.

"Mother, I'm not put together," Erisha pleaded in a whisper. "I don't know if I should be here in such a state of disarray."

"You look wonderful," Lady Semirra said, kissing her cheek. "It is good to see color in your cheeks."

Erisha had to smile at such a comment no matter how put out she was. The side door on the other side of the Hall opened and Esirim, who had left quickly after helping Erisha into the throne, returned with Dumur and Mita in tow. Dumur raced over and Mita followed him at a slower pace.

Dumur hugged Erisha. He stepped back slightly and searched her face. "You are well?" he demanded to know.

Erisha smiled. "Yes, other than being a little annoyed and cold," she said with a quiet laugh.

Mita stepped forward and Erisha welcomed her hug.

"I'm so glad you are here and alright," Erisha said to her.

Mita smiled. "I am still weak, but I'll be alright," she agreed, "Thank you for looking after me," Erisha said.

Mita shook her head. "You looked after me," she said softly. "It was the least I could do."

Erisha smiled sadly. "I am sorry about Lu," she whispered. "It was abominable."

"Thank you," Mita said quietly, looking down.

"You cannot blame yourself," Erisha ordered her.

Mita met her gaze. "I am to be Stewardess of Felrisa one day," she said, standing tall. She reached out a hand to the woman that Erisha did not know. "This is my mother."

Erisha inclined her head to Madam Kusignirgal as the tall, kindly-looking woman bowed.

"My parents will officially act in my stead until I marry," Mita said. She glanced at Anarim who was speaking to Abkur and Lord Ansira, "according to the King's terms."

Erisha looked from Anarim back to Mita. "Then you will head back to the Mountains," she concluded flatly. Her attention was momentarily grabbed by Girisu who bowed to her from where he spoke speaking to Dumur. She smiled gently.

Mita hesitated. "Yes, I suppose so," she admitted. "Now that you are awake."

Erisha paused, dispirited. "Where is your father?" she asked.

"He led the warriors back to Felrisa two days ago," Mita informed.

Erisha nodded slowly.

"But they will not leave before we have a village-wide meal in celebration of your recovery," Lady Semirra cut in, "and in celebration of the victory."

Conversation quickly turned to the battle and the details were recounted for Erisha. She heard of those who proved themselves significant heroes on the field, those who had fallen, and how many warriors each realm had lost. Lord Kankal's death was told to her from Esirim's perspective, and the atmosphere became very somber for a few moments as he related the story. Dumur took over the story after the battle had ended.

"They scoured the field for survivors and wounded and they found us," Dumur explained. "I was unconscious when Esirim and Anarim came to us, but Esirim's attempt to carry me woke me. I was uncertain where I was and what had happened but otherwise alright. Esirim helped me to my feet while Anarim carried you." Dumur gestured to Erisha but was distracted by a pointed look from his mother. "Sorry, I meant his Majesty."

Anarim grinned while Girisu stifled a laugh.

"Well, Esirim was going to try and carry me, but I wasn't about to be humiliated so I had them put me on Sisi," Dumur continued. "I wanted to walk when we got to the village but as the King was on his horse with you and Father was on a horse and Esirim was on a horse I had to be on a horse apparently. They all thought I was going to faint, but I'd never felt better. By then I was absolutely fine."

"You're always fine," both Erisha and Mita grumbled simultaneously.

Dumur flashed a grin. "Don't worry. Being injured is far more interesting."

"It is not," Erisha declared and Mita agreed. Erisha wondered how much Dumur knew and, if he did not, decided to tell him as soon as she could do so privately.

But Dumur sobered. "It is a gift I'm alive actually," he admitted. "I knew that and I'm grateful." He glanced at Anarim.

Erisha was pleased and relaxed back against the throne.

"We were all worried about you," Dumur said, continuing the story. "You were immediately placed in your room and your state seemed dire. The physicians examined you and warned us against false hope. You fell into a raging fever, but your wound improved. Your fever broke last night, I think, and here you are."

Erisha laughed. "Just like that," she said.

The group all smiled.

Lady Semirra went over to her husband. "Shall we have a celebratory meal tonight for dinner?" she asked. "Open the Hall?"

"Whatever you wish," Lord Ansira said with a smile.

"Then I'll be off to the kitchen to tell Cook," Lady Semirra said.

"Poor Cook," Lord Ansira said. "Never a day's rest."

"Is there any way I can help, my lady?" Mrs. Kusignirgal called after Lady Semirra.

Lady Semirra stopped and turned about. "Of course," she said. "Come with me if you'd like."

Mrs. Kursignirgal went after Lady Semirra as Girisu neared Erisha.

"Hello, Girisu," Erisha said kindly.

"Hello, Erisha," he replied with a smile. "It is good to see you up and about."

"Thank you," Erisha said. "I'm sorry about Sidukur," she added quietly. "I was with him... when he died."

"Were you?" Girisu asked lowly, eyes widening. He smiled again. "I'm glad you were. It is good to know he was with a friend. I miss him, but I hope he is happy on his next adventure."

They smiled at each other, and Erisha reached forward and took Girisu's hand. She squeezed it fondly. He nodded, grateful for her comfort.

"He made me promise to check in on his family every day," Erisha said. "I've already failed him for the past four days. I don't know how I'll be able to keep the promise though I have every intention of figuring out a way."

"I will look after them for you," Girisu said. "I know Kami and his daughter Siga very well as you may suspect, and I intend to be the one to bring them the news. I will visit them often until you are able to come to Zari."

Erisha sighed. "I don't know if I'll make it to Zari," she said. "My life is here."

Girisu smiled slightly. "Can we tell where life will take us?" he asked. He shook his head. "I do not think so."

"It would be just my fate to go everywhere except Zari though," Erisha said. "Deserved, I'm sure, because I've had quite my share of adventure."

Girisu laughed. He stepped away. "I may ask leave to head for Zari now," he said.

"And not stay for the dinner?" Erisha teased.

"Kami would appreciate news, I'm sure," he said. "You remind me where my duty lies as a friend." He bowed to her then stepped forward to shake her hand.

Erisha laughed happily. "I hope to see you again," she said.

"And I you," he replied before heading over to Anarim's side. He waited while the King spoke to Dumur.

Erisha looked to where Esirim spoke to Mita and Abkur. She studied the old man who had helped her family and her King. She glanced back at Girisu and watched as Anarim turned to him and he spoke into his ear. Anarim nodded after a few moments and Girisu extended a hand to Dumur.

As Dumur chose to hug Girisu instead of shaking his hand, Erisha's attention was captured by Abkur. The elderly man strode up to her and bowed. Erisha inclined her head.

"I owe you many thanks, sir," Erisha told him.

Abkur studied her. "I'm happy to help where I can, my lady," he replied. "Did you enjoy your travels?"

"In some ways," Erisha said. "In some ways not."

"Such journeys are not always pleasant," Abkur agreed, a twinkle in his eye, "but I've heard that you were a good companion."

"I was journeying with many good men, including my brother," Erisha said.

"Would you ever want to adventure out again?" Abkur asked inquisitively.

Erisha sat back and paused. "Would you suggest anywhere?" she asked in response.

Abkur smiled. "Well," he said, "you've visited all the realms except Zari and the Uncharted, is that right?"

Erisha grinned. "That's true."

"I can't pretend I'm not partial to my own realm," Abkur huffed, "but I imagine that the Uncharted realm would be quite the experience."

Erisha laughed. "I would never go alone," she said. "I'm not brave enough for such a feat."

"Oh, no, no," Abkur agreed. "Neither am I."

"Somehow," Erisha answered, "I don't think that's true. You probably have many tales of your wanderings and experiences."

"One or two good ones maybe," Abkur granted. He reached out a hand and Erisha put her hand in his. He tapped it affectionately with his other hand. "I'm here to congratulate you, my dear."

Erisha's brows furrowed, perplexed. "What for?" she asked.

"For many things," the old man said cryptically. "I hope to know you better one day."

"Then you must visit me here," Erisha said encouragingly.

"An old man like me?" Abkur exclaimed. "No, you must come to me in Zari." He stood, eyes twinkling mischievously, and bowed again.

"You leave as well?" Erisha asked.

"I don't know," Abkur said. "I leave with my King. I've decided that much. I have to see if I can persuade him to let us stay for this feast tonight."

"I wish you luck then," Erisha said, amused by such an idea.

"Oh, I doubt it'll be too hard," Abkur mused before walking back over to Anarim and Dumur.

Erisha watched as Mita excused herself from Lord Ansira and Esirim and left the room the way her mother had gone. Lord Ansira came up to Erisha.

"Esirim and I are going to announce the meal tonight to the village," he told her. "It is good to see you up and about."

Erisha nodded. "I'm glad I'm up."

Lord Ansira and Esirim left for the stables, and Anarim walked up to Erisha.

"I believe you've now done your duty to everyone available in this room," he said quietly.

Erisha smiled up at him. "Yes," she said, "and I'm growing tired and cold. Will you help me back to my room?"

Anarim nodded. "Can you stand?" he asked.

He gave her his hands and helped her up. Erisha draped the other blanket over one arm and was supported by Anarim on the other side. Her legs were shaky and weak, but they held her up. She took a few steps with Anarim's help and she felt steadier with every step.

They left the Hall behind and slowly headed to Erisha's bedroom. The carpet felt better under Erisha's feet compared to the wooden floors of the Hall, but the Manor was still cold.

"Are you alright?" Anarim asked.

"Yes," Erisha said, "but I'm not promising my legs won't fail me at the worst time." She laughed. "If I've learned anything from what we've gone through it's that the unexpected will usually happen."

Anarim smiled. "Negatively and positively," he said.

"Oh yes," she agreed. "Not only the bad, but the good, such as meeting Mita."

They entered Erisha's bedroom, and Erisha made her way to the bed without collapsing.

"Thank you," she said as she situated herself under the covers. "You will be staying for the feast, won't you?"

Anarim took a few steps away. "Yes," he said after a pause. "If you'd liked that I'd stay, I'll stay."

Erisha grinned. "Good," she said. "I've done Abkur's job for him. He was going to try to persuade you."

Anarim smiled. "I'll see you tonight," he said, heading for the door.

"Will you send Mita when you next see her, please?" Erisha asked.

"Of course," Anarim agreed, and he left the room and closed the door.

Erisha lay back on the pillows and felt the tiredness seeping through her body. She was arranging herself more comfortable when a sudden thought came to her: Anarim was the King of Alland. He had just executed one of his Stewards. She could not imagine all the arrangement that went into organizing men for battle, how many had to be made to send them home, the plans to deal with the causalities. Anarim had stayed to see if she improved, and it had kept him from his duties. Now, that she was awake and on the mend, he was free to return to Zari and properly care for things. And she had just asked him to stay longer. She felt foolish and ungrateful.

She lay back in her pillows again and berated herself. Who was she to think that the King had time for her? She was unimportant in such a case. He would return soon, she was sure of it, and he would be gone.

A tear slid down Erisha's cheek as she realized that the journey was indeed over. A wave of exhaustion came over her. She sighed and closed her eyes and fell asleep.

CHAPTER SEVENTEEN

A BEAUTIFUL EVENING

Mita was reading in the room when Erisha woke. She smiled when she realized Erisha was awake and brought over a tray of food. As Erisha ate, Mita refilled her water glass and told her of the preparations for the feast.

"Your Cook is frantic in the kitchen and Lady Semirra and my mother are trying to help, but I think at this point it's just causing more chaos," Mita explained. "They're all running around like chickens—"

"Chickens?" Erisha laughed.

"Well, that's what it looks like," Mita said, grinning. "Esirim arrived and told them all that the village had been invited and Cook basically squawked at him."

Erisha held her tender sides as she laughed. "Oh, poor Cook," she said. "She likes more warning than a day's time."

"They're moving along at an impressive pace," Mita said.

"What time is it? How long have I been asleep?"

"It's mid-afternoon now. Some servants are beginning to clean and organize the Hall."

Erisha nodded and continued to eat. Mita chatted with her about the journey, their wounds, and her plans for the Mountain, anything. The young women spoke animatedly until the sun began to go down. Then, Mita cleared the dishes and brought the tray back to the kitchen. Erisha attempted to walk about the room on her own while Mita was gone. She was successful but had to move slowly. Mita returned and helped Erisha change into a warm dress. Erisha was arranged and wrapped up against the cold by the time Lady Semirra and Mrs. Kursignirgal came to visit her.

Lady Semirra had tales of woe from the kitchen, but Erisha and Mita eventually gleaned that everything was advancing well. Lady Semirra insisted that Erisha lay back down. Mrs. Kusignirgal came forward to the bedside. Erisha offered her consolation for Lu and spoke of how courageous the young man had been when he had helped the small company escape. Mrs. Kusignurgal thanked Erisha tearfully and thanked her for befriending and looking after Mita.

"We looked after each other," Erisha clarified, reaching out to Mita.

Mita took her hand as she sat on the bed.

Erisha smiled at her friends even as she saw Mita look uncertainly at Lady Semirra. She squeezed Mita's hand encouragingly. Mita smiled.

"I can't imagine all you and your husband have been through because of Lord Kankal, Mrs. Kursignirgal," Erisha continued. "Your lives must have been so terrible."

Mrs. Kursignirgal nodded, staring off absently for a moment. "All we could do was hold onto the fact that our children were alright," she said, smiling at Mita. "We were so sorry they dealt with so much without us, but we are proud of them."

Lady Semirra stepped forward and put a hand on Erisha's shoulder. "Yes, we are," she said.

Erisha smiled gently. "Thank you," she said.

The two older women left after a while and Erisha and Mita were left to themselves again. Erisha fell back to sleep for a short time while Mita continued reading one of the histories of Alland that she had found in the room. Eventually, Mita woke Erisha and told her that her father had summoned her to come to the Hall to welcome the guests. Mita helped Erisha up and they left the bedroom, arm in arm.

The Hall's many torches were lit, and the tables were decorated with fern leaves and lanterns. Barrells of ale had been brought up from the cellar with many cups, and the high table at the front by the thrones was set to seat the King in the center. Erisha was seated at an end of the table near the hallway to return to her bedroom if need be. Mita was placed beside her with Dumur on Erisha's other side.

The villagers began arriving soon after Erisha entered the Hall. The Steward and Stewardess welcomed everyone as they came through the two front doors. Esirim stood near his parents to smile and comment as needed while Dumur remained standing behind Erisha's chair. The guests would come to greet Erisha and Dumur before spreading out throughout the Hall. Soon, noise and cheer filled the room and Erisha's heart swelled to feel such joy emanating from so many people in one place together.

The King entered the Hall with Abkur from the hallway and Erisha wondered where they had been. The only places down that hallway for them were the council chamber and the private sitting room. The extra bedrooms and weaponry and storage rooms were on the other side.

With Anarim's appearance, the Hall quieted. Murmurs swept through the room as everyone stood. Then there was silence as Anarim headed for his chair at the table. Abkur and Lord Ansira glanced at Anarim as the King stopped behind his chair and Erisha wondered at such ceremony. What was life at the Palace like? Was it always so formal and dignified? A great curiosity filled her, and she wished she might know the answers to such questions.

"Good people of Furun," Anarim said, his voice carrying through the Hall. "I owe you two things: an apology and my gratitude. First, I am sorry that the peace in our kingdom was disturbed, and the conflict led to great loss, especially for this realm. I had failed you and the rest of Alland, and I give you my sincerest apology. I also give you my promise that I will strive to see that no such corruption is allowed anywhere, including in Zari, again. Second, I extend my gratitude to the realm that has always stood with the Askatte house. My ancestors thanked you; my father thanked you; and I thank you." The King looked to Lord Ansira, placed a hand on his chest, and bowed. "You have suffered for my family and our dynasty continues because of your aid and loyalty, past and present as seen on your fields only days ago. Thank you."

Cheers and applause erupted as Lord Ansira bowed lowly to Anarim. Erisha could not stop smiling as she looked from Anarim to her father to the enthusiastic villagers. She clapped along with the rest of Furun.

Lord Ansira raised his hands and the Hall quieted. "Let us eat!"

Anarim sat, Lord Ansira sat, then everyone else. Cook appeared and filled the plates of those at the high table. Then the villagers came up with their plates to Cook and her apprentices to received food as was the practice.

Everyone ate and talked happily. Between Erisha, Dumur, and Mita, conversation flowed easily. Erisha, however, noticed two different messengers arrive during the feast. They each, at their respective arrivals, approached the King and handed him a letter. Anarim would pause and apologize to whoever he was speaking to and quietly read what had been sent to him. He would pocket the letter each time and speak to the messenger in a low voice. Then the messengers would hurry from the Hall and disappear out the doors opened for him by two Furunian guards. The talk in the Hall grew quiet both times, but it did not grow silent out of respect for the King, no matter how curious the people were. The instances solidified the notion for Erisha that Anarim must leave. His kingdom was his first responsibility, and he had already wasted enough time in Furun. She admitted to herself that she would miss his presence greatly, but she would not be so selfish.

As the dinner was being cleared, a boy from the village came up to the high table to where Dumur sat with Erisha and Mita.

"Hello Dumur," the boy said with a quick bow.

"Hello Sanam," Dumur said happily, standing and shaking the boy's hand. "How are you?"

"I'm well. Would you like to come play a board tournament with us?" the boy asked. "Or go outside to battle as the sun sets?"

Dumur hesitated. He looked up as Abkur came over to their side of the table. People were beginning to move about and mingle. "I don't know, Sanam," Dumur said slowly.

Sanam clearly sensed the reluctance. He smiled yet he could not hide his disappointment. "That's alright," he said. "You've just got back. I'll see you."

"See you, Sanam," Dumur said as the boy left to join the other village children.

Erisha looked from Dumur to the other youths he had often played or adventured with. "You should go enjoy yourself," she encouraged.

Dumur looked back at her. "I can't," he lamented, sitting back down. "I can't pretend to be in a battle after being in an actual one. How could I?"

"You can," Abkur said. "Don't give up your childhood so quickly, young man. Life will become dull."

"But I've killed men," Dumur cried. "How can I pretend to best the others or be bested by them now?"

"Not everything in life needs to be taken as seriously as war," Abkur replied. "Such is play. And without play, you could not war. I suppose you played war with these young villagers long before you ever held a real sword, hmm?"

Dumur paused. "Yes, that's true," he admitted.

"Go," Abkur encouraged softly. "The war you've been in will not be the only war you will have to survive. Take the times of joy and peace when they come."

Dumur stood. Slowly, he smiled. He turned and pushed his way through the crowd after Sanam.

Erisha looked up to Abkur. "Thank you."

Abkur smiled down at her. "I'm turning in," he announced. He bowed to Erisha and Mita. "I wish you both a good rest of the evening."

"Will you not stay for the music and dancing?" Erisha said.

"Oh no," Abkur laughed. "I'm an old man. I need my rest and my time to recover after battle."

"Are you hurt?" Erisha asked concernedly.

Abkur shook his head. "Time at this point is my only wound. I'm old," he said cheerfully. "Good night." He bowed again then left the Hall.

Erisha sighed, watching the doorway Abkur had left through. "I wish I knew him better," she said.

Mita laughed. "Yes, he seems like the kind one wants to know," she said. "A man one wants on his side."

Music suddenly began and the tables were all pulled to the walls to make room for dancing. Esirim stood and walked over to the young women. He looked down at Mita and offered his hand.

"Will you dance?" he asked.

Mita slowly put her hand in his. "I can't promise I'll be proficient," she warned.

Esirim smiled. "It's simple," he said. "I'm sure you'll do well."

Erisha watched them go and sat back in her chair, feeling sleepiness creep over her. She turned and looked down the table. Her parents were talking and Anarim looked in her direction. He stood and joined her at her end of the table. He was watching the already crowed dance floor with amusement.

"Do you not dance?" Erisha asked above the noise of the music, dancing, and conversation.

Anarim smiled. "No, I will," he said. "I'd prefer to watch first so I understand the customs here."

"Yes, I suppose dancing is more formal in Zari," Erisha said.

Anarim looked to her. "Rarely," he said with a shake of his head. "Usually, the people all pour out onto the streets and dance freely like this." He raised his hand and gestured to the couples as they spun, jumped, and stamped about.

Erisha smiled. "That sounds wonderful," she said, imagining the streets of Zari filled with people dancing in lines as the sun went down on a beautiful autumn evening.

"Well, I haven't danced in many years now," Anarim admitted. "So, I may embarrass myself either way."

Erisha laughed. "I doubt it," she said.

"And if I do?" he teased.

"I'll laugh," she replied.

He grinned.

Esirim returned with Mita as the dance ended and a new one began. Mita's eyes were alight, and she was smiling brightly. Esirim looked down to Erisha.

"Dance?" he asked.

She shook her head. "I don't think so," she said. "It would not be wise, I think. By the Harvest Moon hopefully."

Esirim nodded. "Very well," he said. "Excuse me." He melded into the crowd and was soon dancing with a young woman from the village.

"Should I ask your mother?" Anarim asked Erisha, looking down the table at her parents.

Erisha smiled. "I'm sure she'd be honored," she said as Mita sat back down.

Anarim stood and the young women watched as he offered his hand to Lady Semirra after speaking for a moment to Lord Ansira. Lady Semirra was taken aback, but then she quickly and happily accepted his invitation. Erisha and Mita grinned as they watched the King direct Lady Semirra onto the dance floor. Lord Ansira rose and neared the young women.

"I'm not dancing, Father," Erisha announced, "but Esirim has just been out with Mita."

"Then I shall ask her," Lord Ansira said courteously.

Mita smiled and put her hand in the Steward's. She looked back to Erisha as she stood. "Will you be alright?" she asked.

"Of course," Erisha assured. She watched as her father led Mita onto the dance floor and danced near Anarim and her mother. Erisha was endeared as Anarim was careful of her mother's injured arm and side. She smiled brightly when her mother laughed as Anarim allowed her to spin him instead.

Erisha's eyes sought her elder brother. Esirim was busy twirling the young woman from the village. Ari was her name, Erisha remembered. She sat back and mused as the young couple smiled at each other.

Dumur appeared suddenly and cut in between Lord Ansira and Mita with a ceremonious bow. Erisha heard Anarim's laugh and looked to see the King watching Dumur with great amusement. Lord Ansira handed Mita off to Dumur and returned to Erisha's side. The music lilted throughout the Hall and out the open doors. The laughter and noise spilled out into the falling night outside. Erisha sat alone for a moment at the front of the Hall at the high table, thinking about everything she had seen in the past sixteen or so days since the beginning of the sporadic adventure that had changed her life. She decided she had never seen a more beautiful scene than this night now.

Lord Ansira sat beside her in Dumur's chair. "He doesn't dance often," he commented.

Erisha looked to where Dumur danced with Mita. "No, he doesn't," she agreed.

Lord Ansira watched the joyous activity with her. "A pretty picture, is it not?" he said with a satisfied sigh.

Erisha smiled. "I was just thinking so," she said. She looked out and observed her mother chatting cheerfully with Anarim as they danced more slowly. Erisha felt her smile fade. She would have liked to dance with Anarim before he left.

Erisha slept fitfully that night although her stomach was full, and she had felt relaxed before she fell asleep. She woke up the next morning feeling disheveled, and she rubbed her eyes in the morning light. Mita's bed was empty and pristinely made. Erisha had had to say farewell to Mita and her mother the night before as they planned to head out before dawn the next day. It was obvious that they had followed through with their plan and Erisha felt disheartened. Everyone would be leaving today. She changed and brushed her hair. As she splashed her face with icy water from the basin, a sudden fear that Anarim and Abkur had left without saying goodbye came over. She pushed the fear away, knowing it to be unreasonable considering Anarim's character and position. Other fears attacked her in response, but she ignored them and continued dressing. She wrapped a thick cloak around her shoulders then thought to check the coolness of the day for certain. She opened one of her windows and stretched out a hand. She felt the breeze wash over her face and blow into her room. It was a warm, pleasant breeze which existed to remind her that winter had not yet set in permanently. She folded up her cloak and left her bedroom.

She took a breath in the hallway and composed herself. She walked down the hallway slowly, her hands around her waist. She dropped her hands before entering the Hall.

She walked in and saw Anarim and Abkur with her father at one of the tables. Anarim met her gaze when she entered. He stood and strode over to her. She met him.

"Good morning," he greeted.

She smiled. "Good morning."

He paused, almost as if he was unsure of how to continue. "Would you be able to walk with me outside?" he asked. "It's warmer today and I'd like to speak with you."

"I think so," Erisha said. She led the way to the other hallway and smiled her greetings to her father and Abkur as she passed. She brought Anarim out the back way past the stables. She noticed that two horses were being prepared by some stable hands.

Anarim offered Erisha his arm and they walked out across the field ahead of them towards the northwest, away from the back of the Manor and away from the village.

"I love walking here where it feels like you're in the middle of nowhere," Erisha explained. "Yet, you can look around in every direction and know that every way leads somewhere."

"While you're still here in the heart of the land," Anarim added.

Erisha looked up at him as the morning sun shone warmly down upon them. "Yes, I suppose that's true," she said. "Furun is the heart."

Anarim smiled down at her.

Erisha looked down as they continued to walk. "I know what you're going to say," she said finally.

"Oh?" Anarim mused.

"You have to leave," Erisha said. "You're saying goodbye. All I can say is that I'm sorry if I've kept you. You have many responsibilities as King, and you must return to Zari."

Anarim was quiet as they walked on. "I think you would like Zari," he said. "It is not the heart of the land, but it's beautiful in its own way. It's hills... well, you've heard about it, I'm sure."

"I would like it," Erisha said genuinely, knowing she somehow would have found a way to love it no matter what. "But it seems unreasonable to hope I'd make it to *all* the realms in my life here." She laughed quietly. "Our recent adventure has been remarkable and quite sufficient."

Anarim studied her then he looked ahead of them as they strolled. "I am returning to Zari," he admitted.

Erisha nodded and pursed her lips, also looking ahead. "I will miss you," she admitted softly.

Anarim looked down at her. "I will miss you," he said. "But I must say goodbye." He stopped and reached for both of her hands. "Yet, not for long, I hope."

She looked up at him sharply.

"Erisha," he said slowly, "will you marry me?" He waited, holding her gaze.

Erisha tried to speak but no words made it past her lips.

He raised his eyebrows, bemused.

She laughed then smiled brightly. "I—" she began, about to protest since she knew nothing about life in the Palace, or in Zari, or as Queen. But she stopped herself and her smile softened. "Yes."

Anarim relaxed in relief. His smile turned into a joyous laugh as he lifted Erisha up and spun her around. They laughed together and he returned her to the ground before him. He took a breath and rested his forehead against her own. "Thank the Heavens above," he said with sigh.

"What?" Erisha asked with a laugh, looking up at him.

"Nothing," he said. "I was just afraid I was going to have to convince you."

Erisha grinned. "Well, you almost had to," she admitted. "And then you didn't, and I just decided."

Anarim laughed. "I'm glad you did," he said, grasping her hands gently, "because I don't want anyone else to be my Queen."

They grinned at each other then laughed.

Erisha hugged him tightly and felt everything within her relax into a calm blissfulness.

"I must go," Anarim said, his chin resting on her head. "But I will write," he promised, pulling back to look down at her. "And you must write to me. We will decide when to marry, and I will return for you. I will dance with you at Furun's Harvest Moon festival."

Erisha smiled. "Yes," she agreed. "That would be wonderful. And I will write, I promise."

"Good. I enjoy receiving letters from you," Anarim said.

Erisha laughed. "You've never received a letter from me."

Anarim grabbed for something under his coat and brought forth a letter. "I believe you signed this," he said with a twinkle in his eye.

Erisha took it and opened it to read the note she had written for her father.

"It gave me an inordinate amount of delight to see your signature at the bottom of this letter," Anarim confessed.

Erisha smiled at him. She met his kiss when he leaned down and embraced her for anyone to see in that wide field. Then they strolled back to the stables where Abkur was waiting. Erisha waved them off with her family then she revealed the news to them.

One would think the Sadurras and Furun would be tired of celebrations but, no, Cook was told and off to work she went again. Cook, however, was too surprised and too pleased to grumble this time. Erisha excused herself after being hugged by her mother multiple times and after having to declare the news over to every servant in the Manor individually. She escaped to her room and shut the door behind her. She sat on her bed where she cried happily for a few moments. After, she fell into a peaceful, much-needed sleep.

CHAPTER EIGHTEEN

A NEW DAWN

E risha woke early the next morning. She sat up in bed and looked out her windows into the grey stillness of the dawn. The previous day had been chaotic as the news of her betrothal passed around the village. People had come rushing to the Manor only to be graciously turned away. It looked to be chaotic again today, everyone in a tizzy for no reason since nothing could be decided upon or planned without Anarim.

Erisha laughed quietly to herself. She dressed and left her bedroom to walk through the hallway. She entered the Hall. The dinner Cook had made for the family and household the night before had been marvelous. Cook had even been convinced to sit with them all, and everyone had been merry and had congratulated Erisha continually.

Erisha walked through the Hall and stepped outside. She strolled past the stables and followed the same path she had taken with Anarim. She breathed deeply and her breath came out as a white, warm cloud in the cold air. She pulled the heavy shawl she had chosen high up around her shoulders. She looked to the East as the sun began to rise and bring color into the world. She did not quite know why she had woken so early and felt it necessary to go outside, but she had. She deeply enjoyed viewing the sunrise she was witnessing now.

The air shimmered beside her, but she felt his presence before she saw him.

She waited then looked over at Kas. He was dressed more warmly than she had seen him before. Otherwise, he looked the same.

"I was wondering if I'd see you again," she said softly, looking away from him and back at the sun as it crept over the Igi Mountains.

"It will be the last time," Kas told her. "I was allowed to say goodbye."

Erisha's smile faded quickly, and she nodded. "I'm glad," she said.

"As am I," Kas said. "And I'm happy you will not need to say farewell to all of our company."

Erisha looked up at him and met his gaze.

"I've been sent to congratulate you," Kas said, "and I myself also congratulate you. Your forthcoming marriage has been blessed."

Erisha smiled. "Thank you."

Kas glanced at her.

"And please thank your Master for me," Erisha corrected herself.

Kas smiled in the growing light. "I will. I must also tell you that Anarim and you have gained a special approval. You particularly are in high favor. The dynasty that will extend from you will decide the fate of Alland."

Erisha stared at him. "That sounds ominous," she stated.

Kas shook his head. "It doesn't have to be," he comforted. He looked down at her. "You've done well. They are pleased with you. Your name will be remembered by the people and by the land. The land already has a connection with you."

"I don't quite understand."

"It is beyond me as well. I am not told every reason and plan." He hesitated.

There was a short period of silence. The world was quiet and peaceful, and Erisha did not feel as unhappy as she believed she should be at such a goodbye. Kas sighed and began to speak.

Before he could say anything, however, Erisha spoke. "Thank you," she said. "For Dumur. For warning Anarim. For everything."

Again, Kas shook his head. "I am only the messenger," he said quietly.

Erisha looked into his eyes and saw a sadness there that distressed her. The wind rose, however, and a cold breeze brushed against their faces. Erisha gripped her shawl and looked up at Kas. His face had softened. He looked up into the sky, nodded, breathed in deeply, and smiled.

"Goodbye, Erisha."

Erisha took a steadying breath. "Goodbye," she said. "I will never forget you."

Kas continued to smile as he began to fade from sight. "He chose well," he said. "He loves you."

Erisha laughed as her eyes brimmed with tears. "I love him."

"Good," Kas said with a nod. He bowed. "It has been an honor, your Majesty."

Erisha held back her tears, awestruck as he faded and disappeared. She took a shaky breath. An unlooked-for peace filled her.

She stood alone in the field, and the sun, having conquered the mountain tops, shone down on her. A soft, chilly breeze flowed by her, caressing the ends of her dress. The long grasses bent and danced around her in the wind. Erisha's undone hair feathered her face as it swung about in the gust. Then, everything calmed, and the sunlight warmed her. She turned about, looking at Furun.

She looked North. Although she could not see them, she knew the hills awaited her. Soon, she would have visited every realm in Alland. The Uncharted remained unknown, but Erisha was content. She laughed happily, and the wind rose up and laughed with her.

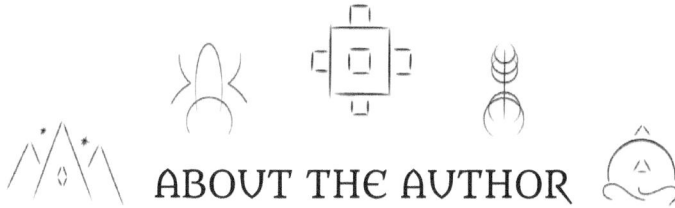

ABOUT THE AUTHOR

A. B. HOLMSTEDT holds a bachelor's degree in English Language and Literature. She enjoys writing, reading, movie-watching, being outdoors, and having fun with her family and friends. She lives in Michigan. *Erisha and the Realms* is her debut novel.

www.ingramcontent.com/pod-product-compliance
Lightning Source LLC
Chambersburg PA
CBHW020352110726
47899CB00006B/1686